MW00629046

Alex,

WESTCOTT HIGH

"Don't do it like them, do it like you!"

All my love,

SARAH MELLO

Sarah Mello

—

*I dedicate this book to my twelfth-grade
English teacher, Mrs. Verrone, for telling me
I'm a writer. Maybe you were right.*

Copyright © 2019 by Seven Plus Five Publishing

All rights reserved. No part of this publication may be reproduced, distributed, or transmitted in any form or by any means, including photocopying, recording, or other electronic or mechanical methods, without the prior written permission of the publisher, except in the case of brief quotations embodied in critical reviews and certain other noncommercial uses permitted by copyright law. For permission requests, write to the publisher at sevenplusfivepublishing@westcotthigh.com.

This is a work of fiction. Names, characters, places, and incidents either are the product of the author's imagination or are used fictitiously, and any resemblance to actual persons, living or dead, business establishments, events, or locales is entirely coincidental.

First Printing, 2019
United States of America
ISBN 978-1-7331743-0-5 (paperback)

Author: Sarah Mello
Editor: Andrea Reimers
Book Cover & Interior Design: Olivia Heyward

www.westcotthigh.com

CONTENTS

1

HE'S BACK

I'm going to tell you a story. I know—such a cliché, recurrent one-liner no longer appeals to the masses. But there are three things that do.

One, a story about love. Because whether you've fallen in love, or have recently fallen out, one truth prevails—love is the unsurpassable act of will that everyone aspires to have, and we will do anything not to lose the feeling it gives us.

Two, a story about tragedy—quite possibly the most bittersweet story. It's the one thing we try to avoid—because no one likes being the tragic kid—but it's inadvertently who we all become at some point in our lives.

That's the bitter part. The sweet part is knowing you won't stay that way—if you're lucky anyway.

And number three, the most alluring one of all, a story about friendship, and the lengths we are willing to go for those most important to us. I guess that's where my story began.

Tucked away in a secluded, sinister town in the suburbs of California is one of the nation's most prestigious private schools: Westcott High. I only wish I were being dramatic when I liken the surrounding town to an eerie, evil playground—but underneath the Botox and Teslas lay a bag full of scandals, secrets, and cover-ups. And it all started with one event—one that would leave behind a shoddy legacy across three states.

The Crescent Closedown. Years ago, the esteemed Westcott High didn't stand alone. It was one of three top private schools in a powerful union—the AWB Crescent. If you connected the dots on a map, the outline of the schools resembled a crescent moon. On one end, you had the Archwick Academy in Oregon. On the other—Bella View Day School in Arizona. And the big school in the middle— in California—was Westcott High. With cutthroat curriculums, competitive fine-arts departments, and elite athletic programs, students at these schools were either extremely intelligent or talented—or both.

Typical kids spent their high school careers attempting to get into a decent college. But AWB Crescent students weren't typical. Every student in the Crescent was there for one reason: acceptance into an Ivy League school.

There was no other option.

Archwick, Bella View, and Westcott were feeder schools pumping out the best and brightest for Ivy Leagues. You can imagine the astronomical pressure in those hallways, especially given the amount of competition around every corner. At those schools, your means to success boiled down to one thing: what you were willing to do to get to the top.

But one day, toward the end of my freshman year, a scandal occurred, and it shook the Crescent to its core. Archwick and Bella View closed, forcing hundreds of angry students into subpar schools. The true cause for the shutdowns was the Crescent's best kept secret, though everyone suspected that pushy wealthy parents facing full waiting lists had something to do with it.

Only one Crescent school survived the scandal—my school, Westcott High.

In an effort to distance itself from the Crescent's corruption, WH was determined to do things differently. The administration would not stack the school with the state's wealthiest kids or overlook what the less fortunate had to offer—diversity. The new Westcott High was about fairness. So, the following school year, as a goodwill gesture to the community, the principal presented an opportunity to kids who wouldn't normally afford a school such as Westcott.

The WH Lottery.

Eighty percent of the school was made up of students whose parents paid steep tuition. Twenty percent was opened only to low-income families, and applications were tossed into a lottery pool once the applicants passed the entrance exam. Those lucky enough to be chosen would enjoy a tuition-free ride at the nation's most elite private school. (Well, free to them. Westcott raised tuition to cover the twenty percent.) Nonetheless, the old and the new would climb their way to the top. Together, they would start a new era—one based on academic equality.

That was, of course, until the student body created a division based on color—and I'm not talking about race.

Cobalts and Violets—aka blues and purples. The eighty percent, those fortunate enough to reside in the distinguished hillside neighborhoods of Westcott, called themselves the Violets, to be known as royalty in the halls of WH. One of the seniors pointed out that you can't get Violet without mixing in a little blue. Just about twenty percent. Hence, the Cobalts, who lived in the valleys, the less distinguished part of town. Everyone claimed it was just an innocent name game, but over the course of my sophomore year, it became an adopted truth of Westcott; the Violets were the favored students from influential wealthy families in the community, and the Cobalts were there by the luck of the draw.

But not all Violets were the same.

Lana Carter. To understand me, you must first understand my sister. And everything that happened to her, and all the things that didn't.

"How was your first day without me? Is being a junior everything you thought it would be?" Lana's sarcasm poured through my cell-phone speaker.

I grabbed my keys out of my book bag as I walked down the sidewalk toward my car. "Apparently, managing my expectations early on to avoid disappointment was in fact a good idea," I said, my eyes tracing the dark red brick that made up the school. "And where are you? It sounds like you're in a tunnel."

"That would be my luxury shuttle service. Mom was not lying about the infamous subway smell, by the way. It's a real thing."

I unlocked my car door with my key. "How lavish."

Lana was a Violet. She had planned to study biochemistry, specifically at Columbia University. That was, of course, until she met our temporary history teacher. Mr. Hill, a tall, young, and incredibly dapper substitute teacher, was filling in for Mrs. Davenport while she was out of the country for five months. Every girl in the school took notice of his charm—Lana especially. Sooner than later, the news broke that she and the sub were caught in a compromising situation out in parking lot B, and it spread around Westcott like a wildfire.

"And let me guess, you're currently walking through parking lot A?" The city commotion competed with Lana's voice.

"How'd you know?"

"Well, parking lot C is reserved for overflow, and I hear parking lot B is reserved for harlots like me. You fit the bid for neither of the two."

I opened my car door and sunk into the driver-side seat, the faithful California sun beating through the windshield.

"If only there were a parking lot reserved for the younger sisters of said harlots," I said.

"That sounds like a request for the school board," she replied. "A genius one."

Once the scandal made its way through the school, Lana was blacklisted for months. Even I, a sophomore at the time, was afraid to align myself with her. But I never quite understood why Lana was demonized the way she was, knowing she likely wasn't the only girl having relations with Mr. Hill. She was, however, the only one who got caught.

Allegedly, Cliff Reynolds, also a Violet and inarguably the most popular guy at Westcott High, was the snitch. Purples aren't supposed to rat on purples, so he tried hard to convince everyone a random bystander must have caught the two kissing in Mr. Hill's car and then leaked a video to the entire student body. But everyone knew he couldn't have been innocent.

"So," Lana said, "did you see him today?"

I looked through my window. Cliff and a group of block-shouldered guys were strolling toward the football field, casually tossing a football around on their way. Cliff's blond hair, swept perfectly to one side, almost bounced as he walked—and his bright smile was captivating. In a town with copious amounts of button-up shirts and quintessential wealthy teenagers, Cliff Reynolds was the poster child.

"No, I didn't see him," I said. Cliff's condescending smile hit my windshield like a rock. "Not today."

Nobody understood why Lana had started dating Cliff, a sophomore at the time, the beginning of her senior year. Although attractive and well respected, Cliff was as shallow as it came. Perhaps being Westcott's star quarterback was to blame for his egotistical nature. I, however, believed his parents' relentless pressure to succeed made much more sense. Being raised in a house with no siblings—and more awards than family photos on the walls—would suck the human out of anyone.

"I'm assuming he hasn't admitted to leaking the video?" Lana asked.

I started my car, breaking eye contact with Cliff. "Not exactly."

After Lana's reputation was nearly destroyed, we all assumed that her dream of attending Columbia was slowly floating away in the hollow clouds of unclaimed destiny. But then, one day out of the purple—it all just mysteriously went away. Much like many scandals in this town. Mr. Hill was released, the rumors were shut down by the principal when they claimed the girl in the video was none other than Mr. Hill's girlfriend, and Lana received an acceptance letter from Columbia. But much to everyone's surprise—Lana declined. After graduation, she cashed in on an internship at a modeling agency in New York and hightailed it out of town faster than you could say *congratulations*.

No one understood why.

"Cliff's silence doesn't surprise me," Lana said. "Admitting he's the rat would be admitting he has blue blood running through those ice-cold veins of his."

"Well, Cliff is all purple, if nothing else."

"If nothing else," Lana said. "I like that one. It sort of indirectly says it all."

"Agreed. It's the best way to end a sentence if you ask me." I mindlessly ran my fingers through the holes in my jeans, staring at my chipped nail polish hanging on by a thread. "Why do you ask anyways? Have you talked to Cliff?" I backed out of my parking spot and began my long drive toward the main road. The rows of luxury vehicles, each looking more ostentatious than the last, acted as walls.

"I think Cliff stopped calling when he realized his arm candy didn't go Ivy League," Lana replied.

Shortly after Lana accepted the internship, she and Cliff broke up. No one knew the real reason for the split, or who to believe. Cliff claimed Lana ended the relationship because she was leaving. Lana swore he dumped her because she was a cheater who didn't go to an ILS. But I had my doubts. Because despite Cliff's obvious personality flaws, he loved Lana. Loving my sister was perhaps the only good thing I had known him to do. Well, one out of two. That's for later.

"Which was so selfish of you not to consider how that would make him look," I said.

"Beyond." Lana's voice was filled with sarcasm. "He's incredibly disadvantaged."

A smile began forming on my face as I gazed out my window and tried to imagine Lana's new life—a life that was worlds away from Westcott.

Sometimes, on my weakest days, I envied Lana. Some days, I wished I had the ability to be unapologetically me—regardless of what others thought. But the subversive rebel look suited Lana far better than a reserved journaler like myself.

Writing was my one true passion in that maniacal world. I'd written more unpublished novels than I could count. With my writing, I could lose myself in a world I controlled—and at least temporarily escape from WH's cretinous status rules.

Sometimes I wondered if, given the opportunity, I wouldn't happily trade places with one of my fictional characters—the ones living in a fictional town. A town that was nothing like Westcott. One with greener grass. But that's the tricky thing about acquiring the unknown—sometimes the grass isn't greener on the other side. Sometimes it's only greener where you water it. And sometimes, if not most times in a town like Westcott, it was neither.

"Hey, promise me you'll try to have some fun this year," said Lana. "Put down your journals and put yourself out there."

"I'm out there," I replied. But my wavering voice gave me away.

I'd be lying if I said my older sister's shadow hadn't obstructed me from carving out my own legacy at Westcott.

After all, everyone knew the story of Lana Carter—Sonny Carter's older sister.

"Sitting upstairs and writing about the things you're borderline desperate for doesn't exactly count," Lana continued. "I've read your writing. It's incredible, Sonny. Open yourself up to the possibility of finding those things."

I grasped the steering wheel as our conversation came to a grinding halt. The silence was deafening, and obvious. How could I tell Lana that no matter what I did, people only saw her—as if I were wearing her scarlet letter down every Westcott hallway? I was living the story she wrote—not mine.

I cleared my throat. "I just need to focus on my academics right now, Lana. My future is depending on it. And by the way, I don't recall giving you permission to read my journals."

"I've been reading them since ninth grade."

"Perfect," I mumbled as I approached the end of the winding street, which led to the highway.

"Do we have a deal?" Lana asked. "You know I hate asking you to make deals with me, but desperate times . . ."

As I was contemplating, a very recognizable burnt-orange Mustang slowly rolled into the parking lot, the car's booming bass vibrating the freshly cut grass. Its tinted windows gave shield to the infamous driver, but I knew exactly who was behind the wheel. In that moment, everything became real. And *everything* stood to change.

I slammed on my breaks. "No way . . ."

"What was that?" Lana asked.

I gradually turned my head around, following the car with my eyes as it cruised toward the front of the school. The sparkling silver rims nearly blinded the eyes of the onlookers, mine included.

"Hello?" Panic rose in Lana's voice. "Is everything okay?"

I turned back around and placed my head down, my eyes roaming the car for any sign of clarity.

"Sonny? What's going on?"

"It's JC." I pushed my foot down on the gas pedal. "He's back."

And so it began. I didn't know it at the time, but my junior year was soon to become a production that would make the Lana Carter story seem like a blurb in yesterday's Westcott newspaper.

2

A SIMPLE SMILE

My mother once told me that a simple smile means more than the strongest of handshakes. And I suppose there's some truth to that. Anyone can shake your hand and all the while be repelled by your existence. But will anyone really smile at you if something inside of them isn't somewhat happy to see you? A more damning question: Is anyone ever really happy to see you? I have often wondered: When I grinned at my classmates in Westcott's halls, did that make their day any different than if I had simply passed them by? Is something as minuscule as a smile truly capable of shaping the next twenty-four hours of someone's life? Perhaps the better question is this: Why is something so small capable of making or breaking us in the first place?

"You're awfully cheerful this morning. I'm guessing you didn't hear the newest Tuesday-morning tidings?" Winston leaned against the long row of blue lockers, then ran his fingers through his dirty blond hair.

Winston Banks—a Cobalt. A master pianist. My best friend. Everyone thought he was a bit quirky—but I knew he was. I saw an opportunity to befriend him sophomore year when a group of guys were antagonizing him in the courtyard about his scarf. It was his first year at Westcott, and I was determined to give him a better welcome than that. I didn't know it at the time, because we rarely ever do, but dropping anchor next to him that day would turn out to be the best decision I could have ever made. His neck accessory pulled me in; his sarcasm sealed the deal. We've been exchanging witty one-liners ever since.

"And why do you look like you're wearing the national flag of Sierra Leone?" Winston's eyes expressed disapproval as he looked down at my sweater.

"That's oddly specific." I rummaged through my locker, my eyes traveling aimlessly down the hall. The long, narrow room was filled with a combination of optimism and dread—the first-week-of-school kind of combo.

Polished Violets in white Westcott hoodies passed by me at rapid speed, pairing nicely with the polished white floor and white brick walls.

"You know, I'd never know you're a Violet just by looking at you," Winston said.

"Thank you."

"Not a compliment."

"Sort of a compliment." I closed my locker. "You do know I refuse to let a color game dictate my wardrobe choices, right?"

"Which is so easy for a Violet to say. If you were a Cobalt like me, you would appreciate the status."

"Being a Violet is not as enticing as it seems, believe me."

"Maybe that's true," he replied. "Or maybe that's the sick lie the rich tell us poor people so we settle for mediocre lives."

"You do know we live in the same neighborhood, right?" I covered the Sierra Leone flag with my crossed arms. "In the valleys?"

Winston and I lived in the same neighborhood, which proved to be rather convenient when he decided to crash at my house after scuffling with his parents. We watched love movies together. Ones that most never knew existed and wouldn't bother watching if they did. The flicks mostly took Winston's mind off the strict, rigorous rules back home. He came from a long line of marines who believed in conduct and order. That was tough for an informal, mordant spirit like Winston. I let him be him. Whatever that meant, it worked for us.

"Not on the weekends," argued Winston. "On the weekends, you go to your supposedly not-so-enticing life on the hillside with your dad."

My parents went through a filthy divorce when I was younger. Lana and I never really knew the reasons. We just assumed they fell out of love. Or possibly came to the realization they'd never fell in.

My dad kept the house on the hillside. My mother, who was left with almost nothing after my dad utilized every legal loophole possible, moved to the valleys. I wish that were a play on words. The valleys of Westcott are suited for the blue-collar families, who live in homes twenty times smaller than the mountainous castles on the hillside.

"And I miss your passive-aggressive undertones every second of every privileged day I'm away," I said.

"Mock me all you want. But you're lucky your last name sealed your color."

"Sealed my color." I pressed my lips together. "That almost makes it sound important."

Winston shifted his weight from one leg to another. "So, have you heard?"

"Heard what?" I asked.

"About Mrs. Penn."

"The new English teacher? Don't tell me she was caught with a student."

Winston looked down at his yellow plaid scarf, adjusting it to just the right position. "I wish," he said. "She left six of the Chosen Ten unnamed."

Every year, WH hosted an award ceremony for local families, as well as influential tycoons from numerous Ivy League schools. Between the junior and senior class, ten students, also referred to as the *Chosen Ten*, were carefully selected by the English teacher to present one piece at the event. The piece could be anything—a song, a short film, and fortunately for me, a paper. After the ten students presented their projects to the audience, the faculty selected the strongest piece, and one of the Chosen Ten received an award so highly respected that it guaranteed entry into an ILS.

I didn't think it was possible, but apparently fear *can* physically creep into one's vocal cords. "What? How?"

"I don't know the answer to that any more than I know why Mrs. Penn replaced Mr. Russell. Teachers fly in and out of this school faster than a Violet in 'detention.' " Winston held up his signature air quotes for the end of his sentence.

I tucked my wavy brown hair behind my ear; my irritation was obvious, I hoped. "Who told you this?"

"Mrs. Penn posted it online this morning," he replied.

"She can't do that. We have to know who our competition is. Comparison is the only way to know if we should up our ante."

"Well, if you're asking me, you should always up your ante. But just be thankful you were still chosen after your sister almost completely ruined your family's last name." Winston locked his phone screen. "Not that I care, mind you."

I clenched my jaw.

"Besides, look on the bright side—if your paper sucks, you can apply to Yale and your rich daddy can pay for it," Winston said. "All is not lost."

"That's not how that works," I retorted. "I need to stand out. All of our college applications look the same. The only thing that makes anyone unique around here is winning that award."

"That appears to be bad news for me," Winston mumbled under his breath.

"Why do you think I take being a Chosen Ten so seriously? Winning the award would allow me to exhale, and it would give me a chance to enjoy my high school experience without the pressure of trying to stand out."

"Enjoy your high school experience?" Winston paused. "You almost sounded like you believe that's an actual thing."

Just then, I heard the dreaded, high-pitched voice of the one person I couldn't avoid if I wanted to. "Sonny . . ." Norah's voice traveled across the din of other voices. "Can we count on your paper to be the sequel to your super interesting short film on why milk is bad for your hormones from last year's English class? I hear the cows from the farm on Fourth Street are dying for part two."

Norah Soros—a Violet. Beautiful, with a dark, slightly tortured soul. A Chosen Ten who could paint circles around some of the most notorious of artists.

I glanced at Norah, desperately trying to ignore her cruel comment. But like most of her comments, it wasn't one that quickly rolled off my back.

"What a facetious question, Norah," said Winston. "Tell me—do your fellow cattle know you've escaped the gates and come here for the day?"

Norah learned about the nuances of painting from her father, Mr. Soros—a true artisan. Allegedly a true deadbeat too. Supposedly her father, who moved to Greece following his divorce from Ms. Soros, recognized Norah's raw talent for painting after she shipped him an original piece for his birthday one year. He began requesting that she send him more, so he could *advise*. What she believed to be a blossoming relationship with her dad turned into a shoddy business transaction when Mr. Soros began selling Norah's artwork at local auctions throughout Athens. He cashed in on some of her most impressive pieces, allowing him to move to another city—his whereabouts unknown. Norah told some people her dad was a tortured artist who took off into the night, and she told others her father was dead. I couldn't help but think that in some twisted way there wasn't much of a difference between the two.

"Do you think you could give me a break, Norah?" I asked. "I've been taking your abuse since freshman year."

Norah brushed back a long strand of thick, shiny blonde hair behind her shoulders. "Abuse? I just came over here to remind you that you won't be winning the award."

Winston tilted his head to the left. "You do realize it's considered cheap to intimidate your competition, right?"

"You do realize you're only here because I'm paying for you, right?" Norah said, her blue eyes piercing through him. "Consider it a military special, from me to you."

Winston's straight face remained unprovoked. "Military special? Sounds like something you'd give out underneath the bleachers at one of our basketball games."

"I'd be careful if I were you, Winston. My position here is more powerful than your scrawny little arms could hold."

"Is that because you spent last year unapologetically flirting your way up the football roster?"

"Flirting your way to the top is a thing," she replied. "You should try it."

"No, actually, I enjoy my dignity."

"Says the guy who wears scarves."

I massaged my temples with my pointer fingers. "Enough, you two."

"Did you hear her?" Winston asked, glaring at Norah. "Enough. Now grab your broomstick and head to first."

"Can I borrow the one that's shoved up your—"

"Okay, enough!" I stepped in between them.

Norah reached around me and tugged down on one side of Winston's scarf. "Have a great day," she said, pivoting. Her jeans looked tighter than she was wound.

I often wondered what it would feel like to have your own father use you as profit for his selfish desires. Perhaps that would turn anyone into a crass, bitter human being. Unfortunately for her classmates, Norah never allowed anyone to get to know another side of her.

I yanked Winston back by the arm before he could follow up with another insult as we watched Norah disappear down the hallway.

"You shouldn't talk to her like that, Winston. You're asking for trouble."

"Please. I will never miss an opportunity to drag her after what she put Lana through," he said, readjusting his scarf. "It's one thing for a video to leak. It's another for someone to go on a crusade, relentlessly pushing it in front of everyone's faces. Between Norah and Cliff—Lana didn't stand a chance."

21

Norah had a genuine detest for most people at Westcott, but eventually, Lana made the top of the list. When the video was leaked last year, Norah made it her mission to expose Lana for what she always believed she was: a promiscuous girl with daddy's credit card. Maybe Norah was jealous of Lana and my father's close relationship. Perhaps she wished her own dad was a well-respected, successful businessman. Or maybe Norah couldn't stand the idea of another girl being more popular than her, regardless of the reasons behind the notoriety.

"At any rate, don't listen to Norah. You're going to win that award. Just ask Casey!" Winston grabbed Casey's attention from across the hall by waving.

Casey Langdon. The sweetest, most genuine girl at Westcott. A bookworm, much like myself. A Cobalt, unlike me. Her mission in life was to become a meteorologist; while tornadoes had always intrigued her, any natural disaster would do.

"Ask me what?" Her tired eyes struggled to stay open.

Casey brought a whole new meaning to the word *perseverance*. She moved to Westcott when her mother sent her and her two younger brothers to live with their aunt. Casey's father had been arrested for drug trafficking a year prior, and her mother, too, was unable to stay clean. Realizing Casey was intelligent beyond her years, her mother knew sending her daughter away to take the WH entrance exam was Casey's only shot at opportunity.

"I was just explaining to Sonny that she's going to be the chosen one." Winston cracked his knuckles in preparation for music class.

"Oh, right. The Westcott Awards." Casey pushed her loose glasses up on the brim of her nose. "Is it true Mrs. Penn hasn't released all ten names yet? Mr. Russell wouldn't have dreamed of doing that."

"Does anyone know why she replaced Mr. Russell?" I asked. "He's been at Westcott High for thirty years, and we all know he planned on retiring here."

"Maybe he already retired," Winston said.

Casey looked down at her casual cotton T-shirt. It was off-green and off-brand. "I don't think so. I heard he was fired."

"Fired?" I felt my heart drop. "Mr. Russell?"

"That's what I heard," she replied, repeatedly brushing her flat hands over her wrinkled shirt.

Casey's move to Westcott was by no means an easy transition. Her aunt, although better off than Casey's mother, worked double shifts to afford the valleys. And despite agreeing to take three kids on, she had zero desire for children. On top of being a big sister, Casey became her brothers' mother, tutor, and friend. Between that and the grueling workload at Westcott, staying strong would be difficult for the toughest of girls. *And every girl has their day.*

My eyes wandered to the left as Casey attempted to de-wrinkle the painful truth that was her life. She always tried to look presentable enough to blend in, all the while knowing she never would.

"If you really want to know what's going on, why don't you go talk to Mrs. Penn yourself?" Winston asked, daring me with his eyes.

"I'm with Winston," Casey said, checking her wristwatch. "Listen, I've got to run!"

Winston and I watched as Casey turned around and began walking toward the library.

"Did she tell you?" Winston asked, crossing his arms and staring ahead.

"Tell me what?"

"Her mom came back around," he replied. "She's been visiting."

"Is that a bad thing?" I asked.

"It is when your mom's a junkie."

I paused. "Maybe she's finally clean."

"I don't think so," Winston replied. "Casey's not that lucky."

"Well, maybe her luck's finally turning around."

Casey reached the end of the hallway. She made an abrupt left turn, not knowing she was walking straight into what was soon to be her very own tornado season.

Winston and I watched as she fell back onto the floor. Her glasses flew off her face, and her cell phone went flying from her hand.

We stared at one another.

"And you said comedic timing wasn't your thing," Winston said before jolting down the hall.

I caught up with him but, hearing a familiar voice on the other side of the wall, held out my hand to stop Winston before he could turn the corner.

We stood behind the edge of the brick wall where the adjacent hallway met ours, peeking our heads around just far enough to see.

"Oh my God! I'm so sorry!" Casey patted the tile floor in circular motions, frantically trying to find her glasses. Her hands finally met the clear frames, and she pushed them back onto her face.

Kyle kneeled down and looked into her spent eyes. "Don't be sorry." He handed Casey her cell phone. "It's hard to see who's coming and going in this hallway."

Kyle Winchester, the principal's son. Cliff's best friend and the running back to his quarterback. A Violet by name, a good guy at heart. A Chosen Ten. Casey's tornado.

We grew up together, Kyle and I. He was the brother I never had the pleasure of having. The kind of brother every girl should have. He was my best friend, and everyone's really. Because everyone liked Kyle Winchester. Being likable was perhaps his best quality, and as it turned out, it was also his kryptonite.

"Do you want to stand up?" he asked.

"Sure." Casey tucked her wavy blonde hair behind her ears.

Kyle jumped to his feet and held his hand out toward her with no luck. His eyes expressed confusion. "So, this is typically the part where you take my hand and stand."

"Right." She placed her hand on his and stood to her feet.

"What are you doing?" Winston whispered.

I turned my head toward him. "What does it look like?"

Winston's breath hit the back of my neck. "It looks like you're preventing me from stopping a train wreck."

"Shh!" I slapped the air between us.

"'What's your name?" Kyle slowly pulled his hand away.

She gently made hers into a fist. "Casey Langdon."

"Oh, you're Sonny's friend, right? She's told me a little bit about you."

My heart raced as I watched their conversation.

"Are the two of you close?" Casey asked.

"Very," Kyle said. "I've known her for as long as I can remember. Much like most people in Westcott . . ."

"Yeah, well, I moved here the summer before sophomore year, but didn't really become friends with Sonny until the latter half of the year."

Kyle nodded. "Until the latter? I can see why Sonny likes you."

"Sonny's intellect is hard to match." Casey looked down at her shattered cell-phone screen. "But I try."

"You should really get a case for that thing," Kyle said.

"Yeah, it's, um, it's in the mail." Casey glanced up at him and quickly looked away.

Kyle grabbed the straps of his new backpack. "Well, Sonny and I didn't become friends until after I confessed my love for her in fifth grade. I told her I wanted to marry her, but she, uh, she didn't want to get married at age eleven."

"That's weird," Casey said, smiling a little. "I hear that's when girls really start thinking about that ring."

"I thought so too," Kyle replied.

"So, what did she say when you asked her out? Or, didn't you?"

"Oh, no, I definitely asked." Kyle grabbed his bicep muscle. "She, uh, she punched me in the arm." His voice heightened.

"Perhaps just playing hard to get?"

27

"See, that's what I thought." Kyle pointed at Casey. "So I asked again a week later, but when she turned me down the second time, we decided to be best friends instead."

"Solid foundation."

"It's proven to be," he replied. "I'm Kyle Winchester, by the way."

"Winchester?" Casey's voice cracked. "As in principal?"

He pressed his lips together. "As in principal."

"That's . . . interesting."

"Extremely," Kyle replied.

Casey looked down, picking the bits of glass off her phone.

"Is there a place to exchange the cards life deals you?" Winston asked me, slowly shaking his head. "I thought my life was tragic."

"Hey, there's a repair shop down the street from here," Kyle told Casey. "It's about a hundred bucks, and you're in and out."

Casey put her phone into her pocket and grabbed the straps of her frayed backpack. "Yeah," she said. "I'll look into it."

With narrowed eyes, he traced her informal clothes, which did anything but paint the picture that Casey had a hundred bucks.

"Look, I have to run. It was nice meeting you." She gave Kyle one last stare before turning to walk away.

Kyle stayed behind, standing in the middle of the hallway. "Yeah," he mumbled. "You too."

I slowly brought my head back from the edge of the wall. "Did you just witness what I did?" I asked Winston, slapping him on the stomach with the back of my hand.

"No," he said. "Absolutely not. Don't even think about encouraging this. You know he's—"

"Sorry, what?" I skipped down the hall, lifting my hand to my ear. "I'm having a hard time hearing you over the endless possibilities floating through the air."

Winston lifted his chin. "We agreed we wouldn't be the friends who meddle!"

"I'm sorry, when did we agree to this? Was it before or after you insulted my wardrobe choices?"

"That's not meddling!" His voice echoed. "That's caring!"

The rooms at Westcott were all a bit somber, but none of them held a candle to Mrs. Penn's English class. There was a splash of unfamiliarity in the air as I approached the classroom. The closed wood door felt foreign; Mr. Russell had always kept it open so students could stop in before the bell rang.

"I'd be careful if I were you." An unknown male voice rolled into my eardrum from behind.

I turned around to find a stranger close to my age standing in front of me. A spine-chilling kind of stranger. The kind you aren't sure you should get to know, but you do it anyway. The kind with brown vortex-like eyes that pull you in and then toss you back out.

The stranger ran his hand over the top of his messenger bag, and I couldn't help but notice the tanned muscles emerging from his black shirt and the scars lining his forearms.

I gazed into his eyes, completely lost in the intensity of his stare. "Excuse me?"

He pulled his black beanie down over his curly brown hair. "I hear she's in a horrific mood," he said. "As in the first-week-of-school kind of horrific."

I examined the classroom door and then looked back at him. The stranger's clothes were casual and possibly a bit dirty. And although his demeanor was intimidating, his dimples and perfect white smile offset his daunting stare. He was alluring. Then again, I suppose bad boys always are.

"That's understandable," I replied.

"If you're the understanding type." He looked at me, and I at him, in a kind of staring contest. Who would blink first?

"What's your name?" he asked.

I took a few small steps back, my body hitting the door behind me. "What's yours?"

He smiled through his eyes, as if his lips were too lazy to make a move. "Good luck in there," he said. "Something tells me you're going to need it."

I slowly broke away from our irrefutable connection, knocking on the door and eventually walking inside. I was happy for the barrier between this stranger and me, even if on the other side of the barrier was yet another stranger.

I stood inside the classroom and stared at Mrs. Penn. She was sitting at her desk, looking at me over a pair of emerald-green glasses. The blinds behind her were closed, and she sat in an oversized leather chair in the shadowy corner of the room. I wanted to turn on the lights, but I didn't get the impression they were wanted.

She suddenly leaned forward in a black dress so fitting you'd think it would be deemed inappropriate. "Can I help you?" she asked. Mrs. Penn's voice was hurried and sharp.

I stepped back a little. Her tone was intimidating to a girl like me, who spoke slowly with deep meaning behind each word.

"Sorry for the interruption. I was hoping to speak with you about the Westcott Awards," I said.

"I presume you're Sonny?" Mrs. Penn smoothed down the hair on the top of her head with bony fingers. "I figured you'd come knocking." She gestured toward a chair. "Have a seat."

I slid into the chair, clutching my book bag to my chest like a shield. "I'm guessing you know Mr. Russell?"

"Not exactly," she replied. "He left in a hurry, but it certainly wasn't difficult to figure out who his favorite student was." The sunlight crept in from between the blinds, reflecting off Mrs. Penn's papers and making her eyes look like the recesses of caves.

"Why did he leave?" I asked.

Mrs. Penn leaned back in her chair and handed me a cavernous glare. "You mentioned something about the award ceremony?"

I swallowed my question. "I was wondering why there are six unnamed students on the Chosen Ten list. Mr. Russell started this program and was very strategic about allowing everyone to gain insight into their competition. It only seems fair."

Mrs. Penn popped the lid up and down on her ink pen. "Nice pitch."

"I'm sorry?"

"You're Lana Carter's sister, no?"

I sat back in my seat, heavily aware of what was coming next.

"Ms. Carter, do you acknowledge that your sister almost single-handedly destroyed this school's reputation by playing house with a temp last year? Do you know what that could have meant for Westcott? If your father wasn't who he is, I doubt highly that you would still be a student here, much less one of the Chosen Ten."

"Wow. You seem to know a lot for a new teacher," I said.

"I've been filled in." She smirked. "If I were you, Ms. Carter, I would think very carefully about questioning me and my decisions. This is my program now." She paused. "Be thankful I picked you."

I tensed up. "Just seems pretty secretive, that's all."

Mrs. Penn clasped her hands and placed them in her lap. "I've come to realize that secrets are somewhat of a thing around here." She leaned forward. "Looks like I'm in good company."

I stared into her black eyes, trying hard to remember to breathe. It's no easy task when your mind is running wild.

Just then, the door creaked open. Mrs. Penn broke eye contact with me and glanced toward the side of the room. "I presume you're lost again, Mr. Harrison?" She spoke over my head, which was sinking deeper into my chest.

I twisted in my chair and looked at the doorway. Standing behind me was one of the most handsome guys I'd ever seen. And that was saying something for Westcott. He was unquestionably the new kid—at least one of them anyway. His eyes were hopeful. His hair was messy. His demeanor was ready.

"Yes, ma'am, I am," he said.

"Ms. Carter will walk you to class." Mrs. Penn looked pointedly at me through her glasses, and I knew she wanted me to leave.

There was a long pause as I scrolled through the rolodex of excuses in my mind, searching for a valid reason as to why I shouldn't oblige. Nothing stuck.

"Sure," I said.

If only I had listened to the stranger in the hallway, I could have avoided that unsettling interaction with Mrs. Penn—although something told me it would have found me eventually.

I stood, threw my book bag over my shoulder, and walked to the doorway where he stood waiting.

"Ms. Carter!" Mrs. Penn's cutting voice sliced me from behind like a sharp blade.

I slowly turned my head back toward her.

"Just in case it wasn't obvious—I don't play favorites."

I nodded in her direction before I walked into the hallway.

"Yeah," I mumbled under my breath. "It was pretty obvious."

"I'm Jacob," said the new kid.

His voice carried the laidback ease of someone much older—as if he knew without a doubt he belonged anywhere he went. Even the relaxed curve of his shoulders and arms suggested a comfortable readiness for anything life threw at him—something I'd never felt.

The gray cotton T-shirt he wore fit him like a glove. You couldn't ignore it if you wanted to, and I wasn't sure anyone would.

"Sonny," I replied, giving him a quick stare down. "What's your first class?"

We glided into the hallway. The white floors were blinding, or perhaps my eyes had adapted too well to Mrs. Penn's cave.

He looked down at his schedule. "Looks like precalculus for me."

"You must be new here?" I asked.

"Is it that obvious?"

"Well, you're carrying around a schedule, and you mentioned you're lost."

"I guess that gives it away, huh?"

I put my hands into my jean pockets. "Trying to hide it?"

"Nobody likes being the new kid, right?"

I shrugged. "Set the scene."

"Okay," he said. "The scene is a slightly menacing school with a boatload of incredibly standoffish teenagers, most with permanent panicked looks on their faces."

"You mean Westcott?"

"Yeah," he replied. "That rings a bell."

"Oh, no, nobody likes being the new kid there."

"Well, I guess moving here was a slight oversight, then."

"Guess so," I replied. "Where are you from?"

"Long Beach." He shook his tanned hand through his brown hair. "We just moved to Westcott over the summer."

"How did you get into WH if you just moved here?" I asked. "The waiting list is a mile long."

"My dad's job relocated him and they made room for me."

"Your dad must have some serious pull to get you in here before the left wing opens."

"The left wing," Jacob repeated. "I'm assuming that's for expansion."

"Wow. Lost and smart. I didn't think you could be both."

"I guess I'm the exception." He smiled. "Do you like it here?"

I glanced into his optimistic eyes. I didn't want to be the girl to crush his positivity, because I knew someone else would soon enough, so I withheld the truth. Talking to the new kid was always a good time to be unforthcoming.

"It's cool."

"Great," he said. "Thank God I'm going to a *cool school*."

"You wouldn't want to be one of those loser kids going to a loser school, would you?" I asked.

"Oh, no. That'd be social suicide."

"Perhaps even more so than carrying around a schedule."

Jacob looked me up and down, and although I couldn't be sure, it wasn't to judge my wardrobe choices like Winston.

"Hey," he said. "What's this whole purple-and-blue thing I hear about? Someone told me before school started that I'm officially a Violet."

"A Violet, huh? You must have a nice house."

"It's not a shack," he said. "But what does my house have to do with it?"

"It's a stupid color game that started last year. The rich kids are Violets, and the less fortunate kids are Cobalts. Some people will try to tell you it's more complex than that, but that's truly all there is to it."

"Isn't every kid here somewhat fortunate?" he asked. "Just to be here?"

"The Cobalts are very fortunate," I said. "They get in through the lottery, and they get a free ride."

"I'm sure they don't appreciate being lumped together as the broke kids." He shook his head. "Do we have a choice not to play?"

We drew nearer to the classroom door. "Not exactly."

"Well, that seems unfair," Jacob said, rolling his schedule into a cylinder.

I placed my hands on his shoulders. "Welcome to your new cool school."

He looked down at my hands and exhaled slightly.

His shoulders were broad, and although my hands could possibly find their home on such a surface, I knew I had to get to class.

I removed them slowly and turned around to walk toward the other end of the hall.

"Hey," he said, stopping me before I could get too far. "What color are you?"

I stopped in my tracks and begrudgingly made a U-turn. "I don't play." My voice was filled with conviction.

"I thought you said—"

I shook my head. "I don't play."

Jacob smiled, giving his schedule a few taps before walking into the classroom.

A simple smile. Such a standard concept with unlimited meanings. Maybe it's the socially acceptable way of politely ending a conversation. Or maybe, if you're really lucky, it's the first step toward the start of something new.

3
DECISIONS

Decisions. We make them all day, every day, subconsciously and consciously. Maybe a world without them would be robotic and meaningless, but I'd be lying if I said I didn't wonder what it would look like. Perhaps it would strip away the very things that make this universe colorful and unique. And maybe it would change everything. Because every decision impacts everything that follows. Especially the wrong ones.

"I saw you and the new guy walking down the hallway this morning. Tell me everything," Winston said as we sat down in the crowded lunchroom.

I looked down upon the long, rectangular table in front of me, brushing my fingers across the cold surface. "It's strange sitting here," I said.

"Yeah," Winston replied. "I know what you mean."

The cafeteria at Westcott was famous for far more than its fancy mobile-stool units and vegan menu. To understand why was to understand one of my old friends.

Jeremy Coleman. JC for short. A Violet, although most would say a fallen Violet. *The orange Mustang.* Westcott High's star wrestler—my father's favorite. I'd never been thrilled that my dad was amongst the crowd at WH, but since he was one of the most respected wrestling coaches in the state, it was only fitting his home was at Westcott. My father, Dirk Carter, was said to produce more star athletes than anyone in his direct line of competition.

And JC was one of them. He was talented, even as a freshman. His goal was to earn a scholarship to Princeton University, and with the amount of drive he possessed, it was inevitable he would receive one. But unlike many young hopefuls at Westcott, he let his vision fall secondary to an alluring Violet: Piper Clemmons. The assistant principal's daughter. The musical talent at WH. A Chosen Ten. A chosen everything. Piper's dream was to become a violinist, specifically at Princeton. Her talent—unmatched. She was one of the hardest working students among us and wasn't afraid to be that, regardless of what she had to sacrifice—even if that meant dating.

JC took notice, and like most guys who can't get what they want, he only wanted Piper more. He began relentlessly pursuing her in all the wrong ways, even asking her out twice in one day. He spared no expense at trying to get her to notice him—and was happy to risk embarrassing himself in front of everyone to make her feel desired. Luckily for him, Piper thought public humiliation in attempt to win a girl over was cute. And although she tried not to, halfway through the ninth grade, she fell in love.

"I wonder what they could have been." I looked over at JC, who was sitting alone in the corner of the lunchroom.

He tossed his hood over his head and placed his bright orange headphones over his ears. I was jealous of JC's ability to shut out the world, although upon second glance, it didn't appear as if it were something he *wanted* to do.

I continued to stare. "Have you talked to him yet?"

Winston stared with me. "Has anyone—?"

Just like Kyle and me, JC and I pretty much grew up together. In middle school, he'd spend his time trying to convince everyone he would one day wrestle for my dad. Being the tall, lanky kid he was, nobody took him seriously. And knowing how cutthroat my father was, I certainly didn't. But JC had passion. Possibly too much. His slightly irascible, won't-take-no-for-an-answer attitude

43

landed him on the team—freshman year. He and my dad would hold private practices in our home gym every weekend, and JC would stay afterward to hang out. We became close. As close as you could get to a guy like JC. He was untouchable, and just hitting the surface of what life had to offer a talented Violet like himself. But little did JC know, home-gym practices were about to take on a whole new meaning.

"I heard he got to come back this year after agreeing to finish sophomore year at home," Winston said.

"I'm just shocked they let him come back to Westcott after finding what they did." I stared down at our table. "What's even more shocking is Piper turning her back on him."

"And how is that shocking?" Winston asked.

"They've been dating since freshman year," I replied. "Plus, both of their parents got divorced that year, and they helped each other through it. Things like that bond you."

"Bond you?" Winston's eyes widened. "The only thing Piper cares to bond with is her perfect reputation."

Despite agreeing to date JC, Piper was uninterested in doing much more than holding hands until she graduated from Westcott. JC respected her wishes, regardless of how big of an adjustment it was for him. Physicality seemed to fail in comparison to his raw feelings for her. Everyone noticed the change in him, and eventually everyone fell in love with their love—even the skeptics.

But that's the funny thing about love. Sometimes love can be deceiving. And sometimes, in the worst cases, *love isn't love at all.*

"Maybe you're right," I said. "Piper wouldn't risk her reputation for JC. She's way too good of a girl."

Winston unpacked his lunch. "Well, she's not *that* good."

"She doesn't even swear," I argued.

"Not true. I heard her yell 'shit' once when she poked herself in the eye with her bow." Winston mindlessly chewed his food.

"Well? Did you take her out back?"

He shrugged. "Just saying."

"And JC? Do you really think he—"

"Oh yeah," Winston interrupted. "He definitely did."

I sighed. "I don't know . . . "

"You know what your problem is?" Winston asked.

I took a bite of my salad. "I'm almost positive you'll tell me."

"You see the good in people before you see the color in them. JC is a Violet to his core. And we all know Violets think they can get away with anything."

"Why are you so convinced he's guilty?" I asked.

Winston unpacked more of his lunch. "Why are you so convinced that he's not?"

I shook my head, dismissing his question. "Did you seriously pack Sour Patch Kids for a meal again?"

Winston was an avid junk-food eater. I was surprised his organs were still thriving. At least I hoped they were.

"And yogurt-covered raisins."

"I'm overwhelmed by your progress," I said.

"It's not my fault. You know I blame my sweet tooth on my grandma—God rest her soul." He signed himself with the cross.

"You aren't Catholic, Wins."

"She baked for me as a kid, and I spent my days in the kitchen eating cinnamon buns while watching reruns of *The Sally Jessy Raphael Show*."

"Yet you're incredibly slender," I replied.

"I blame that on my dad. He made me run laps around the neighborhood with my siblings when we didn't make our beds." Winston paused, staring off into space. "Also, can your mom get me the number to her therapist? I just realized I didn't have a normal childhood."

"I'd be more concerned with your constant need to blame others," I said.

"Twisted upbringings are all some of us have for excuses," he replied. "Just let me have it."

"You're fine, Wins. You don't need therapy."

"That's just what they want you to believe, isn't it? Then you grow up to be Norah." Winston paused. "Also, don't try to get out of dishing on the new kid."

"Have you seen Casey?" I bobbed my head from side to side, searching for her in the crowd. My eyes eventually landed on Jacob, who was sitting with Cliff and the rest of the football team. I watched as they exchanged a friendly interaction and then wondered how, out of all the tables, the new kid ended up at that one.

"I think she's eating lunch in the library today." Winston popped a yogurt-covered raisin into his mouth. "She told me she has to finish her homework so she can take her brothers somewhere tonight."

"That girl never stops," I replied.

I met Casey on *her day*. The day when her responsibilities finally overwhelmed her. She was hunched over the school's bathroom sink, unable to hold back the tears. We weren't expecting to find each other outside the stalls that day, but friendship often finds you when you didn't know you wanted to be found. And that's where ours began—one Winston and I never knew we were missing. I thought she needed me, but as it turned out, I desperately needed her.

"Why are you looking for Casey?" he asked.

"I wanted to see if she could help me think of an idea for my paper." I pulled out my notebook.

Winston rolled his eyes. "Don't tell me you're already starting that. It isn't due until the end of the school year."

"I want to get a head start. Mr. Russell said in the event I don't win the award, a solid original piece would still be an impressive and important part of my Yale application."

"So, what's the new kid's name?" Winston asked, dismissing my comment.

"Jacob," I said as I looked over at him again. This time, Jacob was staring back at me.

"The only thing that threatens to ruin this is if Cliff has already brainwashed him into becoming one of his brocks," Winston said.

"Brocks?"

"A bro and a jock. A brock."

"Colorful," I replied, beating my pencil against the paper.

"What could be worse than a pulchritudinous man like that becoming friends with Cliff Reynolds?" Winston glanced over at their table.

"That's a mighty big word for a Tuesday. And Cliff isn't so bad."

"That's a mighty big load of shit for a Tuesday too. Much like Mike Chang telling Mrs. Bennett he creatively composed a piece that was heavily inspired by Claude Debussy's '*Clair de lune*,' " he yelled as Mike walked by our table and gave Winston the finger. Winston cupped his hand over his mouth and leaned toward me. "The kid thinks if he picks an impressionist from the nineteenth century that nobody will notice his plagiarism." Then he straightened up and waved at Mike. "Love you too!" Winston shouted in Mike's direction.

"Look, there's no proof that Cliff leaked the video. And despite his depthless personality and massive ego, he's harmless."

"Harmless?" he repeated. "Your sister thought differently."

"Can we stop talking about Lana? Mrs. Penn all but threatened my life if I, Lana Carter's sister, had the audacity to question her authority again."

"She did what?" Winston's mouthful of candy made it difficult for him to speak.

"Something isn't right, Winston. First Mr. Russell disappears and is replaced with a newbie who, after two days at Westcott, has the power to leave six of my direct competitors unnamed? That's unprecedented and borderline cruel."

"And you were set off by the word 'pulchritudinous'? You literally speak like you're writing a poem."

I chugged down my water, rolling my eyes to the left of the bottle. "Mrs. Penn is clearly Westcott's new taskmaster. And I have a feeling she doesn't care for me. Not like Mr. Russell did anyway."

"Oh. Hold on a second," Winston said. "I think I spoke too soon."

I followed his eyes over to Jacob, who was now sitting next to JC.

"That could be worse," he said. "That could be way worse."

"What do you think they're talking about?" I continued to watch Jacob and JC's conversation.

"Hopefully you," Winston replied.

Just then, Dean walked in between our view and broke our concentration. He stared at me as he walked by, offering a lazy, shameful grin.

"And him?" Winston asked.

My eyes followed Dean as he took his seat at a table so incredibly foreign to me. He shook his head as he settled in, his messy brown hair falling into place. "What about him?" I asked, making a solid attempt at stuffing my emotions back down.

"Have you talked to him?"

Dean Ballinger. A Violet turned Cobalt. A proficient basketball player—the captain of the team. Undeniably handsome. My ex-boyfriend. After Dean's mom died at the beginning of sophomore year, the family's finances took a hit. Mrs. Ballinger was the breadwinner, and without her income, they struggled to maintain their lifestyle. Somehow, Dean and his dad managed to get by for a while.

But a couple short months later, Mr. Ballinger could hardly pay the bills. That was when my dad brought him in to help manage his company, a high-end sporting-goods store he and a partner owned together. Our fathers became the best of friends, and everything seemed to be looking up for Mr. B.

But all good things must come to an end—and I hear the greatest things tend to end quicker than they started.

"I wonder how Dean felt when he was forced into the lottery pool," Winston said.

Everyone knew Mr. Ballinger had embezzled money from the company. It was an astronomical betrayal, one that my dad was never able to forgive him for. Mr. Ballinger brought the missing funds to my dad's attention, claiming someone else must have been responsible for the theft. It goes without saying that my dad didn't believe him.

Word got around Westcott, like it does, and Mr. Ballinger's name was completely tarnished before the sun left the sky that day. I heard he began work for some call center. They got by, but eventually moved to the valleys before junior year started, unable to keep up with the demands of living in the hillsides of Westcott. And without his comfortable salary from the sporting-goods store, Mr. B was unable to afford tuition. Hence, how Dean became a Cobalt.

"Well, if his dad never did what he did—"

"Did, didn't. Six of one, half a dozen of another." Winston scrolled through his Instagram.

"I don't think that's how that works," I said. "And are you insinuating you don't believe it?"

"I just can't believe Dean would let their fallout affect your relationship. I know he dumped you. But that was salvageable with a sorry. What was irrevocably damaging was his decision to—"

"Why are we talking about this?" I slammed my pencil on top of my notebook, unaware of how loud my voice had become.

Suddenly, Cliff turned around from a neighboring table with his finger over his mouth. "Shhh!"

I stared at his ghostly smile in detest while everyone laughed.

"Did he just *shush* you?" Winston asked, gritting his teeth.

Cliff looked me up and down before twisting his head back around toward his sea of friends.

I put my head down and picked up my pencil as the laughter began to disappear.

"Look, I didn't mean to upset you." Winston chucked a crumpled-up straw paper at the back of Cliff's head. "But we both know that Dean's decision to date Norah was the worst one yet. How do you come back from that?"

I closed my notebook, suddenly finding it impossible to focus. "You don't."

Up until that point in the cafeteria, I only knew that Dean had started dating Norah a month before junior year began, shortly after breaking up with me. But I hadn't yet seen it for myself. Their relationship was a shock to everyone. No one assumed Norah would ever date someone like Dean, in the position that he was in. Winston was convinced she was a rebound and that they'd be broken up in a week's time. Casey was convinced Dean was just confused about me and everything that was happening between our dads—and simply needed space. I was convinced there wasn't a justifiable reason for him betraying me by dating the one girl who tried to ruin Lana entirely, and there wasn't a point in trying to search for one.

Winston held the bag of candy over his mouth to ensure he got every last drop.

"You didn't save me one single piece?" I placed my hands on the table, turning my body toward him.

Winston's eyes peeked over the plastic bag. "You're on a diet."

"Is that how you justify eating multiple boxes of candy? By pretending I'm on a diet?"

"Yes. It's our thing."

"That's not a thing."

"Look, don't feel bad about Dean. Your dad isn't the only one who doesn't speak to Mr. Ballinger anymore," Winston said, wiping his lips.

Most families in Westcott no longer associated with the Ballingers after the business debacle. I credited that to Cliff's father, Mr. Reynolds. He owned close to a dozen high-end condominiums throughout California, making him one of the wealthiest men in Westcott. In all my years of being privy to threats, I'd never known one to be as pathetic as Mr. Reynolds encouraging his fellow neighbors to stay away from the Ballingers. Most would say that's not what occurred—but I know it was.

And I guess I understood. After the accusations made against Dean's father, I wasn't sure if anyone would want to align themselves with a family who could tarnish their good name. I'd be lying if I said it never crossed my mind as I was falling into a deep friendship with Casey. Luckily for me, my good name was already a bit tarnished—thanks to Lana.

"I wonder what would happen if Mr. Reynolds found out that Cliff is still friends with Dean." Winston grabbed my pencil and started scribbling on his napkin.

"What are you doing?" I asked him.

"I . . . am writing . . . that down." He lifted the pencil to admire his work.

I quickly snatched it back from his hand. "Would you stop trying to come up with ways to blackmail Cliff?"

"It's how I plan to get through high school," he said. "You know this."

I hit Winston in the head with my pencil.

"You know what next Friday is, right?" he asked.

My eyes sunk. "How could I forget?"

"I can't believe it's almost been a year since Mrs. Ballinger passed," he said. "Are you going to talk to him?"

"Maybe." I looked over at Dean, who was now nuzzled up next to Norah. "But probably not."

"Probably not what?" Kyle sat down across the table from us.

Winston looked down at his phone. "Don't do it, Kyle."

Kyle turned all the way left, boxing Winston out of our conversation. "Sonny . . ."

"Kyle . . ."

"Casey?"

"No," Winston interjected, his eyes expressing concern.

"What do you think I'm going to do?" Kyle asked him, tossing a football back and forth between his hands.

"Play her like a fiddle," said Winston. "Become everything she wants but can't have. Rope her in just to hang her with it."

"High praises, Winston. Thanks."

"It's a dark day when you find out what Winston really thinks of you," I said.

"The darkest," Winston added, cleaning up the aftermath of his lunch.

"Look, I'm not a player. I've dated the same girl since tenth grade."

"Exactly," Winston replied. "And we all know you're bound to get back together with Ari."

Ari Ziegler—a Cobalt. Westcott's star vocalist. Desperate for and bad at love. Kyle's ex. The Zieglers moved to Westcott the summer before tenth grade, after hearing about the school's new lottery system. Being a Westcott student was Ari's only chance at attending Brown University. She passed the entrance exam and found herself in the hallways of WH her sophomore year, which is when she would meet the guy who would forever complicate and change her life—in so many more ways than one.

"Ari and I broke up over the summer," Kyle said.

"You break up every week," I replied.

"Plus, you're never really broken up—even when you are," Winston said.

I raised my finger at him. "Good point."

"Can't you just date a Violet so we don't have to worry about heartbreak?" Winston stood up and walked off, his dramatics smacking us in the face.

I chugged some more water. "He'll come around."

"Will he, though?" Kyle flicked my water bottle with his fingers.

"So why did you and Ari break up this time?" I asked, slapping him on his arm.

"We got into a fight the night of Cliff's cookout, and we broke up. I stayed home, thinking she would too, but she went without me."

Every summer, Mr. Reynolds opened a new condominium complex; and every summer, he allowed Cliff to host a cookout at the condo's pool. It was a great way for Cliff to throw a color-biased party for the Violets, while his dad got to show their parents around the condos. The cookout evolved into quite the chauvinistic ritual for the two.

"What was the fight about?" I asked.

"Didn't I tell you?" Kyle leaned in. "I could have sworn we had a two-hour conversation about it on your porch swing."

"Give me a refresher," I replied. "It's hard to keep up with all of your breakups."

"She told me I was smothering her, so I said I would give her some space. Then she accused me of not caring about her. Twenty minutes later—we're done."

"It's all the vaping," I replied. "I think it's messing with her head."

Kyle pretended to laugh and gave my water bottle another flick with his fingers—this time causing some of the water to spew from the top.

I wiped the side of my mouth, catching the water drops before they hit my shirt. "I'm sorry, Kyle! But your and Ari's fights are so juvenile."

"And your and Dean's fights are what?" he retorted.

"Not the same thing," I said, tightly squeezing my water bottle.

Kyle's eyes made their way toward Dean's table. "Him and Norah, huh?"

"Yeah," I replied. "Apparently."

Dean and I began dating freshman year. We were always close friends, but my love for him eventually grew far beyond that of a friendship—a love we both chose to explore. The first year of our relationship was intoxicating. He was the kind of boyfriend every girl deserves to have at least once in their life. The overprotective, overly sweet, way-too-perfect boyfriend. The one who makes your single friends jealous and his own friends pissed that he's changed. We spent our days together, under the sun. And our summer nights were spent under the stars.

But sophomore year brought rainstorms—and we simply weren't prepared. His mother's passing changed him, understandably so. I loved Dean through it to the best of my ability, but once the broken relationship between our fathers rubbed off on ours, Dean's love for everything, and everyone, slowly dissipated—including his love for me.

My eyes made their way back to Kyle. "That . . . um . . . that fight between you and Ari doesn't sound so bad," I said. "I'm sure you'll work it out."

"Maybe," he replied as he looked down and twisted his thumbs. "Have you heard the rumor?"

"Rumor?"

Kyle stared at me longer than usual. "About Ari and Cliff. About what happened the night of the cookout."

Every decision impacts everything that follows. But some decisions aren't always ours to make. Sometimes, in the most unfortunate circumstances, our fate is sealed by the decisions of another.

4
TRAGEDY STRIKES

Every now and then—tragedy strikes. There's not always an explanation, like they'd have you believe, or a laundry list of reasons as to why you ended up in the situation you're in. There's not always a person to blame or a crucial event that shifts you into the perfect spot for irrevocable wreckage. Sometimes, things just happen. Things that will change everything. Things that change you.

"I cannot believe Mrs. Penn threatened you," Casey said as we unpacked our bags and sat in our semicircle of desks.

The last period of the day was study hall, the one and only class the Westcott teachers didn't take very seriously. We were supposed to take advantage of the hour-long block of time to study, but we mostly just caught up on the latest Westcott ongoings.

"Who threatened who?" Buckets asked, rolling his watch around his thin wrist as he leaned back in his chair.

Billy Poland, aka Buckets. He got the nickname Buckets from collecting and dumping gossip to everyone in school. Buckets was creative, witty, slightly devious—and most definitely a Cobalt. He lived in a two-bedroom apartment with his parents and little sister—a life that was a far cry from most of his fellow classmates. Especially the Violets. He sometimes, however, received special attention from them—mainly when they needed him to do their dirty work.

Casey gave me a frightened stare through her glasses, as if to suggest I shouldn't say anything incriminating.

"Hey, Buckets, do you know anything about the new English teacher?" I asked.

"That depends. What do you need to know and why?"

"Where did she come from? Why is she here? When is she leaving?"

He rolled his neck from side to side, his blond hair staying perfectly intact.

"Come on, Buckets, you owe me."

Buckets cocked his head to the side to glare at me. "Are you seriously going to hold the Lana story over my head the rest of our time here at Westcott? I've told you—I hated that for her. I just did what I had to do."

When he came to Westcott through the lottery, everything started as a lighthearted hobby for Buckets. That was, of course, until he realized he could turn his hobby into a business—a business based on favors. He began leaking photos and videos for his fellow classmates at WH in exchange for a casual camaraderie with the Violets. An interesting, slightly pathetic strategy, but it worked for him.

"You don't have to leak videos for people; you choose to," Casey argued. "And you never should have released that one. It ruined a lot of people's lives."

I leaned forward. "How about this? If you give me the lowdown on Mrs. Penn, count it all water under the bridge," I said.

"Count what for what?" Kyle descended quickly into the neighboring desk.

Buckets jumped. "Jesus, Winchester!"

"Sorry." Kyle ran his hand through his dark hair, his bicep peeking out from his sleeve. "Didn't mean to scare you."

"I'm trying to convince Buckets to give me some information," I said. "That's all."

"Not about Cliff?" Kyle wrinkled his brow. "I told you, Sonny; he didn't do it."

"No, not about Cliff. And you don't know that. Buckets is the only person who can tell us if Cliff handed the video of Lana over to him."

We all glanced at Buckets.

He held up his hands. "Absolutely not. I don't reveal my clients' identities under any circumstance."

"Well, I can assure you," said Kyle, "that Cliff wasn't responsible for the leak. As much as he hated Mr. Hill, he would never do that to Lana. He loved her."

"Cliff loves himself," Buckets said.

Kyle glared at him, his eyes eventually landing on Casey's. "Hi," he said with a smile.

Casey waved at Kyle from across the circle.

"If I tell you what I know about Mrs. Penn, you'll let this Lana jumble go?" Buckets asked.

I held up my hand like I was swearing. "You have my word."

"Mrs. Penn? The English teacher?" Kyle leaned forward in his seat.

"You know her?" I asked.

"No, but I heard she moved here from Florida to take Russell's position."

"And her son, Guy, is trying out for the wrestling team," added Buckets. "Supposedly, he's a pretty tough guy."

64

"That explains all of the scars," I mumbled under my breath as my mind flashed to the stranger in the hallway. "That must have been who I met outside of Mrs. Penn's classroom this morning." I rubbed my arms and shifted in my seat.

"Did he do something to you?" Kyle asked, reading my expression.

"Not exactly," I replied. "He was just a little strange."

"Like mother, like son," Buckets said.

Kyle reached into his book bag and pulled out a thick binder. "I don't know anything about Guy. But my dad told me Mrs. Penn came highly recommended. Oh, and also, she's a total hard-ass."

"Yeah." I nodded. "I've gathered as much."

Suddenly, Winston plopped down in the empty desk beside me.

"Where have you been?" I asked.

"Culture Club meeting. I'm the founder, remember?" Winston stacked his books in front of him.

"Don't you have to be an impressive human to be the founder of such a club?" Buckets asked. "Or at the very least, semi-cultured?"

"As it turns out, you can be an impressive human just by *saying* you're cultured," Winston replied.

Casey took her glasses off her face, breathing on the frames and wiping them against her shirt. "Innovative."

"We still don't know why Mr. Russell was allegedly fired," Kyle said.

I rapped my knuckles against the desk to get everyone's attention. "We have to go visit Mr. Russell. Today. We have to ask him what happened."

I looked around the circle, waiting for a pushback. It came quicker than I thought.

"Hell no," Buckets said.

"Come on, Buckets! Don't you want to know what happened? How many times did he stay after school to help you edit your photos? Casey, Mr. Russell always gave you extra-credit opportunities, and extra time to finish them when you had to attend to your brothers. And Kyle? He always extended your deadlines after a long week of football practices. Winston, I'm sure he did some nice things for you."

"Not really," he replied, examining his fingernails. "I only knew him for a year."

"Look, if it hadn't been for him, I wouldn't even be one of the Chosen Ten," I said. "Mr. Russell inspired me to start writing."

"All the more reason not to go on a scavenger hunt," Kyle said. "You and I have a lot to lose if we get caught starting an inquisition at an ex-teacher's house." He spun his pointer finger in the air. "We all do."

"Something tells me you have nothing to worry about, *Winchester*," Winston said.

Kyle leaned in. "You might think my dad gives me special treatment, but he doesn't, okay? We aren't close. At all." He looked around the circle, seemingly embarrassed by his distant relationship with his dad. "Don't think for one second he wouldn't write me up if he had to."

I glanced at Kyle as he fell back into his chair, his eyes facing downward toward the top of his desk. Everyone always assumed he and his dad were close, but after his parents split when he was ten, his dad moved out and their relationship took a turn for the worse.

"You kids do what you want." Winston flipped through his books. "I'd rather stick my head under the piano keys while Mike Chang plays another plagiarized composition than go visit Mr. Russell."

"You're going," I said.

"Fine." Winston closed his book and locked his hands. "My demands are simple. I want a 7-Eleven pit stop on the way there, not on the way back. And I get to sit in the front seat with full control, not partial, over the radio."

"Ladies get the front seat in my car," Kyle said, staring at Casey.

"You are shameless, you know that?" Winston asked him.

"Put your dukes down, children," said Buckets. "We can't go."

We looked over at Buckets, who was looking down at his tablet lighting up like a Christmas tree.

"Why not?" I asked.

Buckets held up the bright screen toward our faces, shining the darkest of news.

There's not always an explanation when tragedy strikes, because how could there be? Sometimes, things just happen. And the most tragic thing of all is that you rarely ever see it coming.

5

SECRETS

Secrets. We all have them; we all tell them. Some tell secrets to protect others; others tell secrets to protect themselves. My mother once told me there's nothing worse than being someone's secret. My father tells me there's nothing harder than keeping one. I happen to think the worst of all is knowing a secret is being kept from you.

News of Mr. Russell's suicide took the entire town of Westcott by shock. Principal Winchester closed school for the rest of the week so the students and staff had time to "process and reflect."

Coming back to WH the following Monday was a bit of a drab to say the least. Rumors were flying around the halls at rapid speed. Most of them were centered on Mr. Russell's undeniable depression and stress caused by the loss of his beloved job at Westcott.

I held my locker open, staring blankly inside. Suddenly, the smell of musty cedar wood overwhelmed me.

"I'm really sorry to hear about Mr. Russell. I heard you two were close." A male body leaned against the neighboring lockers.

I slowly tilted my head back in fear and glanced to the right. "Oh. It's you."

"Expecting someone else?" Jacob asked.

"Hoping it wasn't a certain someone."

"Anyone I'd know?"

"Guy Penn?" I yawned.

"Doesn't ring a bell," he said. "Why were you hoping not to run into him?"

"I don't know," I replied. "I had a strange encounter with him. And his mom." My suggestive eyes were hopefully communicating what I couldn't say regarding my feelings toward Mrs. Penn.

"What did he say to you?" Jacob asked.

I yawned again as I closed my locker. "It's not important."

Jacob placed his hand on my left shoulder. "Are you okay?"

His touch was strong. Or maybe I was weak.

"I'm just tired." I rubbed the back of my neck, which felt tight as a knotted rope. "I haven't slept since I heard the news. I'm also trying to work on the most important paper of my life."

"So things are going smoothly, then?"

"Very," I said, digging my fingertips into my skin.

"The Westcott Awards. That's a big deal here, right?" Jacob propped his arm up on the lockers and leaned into our conversation.

"The biggest," I replied, my eyes roaming his chest.

"Maybe I can help. What do you want your paper to be about?"

I paused, giving thought to his question. "I think I want to write a memoir. A 'pocumentary' of sorts."

Jacob smirked. "What the hell is that?"

"A documentary but in paper form. A pocumentary."

"What is it with kids at this school and their abbreviations?" he asked. "I heard someone say 'brock' earlier. A bro—"

"And a jock." I nodded. "Yeah, yeah."

"What about me?" he asked, gesturing to himself.

I looked down, tracing the floral pattern on my shirt with my eyes. "What about you?"

"I've got a good story," he said.

I shook my head aggressively, unsure of whether I thought his suggestion was ridiculous or if I was just extremely agitated. "I have to write something impactful."

"Are you saying I'm incapable of making an impact?"

"You're sixteen," I replied. "How deep could your story possibly be?"

"You know, if I were like most guys, I'd tell you about the time I saved a damsel in distress from a burning building, while on crutches, which resulted in two hundred thirty-six scars on my body."

"Man." My eyes left the light blue flowers on my blouse and locked in with his. "That's incredibly cringy."

"Really? I thought you'd be impressed."

"You're just one scar shy." I attempted to smile through my weakened state.

Jacob held up his hands. "Whoa, hold on. Is that a smile?"

"I think the correct term is half smile." I slung my backpack onto my other shoulder.

"Are you sure?" He studied my face with exaggerated focus. "It looked a whole lot like a full smile."

"Or—it could just be a slightly delirious grin caused by the result of sheer exhaustion."

"I can work with that," he said.

My eyes widened. "High standards."

"You know, you're right. I don't know if you could write an entire paper on me." He coughed. "You could on my dad."

"Yeah? And why's that?"

Just then, a commotion from the other end of the hall caught my eye. JC was engulfed in what appeared to be an intense conversation with Mrs. Penn. I watched as the two went back and forth with one another.

"He's a pretty famous lawyer back in Long Beach."

I returned my full attention back to Jacob. "Wait a minute. Harrison. Is your dad Ron Harrison?"

"My dad is Ron Harrison," Jacob answered.

"He was the lead criminal defense lawyer on the Farrah Klein case." I straightened up, bouncing on the toes of my Converses. "The girl who was wrongly convicted of murdering her sorority sisters, only to be found innocent two years later. Your dad helped set her free. I followed that case from start to finish. It was one of the biggest turnaround convictions in history."

"That's him." Jacob crossed his arms in front of his chest. "But he's since retired."

"What does he do now?" I asked.

Jacob looked down and flicked his thumbnail against his middle finger. "Mostly just PI work."

"Do you think your dad would let me interview him for my paper?" I stared at him with begging eyes.

Jacob stared into my eyes, smiling with his, then dropped his head—and his smile. "I think I could pull some strings. You have to do something for me, though."

I suddenly had a more willing attitude. "Anything."

"Is there any chance you could introduce me to Norah Soros?" he asked.

And then, just like that, my willing attitude took a nosedive. I gave him a blank stare as my face began to burn. It was at that moment I realized the flirtation between Jacob and me must have existed only in my head—and how incredibly wrong you could be about a person, regardless of how right it felt.

"I heard you know each other pretty well."

"Who the heck told you that?" I asked.

He pointed his thumb behind his shoulder. "Winston. The kid who wears the scarves."

"I see you don't pick up on sarcasm as well as I thought."

"So you don't know her?"

"Sort of," I replied, wrinkling my nose. "But why do you need my help with that?"

"Well, I heard she's dating someone. I figured it'd be less creepy if someone else casually introduced us."

I clenched the straps of my book bag so tightly that my fingers hurt. "You do know it's slightly unbecoming to hit on someone who has a boyfriend, right?"

"I'm not going to hit on her. I just figured she'd remember me if they were to break up. I heard they were on-again, off-again."

"Why are you so sure you want Norah to remember you? Because believe me, that doesn't always work out in your favor. Besides, you don't even know her."

"Actually, I do," he replied. "Well, sort of. I saw her over the summer."

"Where?" I asked.

"At a house party some guy in my neighborhood was throwing. She looked so beautiful. She was wearing this red dress. I'll never forget that dress."

I rolled my eyes at the thought of a simple red dress having such power.

"I was sure she had to be some years older than me, but when I saw her here at Westcott—I don't know—I thought it was fate." He paused. "I just figured she'd save my number in the event she becomes single any time soon. That's all."

"That's quite presumptuous," I said.

Jacob exhaled slightly. "So, will you introduce me?"

"Absolutely not."

"Come on!"

I placed my hand in between us. "If you want a go at Norah for reasons I can't understand, you'll have to get in line and fend for yourself like any good Violet would do."

75

"That's too bad," Jacob said. "By the looks of it, you might be trailing behind most of the Chosen Ten."

"More like the chosen four," I mumbled under my breath. "And how would you know that?"

"Because there's some serious competition this year. I'm sure a one-on-one, in-depth, exclusive interview with a famous criminal defense lawyer would put you a step above the rest. I can even get you that interview as early as Saturday morning."

"Saturday?" I asked, considering the trade-off.

Jacob nodded. "But if you're not interested . . . ," he said, luring me in.

Although I wanted to say no, nothing meant more to me than writing a good piece for the awards. Not even keeping what was left of my dignity. "Fine." I relaxed my shoulders. "I'll introduce you. But that's it."

He put his hands up in front of him. "That's all I'm asking."

"Excuse me for a minute," I said, slowly brushing by him.

"See you Saturday?" he shouted as I walked down the hallway.

I reached the opposite end of the hall and cautiously approached JC, who was leaning up against the wall near the faculty break room—an unlikely place for a guy like him to hang out.

"You in trouble with Penn?" I asked him.

He rolled his head against the brick wall, his orange headphones hanging from his back pocket. "What's it to you? And are you sure you want to be caught speaking to me?"

"You do know my sister is Lana Carter, right? I'm no newcomer to scandals."

"What do you want, Sonny?"

"I wanted to welcome you back," I said.

"I'm not welcome," he replied. "And I don't need you to pretend like I am."

"Look, I just want to know what you and Mrs. Penn were talking about."

"Why do you care?" JC asked.

"Because I care about you," I replied. "We're friends."

"Oh, right. I must have missed your friendly texts and calls all summer."

"JC . . ."

"Save it, Sonny."

"Look, I may have kept my distance until things cooled down, but I never stopped caring about you. None of us did."

"You just can't speak to me, right?"

I paused, took a deep breath, and exhaled loudly. At Westcott, aligning yourself with the right people could make or break you. So, when a fellow classmate went

77

under, it was expected that everyone would scurry like cockroaches at the sight of a scandal. And when JC's incident occurred—everyone did exactly that.

"I'm speaking to you now," I said. "Doesn't that count for something?"

He sized me up for a solid minute, clearly unsure of whether or not he could trust me. "Look, I can't talk about this. Not here. Meet me at the country club after school." He shifted on his feet as his eyes scanned the hallways.

"Okay," I replied. "I'll be there."

The Westcott Country Club. Home to self-proclaimed professional golfers, tennis stars, and one of the hardest working waitresses on the planet—my mother, Darcy Carter. When I was a kid, her name had a special kind of ring to it. But when I got older, it was hard to believe how dull it started sounding.

"You two let me know if you need anything else, okay?" Mom placed our drinks down on the table.

"We will," I said as we watched her walk back into the kitchen.

"Your mom works here?" JC asked.

I studied him. "Yeah. They let women work now." I grabbed my green tea and pulled it toward me. "It's sort of a thing that caught on."

"That's not what I meant, smart-ass. I thought she was a registered nurse."

I tried getting comfortable in our off-white booth, although I was beginning to realize comfort wasn't a word in the design plan. "She quit six months ago."

"To work here?" he asked.

"I was just as shocked as you are," I replied. "I think it's a midlife-crisis type of thing."

"Why didn't you tell me?"

"It's not exactly something that rolls off the tongue in a town like Westcott. Especially while talking to you. Your mom's day consists of massages, salads, and Pilates."

"I would never want my mom working at a café, serving perverted old men their Reubens and rum all day." JC took a sip of his soda, which had a fancy cocktail umbrella in it—with the club's emblem on both sides. "No offense."

"What about that sentence made you think I'd take offense?" I asked.

"Sorry," he said. "My mom also walks the dog a lot. That's something . . . else . . . she does. . . ." JC took the cocktail umbrella out and tossed it to the side.

"She's lucky your dad took care of her after their divorce," I said.

"I think it was a no-prenup type of thing."

I nodded and took a sip of my tea. "So, what were you and Mrs. Penn talking about earlier?"

JC cracked his neck to relieve some pressure. "She was pretty pissed at me."

"And why's that?" I asked.

"I may have pointed at my headphones when she tried speaking to me in the hallway this morning."

"JC!"

"What? She was just reminding me to get to class. I still had five minutes before the bell rang."

"That's pretty disrespectful," I said.

"One could say it's disrespectful to come between a guy and his Led Zeppelin songs."

I raised my brows. "One could say you're pushing it."

He ran his strong hand through his curly brown hair. "What's the point in trying to be the nice guy anymore? No one thinks it." JC's voice softened. "And with this stupid one-year ineligibility, wrestling is off the table for me."

I rolled my hands into a ball. "You're lucky it's only a one-year suspension. You know how strict the SCC is."

The Westcott High SCC, aka the *student conduct contract*. Those daunting papers that hung over our heads like thousand-pound weights. Every student had to sign one upon entering the school. It was essentially a rule book mapping out the various regulations us Westcott kids were required to follow—in and outside of school. If you broke any of the rules, even one, you got written up. And if you got written up more than once, you got kicked out of Westcott. No questions asked. No second chances. No mercy.

JC picked up his glass and started swirling the ice cubes around. "Have you talked to Piper recently?" The ice cubes clicked against his glass.

"No. She doesn't talk much anymore—to anyone."

"Especially not to me."

I leaned in. "Can you blame her, JC?"

JC stared off into the room, the weight of his suspension showing across his face. It looked like he'd been awake for months. He seemed tired—but the kind of tired innocent people feel when they've been wrongly accused of something.

"What if I could?" he asked.

My eyes left the tabletop and shifted toward his. "What are you talking about?"

JC looked side to side and then back at me. "What if I could blame her?"

I poked my head toward him. "For?"

"During one of my practices last year, I saw Piper walk into the gym. She discreetly walked by me and sat on the bleachers."

"Yeah. So?"

"A little strange," he said, "considering she's typically too busy to text me back—much less come watch me wrestle. But I brushed it off, waved, and went on with my practice." He took a sip of his soda, collecting ice cubes in his mouth. "She didn't look like she normally does, Sonny. She looked disheveled. Nervous. She was wearing a baggy T-shirt and biker shorts."

"Piper?"

"Exactly," he said. "Next day, your dad's suddenly picking me up by the back of my shirt and escorting me out of the cafeteria for a bag search." He shook his head. "It was the last day I saw any of you—because after they ransacked my bag, I was suspended."

"I remember," I said, dropping my chin to my chest. "But what did any of that have to do with Piper?"

"Nothing." He shifted in his seat. "Until I remembered she slipped something into my bag before leaving the gym that night."

Suddenly, I sunk into the uncomfortable booth.

"I thought it was a note," he continued. "We did that sometimes . . . wrote letters back and forth. We exchanged a quick smile, and then she walked out of the gym. I thought nothing of it, and I forgot to check my bag after practice, but a week into my suspension . . . it hit me."

I leaned in. "What are you saying?"

"It was Piper," he said. "She planted the answer key in my bag."

At Westcott, there was one thing more frowned upon than cheating on your boyfriend with the history teacher— and that was getting caught cheating on a test.

"Seriously, JC?" I was repulsed by his accusation. "That's your position? Piper framed you?"

He rolled up his sleeves, his veins bulging from his arms. "It's not a position, Sonny. She did it. How else could that paper get into my wrestling bag?"

"Maybe you put it in there," I said.

"Jesus." His taut voice stepped forward. "Do you really think I'm that stupid? Why would I risk my wrestling career by cheating on our end-of-year exam? How would I even have access to the answer key? And if I did, I'd never carry it around in my gym bag for anyone to see."

I gave him a suspicious look. "Did you tell your dad you thought Piper framed you?"

"Not exactly." He gently flicked the table with his finger.

With narrowed eyes, I waited patiently for his follow-up statement.

"I told my dad it was mine," he said. "That I stole it."

"Why would you do that?"

JC stared down at the table in a daze. "Because I refuse to rat on Piper. I can't do that to her."

"So you take the fall for something you didn't do?" I asked.

"Look, Sonny. I don't know why she did it. But there has to be a reason. If I accused her of framing me, it could start a war. And nothing is worth never getting to see or talk to Piper again. Not even saving face."

"Why would you want to speak to her again? If what you're saying is true?"

"Because she means everything to me, Sonny. She's my life. We planned to go to Princeton together, and I don't want to go without her. I don't know what inspired her to turn on me, but I need to be here when she's ready to come clean," he said. "I need to stay. For her."

"Come on, JC. Piper aside, I find it hard to believe you'd put your tail between your legs and take on these accusations."

His eyes sunk. "Hey, I love that little lady. I got to be her fool."

"What?"

"The Led," he replied.

I rolled my eyes. "Do you realize how ridiculous this sounds?" With crossed arms, I leaned forward. "Why would Piper plant the answer key in your backpack, tip off my dad, and ruin your wrestling career?"

He shrugged. "Let me know if you can figure it out. Because I've spent all summer trying to wrap my brain around it, and I still can't understand why." He reached into his back pocket and pulled out a dirty white envelope, tossing it onto the table. "And while you're at it, let me know if you can figure this one out too."

I removed the folded piece of paper from the envelope, ironing it out in front of me with flat hands. "What is this?"

JC cracked his knuckles. "It appears to be a riddle."

" 'No one is safe at Geraldine's,' " I read aloud. "The coffee shop on Nelser Street?"

"I guess so," he replied.

"Who gave this to you?"

JC took a deep breath. "When I got suspended and was sent home to finish sophomore year, I nearly lost my mind. I still wrestled, sparring with my brother in our gym, but nothing was taking my mind off of Piper. So I started running. I ran for miles, every night, through my neighborhood and down the boulevard. I got pretty good at it too, for a wrestler. And then one night, a week before I came back to school, I went on a long run to mentally prepare myself. As I approached the tail end of my run, I saw an SUV parked outside of my house. I was pretty far back, and it was getting dark, but I recognized the car. I started picking up my pace, but the taillights lit up and the car sped off into the opposite direction before I could get to my driveway."

I scooted to the edge of the booth's seat, completely fascinated and petrified by his storytelling.

"So I started running full speed ahead, and when I got to my front porch, I saw this envelope. All it said was—"

" 'Jeremy Coleman,' " I said, staring down at the envelope. "I've only ever heard one person call you by your real name. He said referring to yourself by your initials is not only a form of laziness, it's also—"

"A missed opportunity to show confidence in who I truly am," JC said. "Which makes no sense, by the way."

My heart began to race as I looked into JC's brown eyes.

"Mr. Russell." He nodded. "That's whose car I saw speeding off down my street."

I fell back against the booth, my head bouncing from the impact. "Wait a minute. Mr. Russell? Why would he drop this on your doorstep?"

"No clue." JC shrugged again. "I tried calling him, but he never answered his phone. I told myself I'd wait to talk to him on my first day back at school, but when I came back, I realized he'd been fired. That's when I knew something was up. I planned to go visit him after school that day, but then I got the news that he was dead."

"Why didn't you show up on the first day of school?"

"It was Winchester's idea for me to come back the next day," he said. "He thought showing up on the first day would cause too much commotion or some BS."

"I saw you pulling into the parking lot when school was over," I said.

"I saw you too." JC nodded. "I was turning in some updated forms."

I looked down at the paper. "What do you think Mr. Russell is trying to tell you?" I asked. "Do you think he's trying to show you why Piper framed you?"

"That's my guess," he replied. "Why else would he give this to me?"

I read the riddle again. "What could this mean?"

"I don't know," he replied. "But until I figure it out, the silver lining is that I'm allowed to stay at Westcott and get off with a write-up."

"One that cost you everything."

"Not Piper." He dropped his head to his chest. "Not yet."

JC's eyes disappeared under his eyelids, reappearing shortly after—even more lifeless than before. And although there were so many uncertainties in the air, in that moment, I knew he was telling the truth.

"Let me look into this." I folded the piece of paper, then placed it inside the envelope and tucked it into my back pocket. "I'll be quiet while I do."

JC took a sip of soda. "Knock yourself out."

I exhaled. "I think you should know Mrs. Penn's son is trying out for the wrestling team."

"I heard." He checked the time on his cell phone. "I have to go. I'm meeting Jacob at the park courts to shoot hoops."

"Jacob?" I sat up straight. "You know him?"

"Sort of. He came to my house for a party over the summer. He lives a couple of blocks down from me."

I blinked. "That was *your* party?"

"Well, it was my brother's. I don't think anyone would have come if it were my party."

I looked down at his cell phone. "Jacob plays basketball?"

"Plays?" He paused. "Yeah, you could say that. He's freaking sick."

"Freaking sick?" I asked. "As in incredibly talented?"

JC wrote his club ID number down on the receipt to pay for our drinks. "As in freaking sick."

"Wait, is he trying out for the team?" I asked.

"That's the plan," he said.

My heart began to beat at an uncomfortable speed as my mind flashed to Dean.

"I didn't see Jacob much that night, though," he said, taking one last sip of his soda. "The night of the party. He popped in and popped out."

I grinned. "Did you slip in the puddle?"

JC gave me a blank stare as he chewed on an ice cube. "I gave up on trying to understand your jokes years ago."

I picked up the cocktail umbrella and threw it at his chest. "I heard Jacob was drooling over Norah all night."

"Norah?"

"Yeah. Norah Soros."

"Norah wasn't at the party," he said.

Confusion crossed my face. "I'm sure she was. Red dress?"

"Sonny. My brother would never invite Norah Soros to our house. I can promise you that."

"Maybe she slid in without you noticing," I said.

"Everyone notices when Norah Soros slides into a room. She wasn't there," he said, shifting out of the booth. "He must have been talking about somebody else."

Secrets. We all have them. We all tell them. Maybe the only thing worse than learning a secret is being kept from you is knowing you aren't the type to let it go.

6
THE FALL

There is one irrefutable truth in life: every girl will fall down. If you're lucky, you'll enjoy a slow, graceful fall. One that's cushioned with supportive friends and loving family. Or one in which your blood dries up before you've broken skin on your knees. That's the kind of tumble you take if you're fortunate. And if you aren't? You become the girl who free-falls. And there are no ledges to grab onto. And there's no one there at the bottom to stop you from calamity. Because some girls don't just fall down; some fall from grace.

On Friday mornings, the student body attended a weekly rally in the auditorium. It was essentially a school-wide meeting where we received information regarding the newest events at Westcott. In actuality, it was a chance for us to engage with one another on a large scale.

"I can't believe Jacob likes Norah. Does everyone like that trollop?" Winston leaned against a navy-blue folding chair.

"Trollop? Who's the poet now?" I rested both elbows on my knees and cupped my hands under my chin. Below a blue-and-white Westcott High banner, Principal Winchester was setting up his microphone in preparation for his speech. The freshly waxed stage on which he stood was as big as his ego.

"And thanks for telling him I could introduce him to Norah," I said.

"It's not my fault. I misread his ability to recognize sarcasm."

"I figured as much."

"So?" Winston asked. "Did you do it?"

"Yes. It was brief and miserable and awkward all at once, and I wish to forget it entirely."

"I'm assuming Norah flirted with him?"

"Of course," I said.

"Conveniently forgetting she's dating Dean?"

"Naturally."

Winston shook his head. "Trollop."

"Can we talk about something else?" I asked.

"Let's talk about your conversation with JC," he replied.

I shot up from my seat. "Keep your voice down! I don't want anyone finding out I'm looking into this."

With narrowed eyes, Winston tilted his head. "You don't honestly believe him, do you?"

"Would you—" I looked side to side and stepped forward. "Shhh!"

"So what's your plan?" He shook his head. "You mentioned you had a plan?"

"You'll find out tomorrow night when we meet with the rest of the gang. I'm calling a meeting."

Just then, I spotted Buckets sitting against the wall on the other side of the dreary room. His legs were extended out in front of him, and his eyes were glued to the tablet on his lap. It was his usual look.

"Excuse me for a second," I said as I slowly walked away.

I pushed through the crowd, eventually landing in front of Buckets. With crossed arms, I stood and waited for him to acknowledge me. He eventually looked up.

"Were you at Dustin Coleman's summer party?" I asked.

Buckets took a sip of his energy drink, keeping eye contact. "Sit. You look suspicious."

I nestled close to him, my ripped blue jeans almost blending in against the navy-blue Berber carpet.

"I see you don't listen," he said dryly. "I thought we agreed to change our investigative ways after what happened to Mr. Russell."

"Were you there or not?"

"What makes you think I'd go to that party?" he asked.

"Because you're Buckets. What good is your nickname if you don't collect information to spill? And what better place to collect gossip than a summer party?"

Buckets sucked in his cheeks. "Wow," he said. "Good work. If I needed an assistant, I'd take your resume."

"So?" I said. "Were you there?"

"I may have stopped by," he replied.

"Was Norah Soros there?"

"I can assure you if Norah Soros was at the party, I would have skipped it."

"So she wasn't?"

Buckets's eyes continually scanned the audience of high schoolers, never settling. "No," he replied. "Not that I know of."

"Why would Jacob lie?" I whispered.

Buckets looked at my lips. "What?"

"Nothing." I shook my head. "Look, I'm calling a group meeting tomorrow night. I need you to be there."

"Group? Since when are we a group?"

My eyes rolled to the right. "Don't fight it." I stood up to walk away, pushing myself off the boring beige wall. "I'll text you the address," I said as I dragged my feet toward the other side of the auditorium.

My mind raced with thoughts of Jacob as I weaved through the herd of students. I wanted to write his fib off as a miscommunication or mistake, but my heart told me something was up. After all, with a guy so outwardly perfect, *there almost always is.*

"Happy Friday," Norah said, stopping me in my tracks. Alongside her stood Piper and Ari.

The three were a confusing trio, but we all learned to stop questioning it when they were still friends as junior year began. Not vocally anyway.

"Happy Friday," I replied, my voice at an all-time sarcastic low.

"Tell me, Sonny. What were you and Buckets just chatting about?" Norah asked.

I began to wonder how much longer I could put up with Norah's relentless snarky remarks and condescending tones. But I decided, for that moment, I'd play along.

"Why is it any of your concern, Norah?"

I looked at Ari as she avoided making eye contact with me. She and I met sophomore year when Kyle introduced me to his new girlfriend. Her dark wardrobe, pounds of cheap jewelry, and emotionally unstable personality were the last things that confused me about her. Because Ari Ziegler was confusing for numerous additional reasons, including why she'd date a Violet in the first place. And why a Violet would date her.

"I certainly hope it wouldn't involve any information from your little lunch date with JC at the club on Monday," Norah said.

"Are you spying on me now?"

"Look, Sonny. Aligning yourself with a guy like JC will tarnish what's left of your pathetic reputation," she said. "I'm just trying to have your back."

"And tell me, Norah, is that before or after you swivel the knife in?"

"Let's just go," Piper softly suggested.

It was almost satisfying to hear her voice. I looked over into her nervous eyes, hoping to feel some sort of connection. It never came.

Norah leaned in close to my ear, her blonde hair brushing my face. "I'd be careful who you speak to."

She turned around; her paint-stained fingers pushed through the air as she walked to the other side of the room.

"What was that all about?" Kyle asked, quietly sneaking up behind me.

His comforting scent swept underneath my nose as I took a deep breath in.

"Just Norah being Norah," I replied. "Hey, I overheard some girls talking about the cookout this morning. The rumor is spreading. Do you think it's true?"

"No," Kyle said, "I don't think so."

"Maybe you should ask Cliff. Just for good measure."

He hesitated. "Yeah, I'll talk to him."

"Kyle . . ."

"I'll talk to him," he said. "I promise."

His doubt was unsettling.

"I need you to meet us somewhere tomorrow night," I told him. "Are you free?"

"I can be."

Just then, I saw Casey darting toward us out of the corner of my eye.

"I can't accept this," she said as she approached Kyle and me, interrupting our conversation. She stretched out her hand, which held money.

Kyle's brown eyes looked down on her unsteady hand. He took a step forward. "Yes, you can. It's no sweat."

"I can't," she said. "Really. Take it." She stretched her hand further.

"I'm not taking it back. It's a gift." Kyle gently pushed away Casey's hand.

"A very large gift," she replied.

"That's a matter of opinion."

"It's too much," she said.

"It's not."

Casey struggled for words. "You really don't have to do this."

He shrugged his shoulders. "I know."

"I—I can't pay you back." She looked down at her dirty pink sneakers; the right toe had a small hole, and the edges were frayed.

Curiosity crossed Kyle's face. "That would sort of be antithetical to the whole gift thing."

I silently applauded Kyle's intellectual reply.

"Why are you doing this?" Casey asked, staring down at the one-hundred-dollar bill.

"Because I want to," he replied.

"Well, what can I do for you?"

"What makes you think you have to do something for me?"

Casey stared into Kyle's eyes.

"Again . . . antithetical," he said.

She folded the money and tucked it into her pocket. "I want to do something."

"How about this? Why don't you get your phone fixed so I can text you sometime?" Kyle looked at me. "If my wife won't mind?"

I gave him a playful glare. "I'll allow it."

Casey's face lit up. Whether it was Kyle's sweet nature or the joke that caused the grin to appear, I wasn't sure. But she smiled on.

Kyle stared at her lips, seemingly in awe. "And you said you couldn't pay me back." He tapped her upper arm and walked toward his seat.

I watched Casey as she watched him walk away—the first of many times to come.

"Everyone find a chair!" Principal Winchester shouted into the microphone.

"Come on, ladies. You heard the man." Winston shoveled us along.

Casey and I scooted toward the middle of our normal row. "I tried calling you last night," I said.

"My mom was over," she replied through her hoarse voice. "I was up all night trying to process the eventful evening." She paused. "Did I tell you she came back around?"

"Winston mentioned it," I replied. "So I'm assuming it went poorly?"

"Poorer than poor."

I climbed over the legs of a few of my peers. "Is she clean yet?"

"What do you think?"

"Do you think she wants you and your brothers to come home?" I asked.

Casey took her seat in a chair, bringing her knees to her chest. "I never want to see her again," she replied. "Westcott is my home now."

I wondered how truly tragic one's life must be to consider Westcott High a home. Then again, when your home isn't your home, I suppose you learn to lower your standards.

"What does a guy like Kyle see in me?" Casey asked.

"A guy like Kyle?"

"A rich guy," she said.

I shifted in my seat. "Money isn't everything, Casey."

"That's what people who have it say."

"Kyle is different."

"Yeah," she replied. "Isn't every guy?"

Principal Winchester continued with his desperate plea to get hundreds of students into order. It was a job I didn't envy. "Everyone quiet down," he said into the mic, his lackadaisical tone falling just short of encouraging us.

"Not to mention he's that man's kid." Casey nodded in Principal Winchester's direction. "He'd never go for someone like me."

"He went for Ari," I replied.

"Ari's cool. And interesting."

"And you're what?" I asked.

"I study tornadoes," she said. "Ari writes and sings music. The two are wildly different."

100

"Look, lighten up on yourself. Just because Kyle's last name is Winchester doesn't mean he's anything like his dad. In fact, I know he's not."

"How do you know that?"

"They don't have a relationship," I said. "Not one like you'd expect. His parents got divorced when he was younger; he hardly knows his dad."

"Are he and his mom close?" Casey asked.

"Very." I nodded as Mrs. Winchester danced across my mind. "She's like a second mother to me."

"I don't know," Casey continued. "I still don't think I'm going to text him."

"Hey," Winston said as he reached for a bag of candy from his backpack. "Three o'clock."

I quickly turned my head to see Dean sitting by himself. A Westcott hoodie covered his hair, but his puffy red face peeked out over the side of the blue fabric. He stared straight ahead as his tears fell straight down.

"Today's the anniversary," Winston said. "That must be why he's crying."

I stared at Dean. "That's not why."

"All right, everyone listen up." Principal Winchester spoke into the mic. "Now I know it's been quite the first two weeks so far. For those of you who may not be aware, our dear friend Mr. Russell suddenly and unexpectedly passed away. I know that many of you were very close to

101

him, and there are resources available to any of you who may be struggling with accepting this loss. Everyone will receive a flyer, on your way out, that will provide all of the information to connect you to those resources—"

"A pamphlet." Winston smacked on his gum. "That's what we were missing."

I slapped his knee. "Quiet!"

"Oh, please. He can't hear us over his tie."

"Seriously, what color is that?" said Casey. "It's the brightest yellow I've ever seen."

"Maybe he's wearing it in remembrance of his *dear friend*," Winston said.

Principal Winchester gave the mic a few taps to ensure everyone could hear him. "Please do not take one if you intend on throwing it straight into the trash can or onto the floor," he said. "Mr. Randolph, that means you."

Laughs broke out all across the room.

"At least he takes a firm stance against littering," Casey said.

Winston slowly clapped. "He's so brave."

I grinned as I looked forward.

"Moving on . . . Since we didn't get to have our weekly rally last Friday, I didn't get a chance to properly introduce everyone to our newest English teacher, Mrs. Penn." He motioned for her to come forward. "Mrs. Penn, if you would, please come say a few words."

I grabbed both of my armrests as she approached the microphone. She wore a tight purple dress that looked almost painted on. Her stilettos clanked against the stage as her thin frame swayed side to side. Someone from the back of the auditorium whistled, and the room broke out into more scattered laughs.

"All right, please keep your opinions to yourself," Principal Winchester shouted as he held his hand in the air.

Winston dropped his head against the back of his chair and closed his eyes. "I'm beginning to wonder if we will ever get through this rally."

I smiled at him and then focused my attention on the stage.

There Mrs. Penn stood, in all her beauty and rigidness, and introduced herself as if she weren't everything that I knew she was. And for a few minutes, she spoke as if she were truly a nice, demure person. Even I was almost convinced—almost.

Casey leaned toward me. "She is so pretty."

Mrs. Penn's eyes suddenly met mine. I took a swift breath as she stared back at me. "I do hope we have a fantastic year together," she said into the mic. "All of us."

Winston leaned his head to the left. "I think she's talking to you," he said, his eyes barely open.

"And perhaps only you," Casey said.

"Thank you, Mrs. Penn. Okay, let's see here." Principal Winchester continued looking through his notes. "I'd like everyone's undivided attention on this matter. Randolph, are you with us?"

"I'm with you, sir," he shouted back from the edge of the room. More laughs followed.

"Fantastic. Now, I know that last year the school went through quite the video scandal—"

"Uh-oh." Winston sat up in his seat while my heart sunk into mine.

"Thankfully, there was no truth to it, but it did shed some light on an even bigger matter here at Westcott. As you all know, every student who walks through these doors is required to sign a student conduct contract. Here at Westcott, we have high standards for our student body. If you attend Westcott High, not only do we expect you to excel academically, but you must also conduct yourselves in a positive, productive manner. However, not every student who has walked these halls has done so."

"Lana!" A voice shouted from behind me.

I closed my eyes tightly and tried to ignore all the laughter.

"Shut the hell up, Gavin!" Kyle yelled from a few rows back.

"What are you gonna do, Winchester? Beat me with your silver spoon?" Gavin retorted.

Principal Winchester glared at his son. "All right, that's enough!"

I stared down at my shoes, tapping them against the chair in front of me and wishing someone would knock me out with said spoon.

"So," Principal Winchester continued, "to prevent any similar scenarios from happening again, we've made a few adjustments to the SCC. As you will all see, if you check the contract that was sent to the email we have on file for each of you, we've implemented a new rule."

Everyone reached for their cell phones faster than you could say *conduct,* because if there was one thing every student took incredibly seriously, it was the SCC.

"You will all see—on page two, section three—that anyone who is directly and/or indirectly involved in any sort of pictures and/or video footage being leaked around the school will immediately be written up." Principal Winchester shifted his tie.

Nervous conversations started roaring around the room like thunder.

"Now, I can't understand why any of you would be involved in spreading vicious rumors about your fellow classmates. But I've come to understand that's becoming far too accepted here. Whether it's blackmail or kids being kids, I don't really know, nor do I care. I do know that if you're caught leaking footage or if you're in the footage doing anything outside of how a Westcott student should behave, you will be written up without being given the benefit of the doubt. Perhaps like many before you."

"But, sir! How can we control this? If someone records us doing something they deem inappropriate, how can we help if it's leaked around the school? And how is that our fault?" a student blurted out from the corner of the room.

"If you think about it, sir, you're giving everyone more incentive to leak videos," another student shouted.

"Well, since no one wants to come forward to tell me who recorded and leaked the infamous video from last year, I have no choice but to assume it could be any one of you and put the hammer down. Unless, of course, someone wants to come forward and give me names." Principal Winchester's eyes circled the room. They were met with silence. "Very well, then. The rule stands."

The room burst out into scattered complaints.

Principal Winchester put his hand toward the crowd. "I suggest you all walk the straight and narrow and stay away from cameras. Everyone be on your best behavior this year, yes?"

More bellowing sighs filled the air.

"That's all for today. Please print and sign the updated SCC and turn it into the office first thing Monday morning. No lingering in the hallways; everyone head straight to class. Thank you for your time." Principal Winchester walked off the stage, and everyone started walking toward the back doors.

"Well, there goes my idea to plant a voice recorder in Cliff's . . ."

We came to the end of our row and I turned my head toward Winston.

"Football . . . bag . . . which I was not going to do."

I nodded, my blank eyes fixed on his. "You were, weren't you?"

Winston tossed a piece of candy into his mouth. "Don't judge me."

"Wow. There are some scared people in this room right now," Casey said.

Suddenly, I bumped shoulders with Ari, who was darting toward the exit. Her face was pale, her eyes were angry, and her hands were shaking. "Yeah," I said. "I can see that."

"We'll see you after first." Winston walked with Casey toward the side doors. "And try not to break the SCC between now and then!"

I watched them walk away. "Yeah," I said under my breath. "I'll try."

The auditorium lights dimmed as I made my way toward the back of the room, where I saw the stranger from the hallway standing against the wall. He was staring into my eyes—and his didn't blink—not even once. In one hand was a yellow pamphlet, and in the other a paper bagged lunch.

"Nice gesture," he said as I casually strolled by.

My heart began beating fast. This stranger had a funny way of doing that to a person.

I stopped in my tracks as students passed by me. "I'm sorry?"

"The pamphlet." He held it up in the air. "It's a nice gesture."

"I guess so," I said. "I'm Sonny, by the way. What's your name?"

"Guy," he replied.

I nodded. "Thought so."

"Sonny," he said. "Did you know that most plane crashes occur during the first three or the last eight minutes of a flight?" He began folding the pamphlet into many different directions. "I always assumed it would happen in the middle—when the scared passengers finally decide it's safe to let their guard down."

His well-modulated voice sucked you in like a vacuum.

"Because that's what life does to us, after all. It waits until we've decided we've finally reached flat ground and then"—he held the paper airplane in front of his eyes, inspecting it as he twisted it around—"boom." He dropped the airplane to the floor. "Everything comes crashing down."

The hair on my neck stood up as his tortured soul showed itself. I looked down at the ground and then back up at him.

"Do you ever feel like that?" he asked.

Just then, Jacob leaned down next to us and picked up the paper airplane.

"I think this belongs to you," he said, holding it in front of Guy's face.

Guy blinked, breaking his serious character. "Ah! A noble, no-littering crusader. My favorite kind of jock." He took the airplane back.

"I'm Jacob," he said as he stood close to me, towering over Guy.

Guy stared into his eyes. "Guy Penn."

"Everything okay here?" Jacob asked.

Guy studied him. "More than okay," he replied. "Gotta run. Ms. Pamela from the front desk has a lot of mail for me to deliver today."

The Westcott High mailman was typically a student who needed extra credit, or perhaps just extra attention.

"You're the school's new delivery boy?" I asked.

He put his hands into his ripped jean pockets and walked backward out of the double doors. "Brownie points," he shouted over the heads of our peers. "They're a real thing."

I watched him disappear, but his eerie voice still hovered over me like a dark cloud that wouldn't roll away.

Jacob shook his head. "Weird kid."

"The weirdest," I replied.

"My dad is looking forward to meeting you," Jacob said. "I'll see you tomorrow?"

"Yeah." I paused. "I'll be there. Just text me your address."

Jacob handed me his phone. "I'll need your number first," he said in a kind tone of voice.

I grabbed the cell phone from his hand, hesitantly typing my name into his contacts. "So you will."

Jacob's eyes bounced back and forth between me and his phone. "Hey, um, can I text you, text you?"

"As in?"

"As in more than texting you my address," he said.

"Like what?"

"Like . . . good-morning texts . . . or something?"

I was taken aback by his question. Mainly because it came from somebody who claimed to like someone else.

My thumb hit the save button; then I glanced up at Jacob. He nervously grabbed his backpack straps as his eyes floated around the room. "Uhh . . . yeah . . . sorry. That's probably weird."

I stretched out my hand, which held his cell phone. I knew I should have asked him about Dustin's party. I should have confronted him about Norah and the lie he told. Because things weren't adding up, and something told me I shouldn't trust him. But you know what they say—the kind voice of a guy almost always overpowers your voice of reason. "I like weird," I replied, shrugging my shoulders.

He blinked slowly as he looked me up and down, then took his cell phone from my fingers.

"So can I?" he asked. "Text you?"

I slid my hands into my back pockets. "I don't know. Can you?"

I turned around and walked into the hallway, making my way toward first period. It was the first time I remembered feeling relieved to go to communications class. Which was surprising, because having to communicate with a classroom full of uncommunicative teenagers was the most brutal class of all. I looked down at the floor, counting each step I took.

Suddenly, my cell phone buzzed. I reached into my back pocket and pulled a text message toward my face. It read: A noble, grammar-correcting crusader. My favorite kind of smart-ass. I stared around the hallway, mindlessly smiling into the sea of students. I saved Jacob's name in my phone, exhaled, and walked to class.

They say when the school bell rings at the end of the day, a Westcott student takes their first full breath. It's also been said when you're chasing a rumor, you almost never get to breathe.

"Ari!" I shouted as I chased her down in the parking lot after school. "Wait up!"

She continued walking toward her car, ignoring my request. Ari reached her hand down to open the driver's side door, the sleeve on her tight leather jacket grabbing her wrist.

I reached my hand out to stop her from getting inside. "Are you really pretending you couldn't hear me?" I asked, panting from my mad dash.

"What do you want, Sonny?" Ari scratched around the choker on her neck, her fingers covered with rings. She flipped her brown hair to the side and raised her eyebrows.

"Why were you so eager to leave the rally this morning?" I asked.

She casually brushed the front of her jacket. "What do you mean?"

"Don't play dumb, Ari. I saw your face. You were upset. Maybe a little nervous? You ran out of the room before the lights were dimmed."

"I had places to be," she said.

"Would it have anything to do with the rumor that's going around about you and Cliff?"

Ari looked side to side before stepping toward me. "Are you insane? Don't even give that life. If that gets around to Kyle . . ."

"Too late."

Her face dropped. "He knows?"

"*Is* there something he should know?" I asked.

"You can't be serious? You think I'd hook up with Cliff hours after I broke up with my boyfriend? Especially at a pool party with an ocean full of Violets?" she asked. "I'm not an idiot."

"I was hoping you'd say you wouldn't do that to Kyle," I said.

"That goes without saying."

"Does it?"

Ari twisted the rings on her fingers. "Look, what do you want from me? It didn't happen. It's a stupid rumor."

"I know a thing or two about rumors, Ari. And I know every rumor that circulates around the school is either true or almost true. And eventually, the truth comes out."

Ari's monotone voice was telling. "Admit it, Sonny. This isn't about Cliff. You never liked me for Kyle. I'm too *edgy* for your liking. Girls like you want your guy friends to end up with replicas of you, so you can be 'couple friends' and do couple things together. Things girls like me wouldn't do. Like road trips to the beach in your string bikinis and high-waisted shorts while blasting a combo of

Drake and Blink 182, all to snap perfectly edited photos of yourselves at sunset to puke all over your synchronized Instagram pages. You can't get that with me. And you hate that."

I put my hands behind my hips. "It was certainly a shock to see the two of you together, but I never told Kyle that I didn't approve of you."

"But don't you, though? Disapprove?" Ari's detestation for me was leaking from her pupils.

"Kyle's my best friend," I said. "I want what's best for him. Can't you understand that?"

"I am what's best for him," Ari replied.

"How do you know that, Ari?"

"Because he fell in love with me."

"So what? Your and Kyle's love came quick. And fast love is dangerous love. It doesn't know how to stop, even when it should."

"Well, I guess that's the unfortunate thing about love, Sonny. You don't get to tell it to go away." Ari's choker shifted up and down on her neck as she spoke.

"So you're going to try to get back together with Kyle?" I asked.

"It's all I know to do," Ari replied.

"What . . . did you want to do something different?"

Her eyes began filling with tears—the angry kind. "Are we done here?"

"Look—I think you need to be more careful with this rumor. Especially now that the SCC changed."

"Me?" she asked. "And what about you, Sonny? I heard that you rallied up a gang of students to find out why Mr. Russell was fired. I'm pretty sure that would break student conduct too." She pulled out a vape pen.

I grabbed it from her mouth and put it in my pocket. "So would this!"

Ari successfully got into her car and started the engine, which shook the pavement beneath my feet.

"Who told you we were investigating?"

She ran her middle finger over her bottom lip, looking into her visor mirror. "Who do you think?"

My eyes wandered around the parking lot. "Cliff?"

Ari buckled her seat belt and turned on her radio, drowning out my voice with indie music. "Is there anything else I can help you with?"

I shook my head. "You're impossible, Ari Ziegler."

She manually rolled up her window, unfazed by my opinion.

"Hey," I said before the glass could reach the top. "I was only trying to help."

She looked me up and down in disgust. "You can't help me," she said. "You can't even help yourself."

Ari sped out of the parking lot, taking her secrets along with her.

I squinted to keep the sun out of my eyes as I watched her drive off. A trail of muffler smoke sailed through the air, breaking apart as it floated up and away.

"Just perfect," I mumbled under my breath as I made my way toward the football field. Cliff and his "brocks" were about to begin practicing drills for their upcoming season. I walked onto the grass and gave Cliff a packed shove from behind. He turned around, abruptly.

"What is wrong with you, Cliff?" I asked as everyone started to stare.

Cliff towered over me. "Whoa, what are you doing?"

"Why are you spreading rumors that I was investigating Mr. Russell?" I asked. "Are you insane?"

"Look, calm down." Cliff tossed the football to another player.

I grabbed him by his jersey. "No, you calm down! Are you trying to get me kicked out of Westcott?"

He looked down at my fist and slowly looked back up at me. I released my grasp.

"I didn't spread a rumor, Sonny," Cliff said. "Kyle told me that him, you, and a couple other people had some suspicions about Mr. Russell's replacement, Mrs. Penn. That's it."

"And you thought it was a good idea to tell Ari? You two of all people should know to keep your mouths shut about things."

Cliff's wet blond hair fell across his forehead. "What's that supposed to mean?"

"What do you think it means?"

He grabbed his lips and let out a nervous laugh. "Don't talk about what you don't know about, kid. Go home."

"I know what one rumor did to Lana. And I certainly hope I can count on you to not mess anything up for me, the way you did for her," I said.

Cliff looked down at the field as he brushed his cleats against the grass. "Whatever happened to Lana after she did what she did was on her. I told you—I had nothing to do with that."

"Yeah, you know, I almost believed you. I thought maybe your days of spreading rumors were over. Until this."

Cliff glared at me with a twisted smile, then sauntered closer. He leaned down so his face was inches from mine. "Look, Carter. You come stomping into my practice, stumbling onto my turf, shove me around, and accuse me of involving myself in petty Westcott girl fights. I'm a Violet. I'm a savage. I do what I want, when I want. You're looking at the most sought-after guy at WH, with more strings available to pull than you could count. Do you really think I care about your dumb-ass investigation? The days of you and everyone else at this school accusing me of leaking the video are over." He brushed his finger across

117

my hair. "I know deep down, underneath this pretty hair of yours, is a massive brain. One that couldn't possibly believe I'd waste my time following a temp around town to take videos of him and my ex-girlfriend, who dumped me to play dress-up at a low-budget school in Yonkers, New York. If I were you, I'd walk off my field and forget you ever came." He stepped away slowly as he cocked a crooked smile.

My eyes began swelling with tears.

"Just a suggestion," Cliff said, holding up his hands.

"What's going on?" Kyle asked as he approached us.

"Nothing." Cliff looked straight at me with his piercing blue eyes. "We're all good."

I slowly looked around the field. The football team behind Cliff stood silently in solidarity with him. And for the first time ever, I recognized that the field on which I stood, the field I thought was a public gathering place, in all actuality belonged to the king of Westcott. It belonged to Cliff Reynolds. And I knew I didn't belong there. I stepped backward, slowly, making my humiliating exit off the bright-green grass.

I turned around and picked up my speed, passing by the football stands on my way back toward the parking lot. To my surprise, I looked up to find Guy leaning against the railing and watching me as I drew near. His beady eyes bounced back and forth between Cliff and me.

"And what the hell are you looking at?" Cliff yelled in Guy's direction.

I stopped in my tracks, wondering the same thing.

"This is a closed practice!" Cliff shouted. "Leave my field!" He paused. "Now."

I turned around and glanced at Cliff, then turned back around to face Guy—not knowing which of the two I was scared of most. Guy didn't say a word. He slowly pushed himself off the railing, giving both me and Cliff one last glare before walking off. I waited until he was out of sight to walk to my car, hoping he hadn't heard too much—but all the while knowing he probably had.

Later that night, Winston and I debriefed at our usual place.

"Can you believe that?" I jumped up to perch on my kitchen counter, my hair trying to stay up in what was left of my messy bun. My white shirt hung off my left shoulder as I reached for a bite of cookie dough.

"Wait, what was it you told me? Let me see if I remember. 'Cliff Reynolds isn't that bad. He's harmless.'" Winston sliced the dough with a dull butter knife. His scarf was wrapped around his head like a turban, so he wouldn't get it dirty.

"Do you need me to say it?" I brought my knees to my chest.

"I'm not ashamed to admit that I do."

"You were right, Wins. You happy?"

"Eh. That felt forced."

"It was," I said.

Winston chucked the last chunk of cookie dough on the baking sheet.

I grabbed another piece. "Have you thought any more about entering your new composition in to Mrs. Bennett's showcase?"

"You mean the knockoff Westcott Awards?" he asked.

"I'd hardly call an end-of-the-year music competition a knock off anything."

"You win a prestigious award; we win cheap medals. The two don't hold the same weight."

I tightened my bun. "You should enter. Winning would look good on your college applications, and your piece is beautiful."

"Maybe I want to pull a Lana and hotfoot my way to New York to pursue fashion," he replied.

"You'd do that?" I wrinkled my nose.

"Not necessarily. I'd love the scandal, though."

"I'm not sure anyone envies the Lana Carter scandal. It almost sunk the school entirely—so I've been told." I glanced over at a family photo and grabbed another ball of dough.

"Would you stop it?" Winston removed the cookie sheet from in front of me. "If you keep it up, we'll be sticking this pan in the oven for one cookie's sake."

I hopped down from the cluttered green countertop and slid the cookie sheet onto the rack.

"But back to more pressing news—I still can't get over your conversation with Ari," Winston said. "Do you think she's lying? Do you think she and Cliff actually hooked up at his cookout?"

I set the timer on the microwave and leaned against the counter. "I don't know. I'd hate to think she would do that to Kyle. I'd be even more shocked if Cliff did that to him. They've been best friends since kindergarten."

"What does Kyle believe?" Winston patted his turban.

I placed my hand on my hip. "What do you think?"

"Why is that kid so naïve?"

"You know how obsessed he is with Ari, Wins. She was his first real love. Sure, Ari's a little crazy and rough around the edges. And maybe they do break up every other week. But Kyle is completely infatuated with her. I don't think that's going away."

"Well, if there's a rumor, there's a reason," Winston said. "I guarantee you it's true."

Just then, my mind flashed back to a conversation I had with Lana. A very specific, telling conversation in which she told me a secret—one that nobody knew but her, Cliff,

121

and Ari. And now—me. Cliff had told Lana about something that happened the summer before sophomore year, when Ari moved to town. Four people knew this shoddy secret. And four people only.

"Regardless, we need to support Kyle in whatever he chooses to believe." I stood there in a daze. "Besides, it hasn't been proven."

"Yet." He licked his finger.

"You have a visitor, Sonny!" My mom's voice traveled through the kitchen from the foyer.

Winston and I glanced at one another.

"Do you typically get visitors at this hour?" he asked.

"Yeah. You," I replied, poking him in the chest.

We slowly made our way to the front door.

"Maybe it's Cliff coming to apologize," I said.

"Please. His dignity wouldn't allow him to make the drive."

"Are you implying Cliff has no dignity?" I asked.

We glided through the hallway, both of us smiling from our mini conversation about Cliff. That was, of course, until we saw who was standing at the front door.

"Piper?" We stopped in our tracks.

One thing I never thought I'd see was Piper Clemmons standing underneath my flickering porch light. Her fingers clutched onto her sweater as if her life depended on it.

"I'll let you three have some privacy," Mom said.

Winston and I walked outside, closing the front door behind us.

Piper stalled. "This is a cozy house."

I could tell her nerves were getting the best of her. "I appreciate that."

"Piper, what in the world are you doing in the valleys after dark?" Winston asked.

"Seriously?" I knocked his scarf off his head. "Piper, what's up?"

"About you and JC having lunch . . . ," she said, tucking her long light brown hair behind her ears.

"Look, Piper. I don't know who could have shared that information with you and Norah. We were the only two in the café that day."

She leaned in, her deep brown eyes expressing concern. "Listen to me, Sonny. You don't want to stick your nose into places it doesn't belong. Believe me. If anyone catches you talking to JC, it'll ruin you. He's tainted. I'm here to tell you that whatever JC told you, whatever he said, bury it. It doesn't matter anymore."

The crane flies swarmed the porch light.

"You do know JC thinks someone framed him, right?" Winston asked her.

Piper crossed her arms. "That's ridiculous."

"Is it?" I asked. "Because I'm not so sure JC would steal the answers to the exam. He doesn't struggle with grades. Isn't it much more plausible that someone slipped the answer key into his bag? Someone who had access to his belongings?"

I could hear her thumping heart beating through her chest.

"Are you insinuating that I did it?" Piper asked.

"Maybe," I replied.

"That's your angle, Sonny? That I framed my own boyfriend? That I what—snuck into my dad's office, got my hands on the answer key, and planted it in JC's bag when he wasn't looking?"

"That's eerily specific," Winston mumbled.

"What would I gain from framing him?" she asked.

"Maybe nothing," I said. "Or maybe everything."

Her innocent eyes turned sinister. "I would appreciate it greatly if you would stop trying to snoop around. I lost someone I really cared for because of his poor choices, and I'm trying to move on."

I wasn't convinced. "Piper, you know you can talk to me, right? You can trust me."

Piper was the definition of brains and beauty. Every teacher praised her. Every girl wished she looked more like her. Every guy wanted to date her. Perhaps it was because she was inaccessible—like an expensive porcelain doll tucked far away on the highest shelf.

But behind the powdered skin and picture-perfect report cards, Piper was just a girl. A girl like me, fighting to define herself in a place where others did it for you.

She stared blankly into my eyes as the flickering porch light made shadows on her face. "You're one of the good ones who still thinks trust exists." She stepped away, beginning to shift toward her car.

I matched her movement, stopping her before she could get too far. "Is there anything you want to tell me, Piper? Anything at all?"

"Like what?" she asked.

"Anything," I said.

Piper paused for what seemed like an eternity. "There is one thing," she said.

I leaned in, desperate for her reply.

"You'll be sorry if you don't drop this." She walked down my porch steps, opened her car door, and turned to face us. "And by the way—this is Westcott, Sonny. You're never the only one anywhere." She slammed her car door and sped off into the stale California night.

"What in the hell was that?" Winston asked.

"That was a cover-up," I replied. "True Westcott style."

Sometimes, girls free-fall. Sometimes it's by choice, other times by mistake. But sadly, once your feet have left the ledge, there's no going back.

Z
SHADOWS

Shadows. Dark areas where light is blocked by an object. When I was little, I loved to skip alongside the silhouette of my shadow down the sidewalks of Westcott. I found it comforting that my shadow always walked ahead of me, or beside me, and I never had to question whether or not it was there, or why it was there. But as I got older, I realized there are other types of dark areas. Ones you can't see. Ones that don't follow you around while you stroll through town like a giddy schoolgirl—but instead stay tucked away in those black, scary places. And those dark areas, you always have to question.

I pulled up my text thread to ensure I had the correct address. Jacob's house was remarkable. It was all white brick, which paired nicely with the glistening green grass. Each sagebrush bush was perfectly trimmed to hit the bottom of every crisp black shutter. The long stone pathway leading up to the porch was welcoming, though I still felt unsettled approaching the tall, dark doorway.

His doorbell played a fancy song.

"You're here," Jacob said as he opened the door.

"So I am," I replied.

Seeing Jacob outside of school felt a bit odd—especially given the circumstances of our arrangement. He was wearing a worn T-shirt and sweats. I wished I felt as comfortable as he looked.

"Welcome to my humble abode." He held out a hand to usher me in.

I walked inside, stepping onto the pristine black marble tile.

"I don't know that 'humble' is the correct word," I said, gaping at the tall white columns in the entryway.

"Yeah, well, I have to keep up with my fellow purples."

"My house does not look like this, I can assure you."

"No?"

"Well, I guess one of them does."

"Oh, so you have two homes?" he asked. "How humble."

I gave him a coy glare. "My parents are divorced. My father lives on the hillside—just about five minutes from here."

"Coach Dirk, right?" He led me into his exquisite kitchen.

I sat down on a white leather barstool, pulling myself closer to the white marble countertop. It had a particular shine to it. "That's him."

"Wrestling, correct?" Jacob pulled out a gallon of iced tea from his stainless-steel refrigerator.

"Right."

"Well, I'm sure you know a lot about wrestling, but what do you know about the basketball team? Do you have any insight on the competition or tryout process?" he asked.

My mind quickly flashed to Dean. "I'd say it's pretty competitive. Every sport at Westcott is."

"Back in Long Beach, being on the team just meant that you're part of a brotherhood," he said. "Something tells me Westcott is a bit more cutthroat."

"Well, you're certainly offered brotherhood. But if you want to stand out, you will have to cut their throats."

Jacob grabbed two glass cups out of a light gray shaker cabinet and placed them on the counter. "You're witty, you know that?" He poured in the tea.

"That's what years of writing will do to you."

"What exactly do you write?" He handed me a glass.

"I don't want to bore you." The cool tea swam through my body as I took a sip.

"I doubt you will," he said.

"Just . . . stuff."

"Stuff?"

"Fiction, mostly."

"Fiction. Mostly." Jacob tossed a crumpled-up paper towel into the trash can five feet away. "You have a way with words."

I tilted my head to the left. "And tell me again why you're worried about the tryout process?"

He smiled. "I heard Norah's boyfriend plays."

At the mention of *Norah's boyfriend*, I sunk into my barstool.

"Do you know him?" Jacob asked.

I paused, likely longer than I should have.

"Sonny?"

"Not anymore," I replied.

Jacob studied me. "Hey, we can, uh, we can wait in my room if you want. My dad is on a call. He should be finished soon."

"Sure." I swallowed my nerves.

His joggers clutching his ankles, Jacob led the way upstairs. I counted the wood steps as I watched his bare feet climb each one. We approached the landing, and Jacob opened his bedroom door. The décor smacked me straight in the face.

"Wow. This is—"

"Underwhelming?" he asked.

"Not exactly," I said, feeling jealous.

Jacob plopped down on his white comforter. The tufted dark gray headboard bounced against the wall behind it. "My mom's an interior decorator. She went a little crazy."

"In general or specifically while decorating your room?" I looked around at the black-and-white artwork covering the walls.

Jacob stared at the ceiling, giving thought to my question. "Maybe both."

"What does it feel like to be such a great athlete?" I asked, standing in front of his bookshelves. I found myself admiring his rows of medals and shiny gold trophies.

"Someone's gotta do it, you know?" He propped himself up against his headboard.

"Well, thank you for your bravery," I replied.

"I actually have a ton more where that came from," he said. "I wanted to build custom shelves to display them all, but my mom said it would mess with the feng shui, so she wouldn't allow it."

"You're incredibly deprived, you know that?"

Jacob tossed a suede throw pillow at my back. "All right, that's two in a row! Enough with your wit!"

Smiling, I kneeled down to pick up the pillow, then walked over to a beanbag chair in the corner of the room and sunk into it.

"I love your room," I said. "It's so . . . clean?"

He stared at me. "Why thank you."

Just then, I spotted a picture frame tucked carefully underneath the big fluffy chair.

"Who's this?" I pulled the metal frame toward my face.

Jacob clasped his hands behind his head and sighed. "That . . . is Claire."

"Is she your—"

"Girlfriend," he said. "Well, she was my girlfriend. From back home."

I ran my thumb over the glass, captivated by this stranger. Her eyes were bright, the kind of eyes I wish I had. Her beautiful dark brown hair fell out of her messy ponytail and lay across Jacob's face. He was nestled into her neck as she smiled into the camera and snapped the photo.

"Bad breakup?" I asked.

"Something like that," he said. "She passed away last year."

I glanced up at him from the floor, taken aback by his reply.

Jacob took a deep breath. "Distracted driver. We dated for a year, and then, just like that, she was gone. She was on her way to one of my basketball games when—" He choked on his words.

I put the picture frame back down.

"I guess basketball hasn't been the same for me since. Trying out for the team would sort of be a big deal for me —if I try out."

I twisted my thumbs, searching for the right words to say. "What was she like?"

Jacob's heavy eyes floated around the room. "Ah, she was smart. Very funny. Caring. She loved to read . . . and eat."

"Sounds like my kind of girl," I said.

"Her favorite thing to do was trying out different brunch spots around town on Saturdays. She'd wake me up at seven in the morning, scared we wouldn't have enough time in the day if we didn't hurry. I'd wake up to her prying my eyes open. Literally. We must have eaten at every restaurant—ever."

"Expensive date."

Jacob stared off into his bedroom and smiled a little. "She was worth it."

I traced my fingers over the pattern on his jute rug. Perhaps I didn't know the first thing about Jacob, or the past he'd been dragging around like thousand-pound chains on his ankles. Maybe he wasn't the type of guy who would go for the prettiest and meanest girl in school. Perhaps he was just searching. Searching for anything to remind him of what he'd lost. Chasing the high of a love he once felt, scared to death he may never feel it again.

"She sounds lovely," I said.

"She was," he replied. "She actually, uh, she actually was a lot like you." Jacob's eyes scanned my body.

"You must be Sonny." Mr. Harrison suddenly appeared. He stood inside of the door frame, then slowly walked into Jacob's room. He moved smoothly in a navy suit and shiny loafers that could blind you.

I broke the intense eye contact I shared with Jacob and stood up to meet him. "Mr. Harrison, I am such a fan of yours."

"I have fans?" he asked. His voice was loud and confident. "And call me Ron, please."

Jacob put his head down. He pressed his lips together and looked up at me from his bed. He was bothered by his father's interruption, and it was painfully obvious.

"I followed the Farrah Klein case," I said. "I knew she was innocent."

"Me too," Ron replied.

"Dad, Sonny would like to interview you for her end-of-year paper," Jacob said.

"Ah, you're one of the Chosen Ten?" Ron asked.

I shrugged my shoulders. "So it seems."

"Impressive. I hear there's some intense competition."

"Which is why I felt telling this story from your angle would produce a powerful paper," I said. "I was two seconds away from having to write about body shaming or bullying."

Ron's dark eyes were hard to read. "Well, who needs that when you can write about a dozen grisly murders?" He paused. "I'd be happy to help. Why don't we head to my office?"

I looked at Jacob. "You coming?"

"If you want me to," he replied, rolling his feet off the edge of the bed.

I nodded.

"Then sure." He stood to his bare feet.

We followed behind Ron as we made our way toward his office. Jacob walked closely beside me down the hallway. His arm brushed up against mine as we strolled. I looked down at his hand, which was swaying slowly by his side. I watched as his hand grazed mine, and they almost met . . . almost.

"Sorry for the mess—working on a new case," Ron said as we eventually reached his office door and walked inside. He motioned for me to have a seat in one of the two brown leather chairs planted in front of his desk. "Sonny, your dad is Dirk Carter, yes?"

"Pops, she isn't here to talk about her family," Jacob said, collapsing into the second leather chair and looking at me in apology.

"No, it's okay." I nestled in. "He is."

"Funny enough," said Ron, "me and a couple of my buddies from my firm back in Long Beach were old customers of his."

"The sporting-goods store on Baron Street?" I asked.

"That's the one." Ron loosened his maroon tie. "I actually purchased my gym equipment from his shop when I realized I was too busy to go to the actual gym and needed a home one. Apparently he had the newest and coolest inventory."

"Newest and coolest." I nodded. "Doesn't sound like him."

Ron cleared his desk, letting out a small laugh as he shuffled his papers. "No?"

"I'm surprised the store on Baron is still around," I said. "The manager embezzled a ton of money and nearly sunk it entirely."

"Wow." Ron sat down in his leather armchair. "Hope your dad tossed him in jail."

I shook my head. "His partner wanted to, but my dad convinced him to let him walk."

"I see," Ron replied. "Your dad must be a good man."

"Yeah." I paused. "He can be."

"I couldn't believe it when I found out he was a coach here at Westcott. I only wish he were the basketball coach, so my son here could learn from the best."

I looked over at Jacob, whose mind seemed to be in an entirely different room altogether. He wasn't present, and it was noticeable. "Jacob just informed me that he's trying out for the team."

"Uh, no," he said, joining the conversation. "I said I'm thinking of trying out."

"Oh, come on, son," Ron said. "Don't be shy. You've been practicing all week."

Jacob bristled, shifting in his seat. "Not really."

"Jacob was the MVP on his team back home."

"Wow, that's an accomplishment for a sophomore," I replied.

"He ran circles around the seniors," Ron said. "He's got some pretty raw talent."

Jacob looked down at his lap, picking the strings on his sweats.

"I hear there are some good players on the team already. I think he's just a little nervous that he won't shine the same way he did back home," Ron said.

Jacob stared out of the office window, the sun hitting his cheeks. "From what I saw the other day in the gym, there's just one guy who'd be my direct competition."

"Dean?" I asked.

He turned back around to face me. "Yeah," he replied. "Dean."

"Maybe Sonny here could give you the skinny on Dean's weak spots. All in good fun, right?" Ron stared at me once again with those hard-to-read eyes, then rapped his knuckles on the desk. "So, Farrah Klein."

After many hours of gruesome stories, Jacob held open the front door, and we walked outside.

"You know, had I known this case had so many layers to it, I'm not so sure I'd have picked it for my paper," I said.

"It's a long one," Jacob replied as we walked to my car. "I can't count the endless hours I've been forced to hear about it."

"Your dad's nice."

Jacob dribbled a basketball down the driveway. "For the most part."

"Hey," I said. "Before I go, I need to talk to you about something."

"Sure." He balanced the basketball against his right hip.

"I heard Norah wasn't at Dustin Coleman's summer party," I said.

Jacob's eyes zoned in on me. "Who told you that?"

"A couple of people," I replied.

He ran his fingers through his disheveled hair. "Okay."

"Okay?"

"Maybe whoever told you that didn't see her." He rolled his neck from side to side.

"No," I replied. "I don't think that's possible."

Jacob exhaled. "What do you want me to say?"

"Did you lie?" I asked.

"Not on purpose."

"So on accident?"

"You think I'm lying about liking Norah?" he asked. "Why would I make that up? I like her." He paused. "A lot."

I quickly looked away, unsure of why his statement caused me to shrink.

Jacob's eyes looked apologetic. "I mean . . . I . . ."

"I get it." I shrugged my shoulders. "Red dress. Fate. All the things."

"Right." He seemed unconvinced. "I'm sorry but I've got to run. I'm meeting JC on the courts."

I exhaled slightly, temporarily setting my suspicions aside. "Okay."

He spun the basketball on his finger. "I'll text you later," he said before walking toward his Jeep.

I walked to my car and opened the door. "Hey!" I yelled in the direction of Jacob before I stepped inside.

He spun around. "What's up?"

"I think you should try out," I said, swallowing my selfish desire to keep him as far away from Dean as possible. "For the team."

Jacob's eyes were heavy, but hopeful too. "Yeah," he said. "I think I will."

I watched him hop into his Jeep. He sped down the winding street, leaving me in a whirlwind of dust and confusion.

They say no good things happen on street corners. Especially things that occur so close to midnight.

The tall metal light post towered over me as I waited in distress. I wrapped myself in my blue jean jacket, kicking the pavement with my dirty Converses. The air was thick, and my nerves were multiplying on top of the sidewalk as each minute passed. I pulled out my cell phone to check the time, my eyes skimming the dark street. It was time for our meeting.

"What the hell are you doing out here by yourself?" Kyle walked down the sidewalk toward the stop sign.

I wanted to scream, but I knew I should whisper. So I did both. "Jesus, Kyle!"

He pulled his tan hoodie off his head. "I'm serious. You shouldn't be standing out here all alone."

I stood close to him, relieved by his presence. "I'm not alone anymore, am I?" I asked him. "Besides, there are other people around."

"Hardly," he replied. "Now are you going to tell me what we're doing here?"

"I can only assume we aren't here to study," Buckets said, coming in shortly behind Kyle.

I looked down at his red-and-white striped pants. "Are you seriously in your pajamas?"

"Oh, right. Had I known we were meeting on a street corner just before midnight, I would have dressed up."

"Unlikely," Winston said as he shone a flashlight in my face.

I held my hand up in an attempt to block the brightness. "Would you turn that thing off?"

He and Casey walked down the sidewalk toward us. "I needed to make sure it was you," Winston replied.

"Who the hell else would it be?" Buckets said.

Kyle stared at Casey. "Hi," he said, smiling a little. "I didn't know you were coming."

Casey ran her fingers through her hair. "Sonny asked me to come."

"Lucky me," Kyle mumbled, continuing to stare.

"What is this?" Buckets's bony finger swayed back and forth between Casey and Kyle. "This thing?"

"Nothing." Kyle's voice flooded with uncertainty.

"Jesus, Winchester." Buckets shook his head in disbelief. "Seriously?"

"Did you tell Kyle about your conversation with Ari after school yesterday?" Winston asked me.

"Yeah," Kyle said. "She told me Ari denied it."

"And you believe that?" Winston asked.

Kyle looked down, his hands in his pockets and his expensive sneakers brushing against the cement.

"Okay, he believes it." Winston shook his head.

"Why wouldn't I? Ari wouldn't do that to me. Plus, I asked Cliff straight up, and he swore it was a lie."

"I never believed it anyways," Buckets said.

"Why do you always stick up for the Violets, Buckets? Don't forget what street you live on." Winston put his flashlight into his back pocket.

"The cookout rumor has never been proven," said Buckets, "and they both adamantly deny it. Unlike the rest of my student body, I don't believe anything until someone places the proof in my hands. Until that day comes, in my opinion, it's just a stupid rumor." He wagged a finger back and forth between Casey and Kyle. "Which makes whatever the two of you are doing incredibly risky." Then he aimed his gaze directly at Kyle. "Especially since you and Ari are likely to get back together any day now."

"Why are we here, Sonny?" Casey asked, changing the subject.

142

I looked into each of their eyes, most of them a different color, all of them filled with curiosity. "This stays between us," I said. "Okay?"

Everyone leaned in.

"JC was framed."

Buckets looked side to side. "By whom?"

"Piper," I replied.

Kyle leaned in further. "Hold on—JC thinks Piper set him up? That's crazy."

"He told me Piper slipped the answer key into his bag when he was in practice one night," I said.

"What makes him think that?" Casey asked.

"Because he saw her," I replied. "He saw Piper put something into his bag before walking out of the gym that night. The next day, my dad did a random bag search. Don't you think that's a bit of a coincidence?"

"Maybe she put something else into his bag," Casey suggested. "A note?"

"That's what JC assumed. He forgot to check his bag when he got home that night, but when my dad and the principals dumped it out, the only thing they found was the answer key. There was no note."

"Piper planted it there and tipped off your dad?" Kyle asked. "Why would she do that?"

"We don't know," I replied. "Yet."

"You're kidding me, right?" said Buckets. "Do you honestly think anyone is going to believe that?"

"I'm with Buckets. Why would Piper turn on JC?" Casey asked. "She loved him."

"I don't know. But JC swears he's innocent," I said. "And I believe him."

"Why?" Kyle asked, crossing his arms.

"I saw it in his eyes," I replied. "I can't explain it, but I know he's telling the truth."

"So you dragged us here to tell us that Piper planted the answer key?" Buckets turned around to walk away. "I have better things to do."

"No!" I yelled, causing him to stop. "I called you here for this." I reached into my pocket and pulled out the envelope.

"What's this?" Winston asked.

"It was left on JC's doorstep," I said.

Casey pulled the paper out of the envelope and glanced down at the riddle. " 'No one is safe at Geraldine's,' " she read aloud.

"What the hell does that mean?" Buckets asked.

"JC thinks Mr. Russell left it behind for him."

"Mr. Russell?" Kyle took the note from Casey's hands and studied it. "This is typed. It could be from anyone."

"Could be. But he saw Mr. Russell's car parked outside of his house as he was coming home from a run one night.

144

When he got back to his house, this envelope was sitting on his doorstep with his name on it. And not just any name. Jeremy Coleman, specifically."

Buckets grabbed the envelope. "Spelled out?"

"Spelled out," I replied. "And inside of the envelope was this riddle."

"What does this mean?" Casey repositioned her glasses.

"I think Mr. Russell wanted JC to find something. To link him to evidence. Evidence that Piper did indeed frame him."

"Did he confirm this with Mr. Russell?" Casey asked.

"He died before JC could talk to him," I replied. "But come on, guys. Why would JC need the answers to the exam? He wasn't struggling in any of his classes."

Kyle rolled up his sleeves. "I don't think we should get involved," he said. "I hate what happened to JC. I don't know what I'd do without football, so I can't imagine how he feels. But we don't know that he's innocent. And claiming Piper framed him is not only unbelievable, it's risky. She's the assistant principal's daughter."

"And none of us should risk anything without proof," Casey added.

"So we find proof," I said. "We find whatever it is Mr. Russell wanted us to find."

"As the resident smart friend—I think we should call this whole thing off," Buckets interrupted. "You heard

Principal Winchester. If anyone gets caught doing anything outside of how a Westcott student should behave—"

"Christ, Buckets, did you memorize that?" Winston looked at him, disgusted.

Casey buried herself into her T-shirt, squirming. "Buckets is right, Sonny. As much as we all feel bad for what he went through, why should we help JC? I hardly know him."

I looked down at my jacket, tracing the buttons with my eyes. "But you know me. JC was my good friend, and I turned my back on him." I glanced at Kyle—JC's other good friend. "Kyle did too."

He exhaled.

"And he didn't deserve that," I said. "He deserves for someone to help him."

"Touching," Winston whispered. "But I'm going on the resident smart friend's boat and sailing the hell away from this mess."

I grabbed Winston's arm. "If Piper did this to him, if she was involved in ruining his life, then she has to go down for it. We have to help him get back on the team. He doesn't have a voice—but we do."

"If you think the five of us, with no evidence, can bring down the princess of Westcott, you're more delusional than I thought," Buckets said.

"The princess of Westcott." A deep, sultry voice snuck up behind us. "Now that's a title."

We all glanced toward the darkness behind the stop sign; the street light above gave off just enough brightness to make the frame of a young woman's body visible.

Kyle stepped forward, the heavy air pushing back against his face. "What are you doing here?"

Maybe some shadows aren't meant to follow us around. Maybe some stay put, providing shelter for people who are lurking in the dark corners on Nelser Street. People like Piper Clemmons.

8

GERALDINE'S

Is everything we see truly ours to discover? How do we know when we've discovered something we weren't supposed to? Perhaps our eyes sometimes fall upon things by mistake, which begs the question—does anything ever happen by mistake? Sure, maybe some things are never supposed to be seen, but in the same terrifying breath, maybe they need to be.

"It's a nice night, huh?" Piper walked toward us.

She was pleasant, but jaded. The kind of jaded you become after experiencing a few things in life. Bad things.

"Are you following us?" Buckets asked.

149

Piper walked past us toward the entrance of Geraldine's. She put her hand onto the coffee shop's glass door, which displayed a chipped teal-blue coffee-cup logo. The shop was located in between a hardwood store and a boutique on a long street. "Following you? You're the ones behind me." She opened the door and walked inside.

We all glanced at one another and then piled in after her. We stepped onto the layers of Bohemian rugs spread across the cracked concrete floor. The room felt vibrant, with large and small picture frames covering the brick walls and multicolored metal tables scattered throughout. Industrial chandeliers hung above us, just low enough to make a statement. The sofas were floral, the fabric chairs were striped—and the charm was priceless.

Piper turned on an orange floor lamp in the corner of the room and nestled into an oversized green-and-black striped chair close to the lamp. "I'm here to study," she said. "It's the only twenty-four-hour coffee shop in town. What are you guys doing here?"

"Sonny is treating us to coffee!" Winston glanced wistfully at the brightly colored coffee mugs behind the counter. "Big, expensive cups of coffee. Whatever we want." He smiled at me and then glanced at Piper. "Isn't that nice of her?"

Piper placed her tablet on her lap. "So nice."

"Let's go find a table," I mumbled to the others.

"Studying on a Saturday night?" Casey whispered as we walked toward the opposite side of the room.

I kept my head down as my eyes paced across the concrete floor.

"And what exactly are we doing at Geraldine's?" Buckets ran his fingers over the dusty picture frames on the wall. "What are we supposed to be looking for?"

"I don't know," I replied. "But there's a reason why Geraldine's was in the riddle."

Everyone took a seat in the scattered chairs around the metal table.

Kyle took off his hoodie and placed it on the back of his chair. His hand grazed Casey's arm as he turned around. "Uh"—he shook his head—"what's the plan?"

I looked down at the small amount of space between Casey's and Kyle's chairs. "To look around." I glanced at Piper. "But we can't draw attention to ourselves or look suspicious."

"Right," Buckets said, softly punching the top of the table a few times with a closed fist. "Because coming to a coffee shop at midnight to solve a riddle isn't suspicious at all."

"We at least need to have drinks in our hands," I said. "I'll go get us some coffee. You guys look around."

Kyle leaned his chair back on two legs. "For what?"

"Anything," I replied as I stood up.

"This is absurd. We're going to go on a wild-goose chase based on secretive lingo left behind by a dead teacher? Count me way out." Winston crossed his legs; his body language was telling.

"I agree," Casey said, her bright burgundy lip balm accentuating the tightness of her mouth. "This seems a little crazy."

"I don't believe JC anyways," Buckets said. "I'm out."

"Would you guys get up?" I whispered. "I need your help. Don't make me call in all the favors you owe me."

"Favors?" Winston's eyes narrowed.

"I don't think I owe you any favors," Casey said.

Buckets shook his head. "I definitely don't."

I exhaled, staring at Kyle with sinking eyes.

He sighed and dropped his shoulders. "Fine," Kyle said. "I'll look around."

I smiled at him and glared at the others, then pivoted and walked toward the counter. "I'll take four black coffees and one big, expensive one," I told the barista, resting my forearms on top of the black-and-gray speckled countertop.

Suddenly, a familiar voice rolled into my eardrum.

"Figures you'd drink black coffee," Cliff said. "But four of them?"

I turned my head to the right, rolled my eyes, and then focused my attention on the barista. "I'm here with some friends."

Cliff glanced behind him toward our table, nodding at Kyle before turning back around. "Interesting group."

"What do you want, Cliff?" I asked him. "What are you doing here?"

"It was either come to Geraldine's or stay home and listen to my father and his drunk football buddies reminisce about the good old days." Cliff grabbed the attention of the barista by placing his finger in the air. "I chose Geraldine's."

"Lucky me," I said, pulling two of the black coffees toward me.

"Their night typically ends with a discussion on how my dad plans to increase rent at his condos, just to clear out *certain* families," Cliff said.

"He would never, would he?"

"You sound like me." His eyes widened. "Only a hell of a lot cuter and still hopeful that people aren't shitty humans."

I shook my head.

"I'll take a chai tea," Cliff said to the barista, then looked down at me. "So Kyle and Langdon, huh?"

I stared ahead and pressed my lips together. "Don't know what you're talking about."

"I think you do," he replied.

"They're just friends," I said. "And it's really none of your business."

"Would you calm down, kid?" He glanced toward the back of the room. "I just find it interesting. That's all."

"Calm down," I repeated. "That's rich coming from you and your recent speech on the football field."

"If you were constantly accused of leaking a video you didn't leak, you'd reach your breaking point too."

"I'll have you know that I'm one of the only people in this school who still questions whether or not you leaked it," I said.

Cliff dropped his head. "And why's that?"

I placed the piping-hot cups into a drink tray. "Because you'd do a lot of things . . . but I'm not convinced you'd do that to Lana."

Cliff rolled his shoulder blades back and cracked his neck, then exhaled. "I just hope Kyle knows what he's doing," he said, abruptly changing the subject.

"And what is that exactly?"

"Come on, Sonny. It's Casey. The girl's—"

"A Cobalt?" I interrupted.

"She's trash."

I shoved the last two cups down into the drink tray. "She's not."

"Kyle's too good for her," he said.

"Kyle's too good for a lot of people," I replied, glaring at Cliff.

We locked eyes for an uncomfortable few seconds.

The barista placed Cliff's tea down on the counter and then rang me up. "Fourteen sixty-eight," she said.

Cliff reached into his back pocket and placed a twenty-dollar bill on the counter. "On me." He took a sip of his tea, giving me one last stare down. He then glanced at the barista. "Have a good one, Ash. Tell your mom I said hello."

I watched Cliff walk toward the exit. On his way out, he passed by Piper, who glanced up at Cliff and then at me. I quickly turned around and walked toward the others.

"What was Cliff doing here?" Kyle asked me as I placed our drinks down on the table.

"Escaping his father," I said.

He nodded.

"Why didn't you come say hello?" I asked.

Kyle took a sip of his coffee. "I don't know. Things are a little weird between us right now."

"The rumor?"

He nodded again.

"But you said you don't believe it."

"Yeah," he replied. "I don't."

"Ky . . ."

"Just drop it." He stood up. "I don't want to talk about it, Sonny."

I swallowed my comment. We both grabbed our coffees and walked toward the back wall where the group was gathered.

"Did you find anything?" I asked them.

Winston held his hand in the air. "I found a pack of unopened gum, a half-eaten panini, and a red ink pen."

"Do you think this is a joke?" I asked him.

"Yes," he replied. "But I'm also hungry, and you never pass up a free pen. Especially a red one."

"We've got nothing," Buckets said.

"Well, there's this." Casey tapped her finger on a glass picture frame.

I walked toward the wall and stared over her shoulder at the frame. In the photograph was a little boy with curly brown hair. He stood in the middle of an empty field, holding a teddy bear in one hand and a blanket in the other.

"That might be the single creepiest photo I have ever seen," Buckets said.

I stared at the sepia-toned picture in a daze.

"There's nothing here, Sonny," Kyle said. "Maybe the riddle was an innocent joke."

"If Mr. Russell had something to say to JC, he could have said it before he killed himself," Buckets added.

"And what if JC is lying?" Winston took a bite of the panini and glanced toward the corner of the room. "I mean,

156

just look at her. Does Piper look like the type of girl who'd have access to an answer key?"

"Yes," Buckets replied.

"Or have a reason to frame her boyfriend?" Casey added.

We watched as Piper lost herself in her books.

"I guess not," I whispered.

Kyle shrugged. "Maybe we should just call it quits."

"Okay." I shook my head. "Let's just go."

We all walked toward the exit, but as I approached the middle of the room, I slowed my pace. "I'll catch up with you guys in a minute!" I waited for the group to pour out onto the sidewalk before walking back to the counter.

"Hey, Ashley!" I grabbed the barista's attention.

She brushed her damp hands over her apron and walked toward me. "What's up?"

"Do you know who this little boy is?" I pointed behind me toward the wall.

"Mmm." She pressed her lips together. "No idea."

"Well, do you know who owns this place?" I asked.

Ashley grabbed a damp towel and wiped the countertop. "Ed and Dorie Williams."

My eyes paced across the wall behind her. "Never heard of them."

"They're pretty cool." Ashley slung the rag over her shoulder. "For seventy-five-year-old retirees who know

157

nothing about coffee. I do most of the grunt work here . . . and all of the decorating."

"Why did they name the shop Geraldine's?" I asked.

"Family name," she said. "I believe Geraldine was Dorie's mom."

I glanced back at the photo. "So this must be little Ed."

"Doesn't really look like him." Ashley scrunched her nose. "But how can you tell?" She put her hand on her hip. "Why do you ask?"

"You look tired." Winston approached me as I walked through the school parking lot the following Monday morning.

"Jesus!" I jumped. "Don't creep up on me like that."

He stepped back, holding his hands up defensively. "Whoa!"

"Sorry," I said, the bags under my eyes weighing me down. "I was up all night sorting through my notes from my interview with Ron."

"Was Jacob there?" he asked.

"He was."

"Did you two—"

"We did not," I snapped before Winston could continue.

"Damn." Winston scowled back at me.

"Speaking of Jacob." I looked around the parking lot. "He told me he saw Norah at Dustin Coleman's summer party."

"So?"

"But I have since confirmed that Norah wasn't there."

"Well, slap an orange turtleneck on and call you Velma!"

I stopped in my tracks. "Are you okay?"

"Are you?!" he retorted. "Would you stop trying to play detective? You're going to burn out."

"But why would Jacob lie?"

"Did you ask him?"

"Yes," I replied. "And he brushed it off."

"There you go," he said. "Maybe it was a misunderstanding."

I shrugged. "Maybe."

Winston cracked his knuckles. "So what's the new plan since we found nothing at Geraldine's? Except my lovely new red pen, of course."

"Why do I always have to come up with the plan? It's not exactly my forte."

"That's true," he replied. "Remember when you planned my birthday party last year? You forgot to mention it was a costume party on the invitation. The only one who showed up in costume was the birthday boy." Winston shook his head.

"You looked adorable."

"No, Sonny. The man in the yellow hat doesn't work without the monkey. I looked like an idiot."

My tired eyes attempted to roll. "An adorable idiot."

"Guys!" Casey suddenly appeared on the other side of me. She was out of breath, and her eyes were as wide as the parking lot. "Did you get my text?"

I reached for my phone.

Just then, Kyle zoomed past us, walking full speed ahead. We all followed, trailing quite a bit behind him.

"What's going on?" I asked, weaving through the crowd of students.

"Something tells me you're about to find out," Casey replied.

Kyle jolted toward the front of the school and approached Norah and Ari. "What is this?" He tossed his phone into Ari's hands.

She looked bewildered by his approach.

"Something tells me if she were to keep scrolling down in those threads, she'd find things that wouldn't paint *you* in such a good light," said Norah as she glanced back and forth between Casey and Kyle. "You sure you want to play this game?"

"Save it, Norah!" Kyle held his hand up. "That's clearly Ari and Cliff!"

Ari watched the video. Her pale face made her wardrobe look even darker than normal.

"And how could you possibly tell that?" Norah asked.

"She's wearing a baggy jacket, a hat, and her back is turned to the stupid rat of a cameraman who filmed this. It's blurry at best. This doesn't prove a thing."

"Ari's jacket," Kyle said. "The one I bought her for her birthday last year."

"So what? Anyone could have borrowed it."

"What's next, Norah? You're a good person?"

"Only on Mondays." The sparkle in her eyes was haunting.

Ari grabbed Kyle's arm. "This isn't me, Kyle. I swear."

Casey took a couple steps back and stood behind me.

"Then who is it?" he asked, swaying side to side.

I put my hand on Kyle's shoulder. "Maybe we should leave."

"What's going on?" Cliff approached the circle; he was wearing a Westcott hoodie, and his blond hair was swept perfectly to one side of his head—his usual look.

I gawked at his arrogance.

"What the hell were you thinking?" Kyle asked, walking toward Cliff.

"Whoa, take it easy, Ky. What's your problem?"

Kyle grabbed his cell phone from Ari and handed it to Cliff.

161

Cliff watched for a minute, his eyes pacing across the screen. He glanced at Ari, then back at the phone. "Oh," he said. "I've already seen it."

"You kissed Ari?" Kyle asked.

"Hold on—Ari? That isn't Ari, dude." Cliff handed Kyle his cell phone. His lackadaisical attitude was convincing.

"Then who is it?" Kyle asked.

Cliff looked around the group as we all waited for his answer.

Just then, out of the corner of my eye, I saw Piper standing near the brick railing. She stood some feet back, just close enough for me to notice her presence, but far enough away to remain discreet. She was hiding behind her stack of books and cream sweater, but I could tell she was eavesdropping. I slowly held up my hand and waved. We made brief eye contact—just long enough for her to feel uncomfortable. She then put her head down toward her pearls and quickly walked up the steps to the front of the school—tossing her coffee cup into the trash can before walking inside.

"It was Lana," Cliff replied.

At the mention of Lana, I jerked my head back toward the group.

"Lana? You expect us to believe that, Cliff?" Casey asked.

"I don't care what you believe, Langdon," Cliff retorted. "Don't you have a floor to mop?"

With narrowed eyes, Kyle stepped forward. "Are you serious?"

Winston pulled out his napkin and new red ink pen. "Bullying . . . the . . . poor," he said, scribbling on the napkin with jerky strokes.

"Would you give me that?" I whispered, snatching the napkin from his hand.

"Tell them, Sonny," Cliff demanded. "Tell them your sister was home that weekend, and she came to my cookout."

I stared into his somber blue eyes as he rocked back and forth on the balls of his feet.

"And because they were both into all that fashion shit, they could have had the same jacket, right?" Cliff asked, desperately attempting to suck an admission from my soul with his intimidating eyes. "Tell them, Sonny. Tell Kyle."

Suddenly, my mind once again flashed back to the conversation I had with Lana.

"I—" I began.

Cliff exhaled. "Jesus, Sonny! Just tell him!"

"I guess . . ."

Kyle's eyes narrowed. "You guess?"

163

"She went!" I blurted out. "Lana was home that weekend, and she went to the cookout. I remember now." I nodded. "I think she came home wearing that jacket."

Cliff rocked back on his heels and smiled the tiniest of smiles. He grabbed Kyle's shoulders and shook him. "Dude, I told you. I wouldn't do that to you. It's just a stupid rumor."

Kyle looked at Cliff, studying his eyes. Eventually they exchanged a fist bump, so maybe that meant he believed Cliff. Or rather, had to.

"Now, can we all move on with our day?" Cliff asked, eyeing everyone as he walked toward the school. Kyle followed after him, giving Ari one last look of disappointment.

Winston grabbed my arm, holding me back so we'd be out of earshot of everyone. "Why the hell did you lie for Cliff?"

"I didn't lie for Cliff. I lied for Kyle."

"Kyle deserves to know the truth, Sonny," Casey said.

"Look, I may have lied about Lana being home, but the video is blurry. That could be anyone," I replied.

"In Ari's jacket?" Winston asked, raising his eyebrows.

"Everyone knows that's Ari," Casey said.

"Well, Kyle's going to have to figure that out himself," I replied, knowing that day may never come.

Winston's eyes skimmed the parking lot full of students. "So, who do you think leaked this one?"

"Why would anyone leak a video after the SCC was changed? Even I'm retiring," Buckets said. "Eventually."

"What about Guy?" Winston asked. "Didn't you tell me Cliff was really rude to him on the football field?"

I shook my head. "I don't think it was him," I said. "I think it was someone who thinks they're a little more invincible than the rest of us."

Buckets crossed his arms. "I'm listening."

"What if Piper did this?" I asked.

"Piper? Why would she leak that video?" Casey asked, balancing a stack of books against her hip.

"Because she knows I'm looking into things," I said. "And she doesn't want me to. She knows I met with JC, and she saw us at Geraldine's. She must have seen me talking to Cliff. Maybe she thought I was dragging him into this."

"Wait a minute," Buckets interjected. "That would make sense. If Piper thought we were on to her, and that we planned on exposing her, her perfect reputation would go to shit when everyone found out that she framed JC."

"And we all know Piper would do anything not to go under," I said. "Even if that meant throwing someone else under the bus to cause a distraction."

"She did come to Sonny's house just to tell her not to get involved," Winston added, tossing his red checkered scarf over his shoulder.

"You really think Piper leaked this video?" Casey asked.

"Think about it. . . . Two days after she saw me talking to Cliff—a video of him was leaked. She's clearly trying to throw us off."

"You think Piper was there the night of Cliff's cookout?" Casey questioned. "And randomly recorded them?"

"Possibly to have something against Cliff, should she ever need it," Buckets offered.

"I don't know," I replied. "But I plan to find out."

Winston looked around the parking lot. "Well, who could tell us if Piper was at the party?"

Approaching Cliff wasn't for the lighthearted—especially when there was leaked unflattering footage of him flying around Westcott. I stood next to him, waiting patiently for him to acknowledge me.

"Yesterday's morning scuffle wasn't eventful enough for you, Carter? Back for round two?" Cliff stood at his locker, packing up his book bag.

"I need your help," I said.

"First you shove me, then you need me? You sound like your sister."

I moved my legs into a wide stance. "Look, are you going to help me or not?"

"What do you want?" he asked.

"I want you to tell me how well you know Piper Clemmons."

"The violin girl?" Cliff asked. "I know that she's Principal Clemmons's daughter."

"I think she went to your cookout over the summer."

"So what? Everyone does—although I didn't see you there." Cliff turned his head to the side, nodding in the direction of his friends.

"I must have been super busy."

"You know, I don't remember Lana ever being this sarcastic."

"I'm not Lana," I said.

"That's too bad. If she hadn't fooled around with a teacher, I'd almost admit to missing her."

"Yeah, it's not obvious at all that you miss her," I replied.

"How I feel about your sister is not really your concern, kid," said Cliff.

I stepped forward, lowering my voice. "You're welcome by the way. Lana wasn't home that weekend, and you and I both know that. Besides, even if she was, she wouldn't be caught dead kissing you at your cookout."

Cliff's ego came out to play. "You sure about that?"

"I'm pretty positive."

"Look, I didn't invite Piper to the cookout if that's what you're asking. Maybe she got wind of it through the country club and decided to stop by. Who cares?" Cliff shrugged his shoulders.

"I think she's the one who leaked the video," I said.

He moved his head to the left. "Of Lana?"

"No," I replied. "Of you."

Cliff stared at me with a straight face.

"You know, the one of you and 'Lana' kissing under the pool cabana." I waved my hand in little circles.

"Yeah, I saw the video," Cliff said. "But why would she leak it? What does that girl have against me?"

"It's complicated," I replied.

His eyes narrowed. "Look, just drop it, okay? I don't care who leaked the video, and I really don't care why."

"Do you care that people still believe it's you and Ari? Do you care that Kyle himself still might believe that?" I asked.

"Do you think I'm a virgin to these types of things? Cobalts try to tarnish my name out of spite all the time. It's not the first video, and it likely won't be the last."

"Piper *Clemmons* isn't a Cobalt. She's a Violet."

168

"I don't care if she's a periwinkle." Cliff slammed his locker. "That video is yesterday's news. It wasn't Ari. It was Lana. I didn't betray Kyle. All is well in the world. Why does it seem like you always want to mess with the natural order of things and ruin that for everyone?"

I paused, and then redirected my focus. "What about what you told Lana? About the summer before sophomore year? If that's true, then this video would make sense."

Cliff smiled a little, his eyes wandering around the hallway. "This conversation is done," he said. "Don't bring that up again."

"You can't possibly believe that everyone is going to let this go?" I asked.

"No. But I do believe you will."

"And why's that?"

"Let's just say if you don't, I'll make sure I pay a visit to my old pal Principal Winchester. He'd probably love to know that you're terrorizing the student body with your detective shit. And I'm sure he'd really like to know that the assistant principal's daughter is top on the list." Cliff's eyes narrowed in on me. "Drop it."

"What, you're gonna rat on *me* now?" I asked.

Cliff smirked, walking backward down the hall. "Everyone thinks I'm a rat anyways, right?" he shouted.

I watched as Cliff turned around and greeted some of his fellow letterman jacket–wearing friends.

Just then, a gust of cold wind blew by the back of my neck. "Can we talk?" Jacob asked.

I swiftly turned around; my flushed face met his.

"Everything okay?" Jacob asked, his eyes expressing confusion.

I nodded, though I wanted to say no. "What do you need to talk about?"

"I went to basketball tryouts yesterday . . . and Dean gave me quite the welcome."

I turned my head to the side. "What do you mean?"

"I can't explain it. He was just . . . giving me the eye."

"Okay." I shrugged.

Jacob's tone became more serious than usual. "It's a look I've given out quite a few times before. He didn't want me to be there, and it had nothing to do with basketball. Do the two of you have something going on?"

"Why would you think that?" I asked.

"Because he sees that you and I have been hanging out. And if he likes you, it would explain why he was mean mugging me from across the gym."

"Or maybe he caught wind that you like his actual girlfriend," I said.

Jacob shook his head. "No. I don't think so. I think it's more than that. He was giving me the eye in science class every time I turned around to talk to you."

I exhaled slightly.

"Sonny?" He leaned forward. "Do you have something going on with Dean?"

I wanted to skip the years of history telling. I wanted to tell Jacob no, but something told me he wouldn't believe me. And even though I wanted him to, something told me he wasn't going to stop asking. I figured now was as good a time as any to fill him in.

"Meet me at the club after school."

"You mean to tell me that Norah's boyfriend is your ex-boyfriend?" Jacob tugged at his earlobe and gave me a sideways glance.

"That is what I'm telling you," I replied.

He sat back in the booth and smiled. "That's why he was sizing me up. He's jealous."

"Of you?" I asked.

"Of us," he replied. "He probably thinks we have a thing."

"Here you go," said the server. "One vanilla shake."

"Thanks, Belinda." Jacob watched her place his drink on the table.

"You come here a lot or are you just good with names?" I asked him.

"Both." He began ripping the paper off his straw. "I come here to get away."

171

"Get away?" I blinked repeatedly. "Why would you want to get away from your house? It seems like paradise."

Jacob stabbed his milkshake with his straw. "Well, perception is not reality."

"You don't think so?" I asked.

"No. I think reality is reality."

"And . . . the reality is . . . your house isn't paradise?"

"It isn't that," he said. "I have great parents. But we don't always see eye to eye."

"On what?"

"Things I can't really talk about," he said. "Or don't want to."

I nodded as I read the room. "You know, I heard only crazy people drink vanilla shakes."

"Who told you that?" he asked.

"Someone who really likes strawberry shakes instead," I replied.

Dean and I would take long walks around my neighborhood a couple nights a week, and he'd always come bearing strawberry shakes. I loathed them, but he cautioned that chocolate shakes are too rich and vanilla shakes are for sociopaths.

"Well, I happen to think strawberry shakes are disgusting."

I looked down at the table between us. It had just been cleaned, and I could see my reflection in it. And for a split second—I saw how heavy my eyes looked when my mind was fixated on Dean. "Yeah," I said, wiping away the bleak reflection with my hand. "Me too."

"So, why did you two break things off?" Jacob asked me. "You and Dean?"

"*We* didn't," I replied. "*He* did. Our dads had a fallout, which ultimately affected our relationship."

"Fallout?"

"Mr. Ballinger was the manager at the sporting-goods store."

Jacob nodded. "Ah."

"Things got too crazy, and Dean eventually ended things with me."

"That seems pretty unfair to you," Jacob said.

The weight of that night forced my head lower. The ugly in both of us had come out to play, and we both said things we didn't mean: about each other's fathers, about money, and about each other. The stress of our dads' business debacle poured into our relationship like leaking gasoline. Unbeknownst to me, Dean was holding a match. And while I thought the argument would blow over by the end of the car ride home, when he walked me to my door, he told me he couldn't do us anymore.

Before I knew it, everything caught fire.

I always thought the worst part of a breakup is when emotions are still raw, and you're wondering if you should

173

run back in to save any remains. Or when you're watching the scaffolds you spent years building being burned to the ground. But as I walked through the ash and felt the depth of the hole in my heart—I realized the worst part isn't the fire. The worst part is when the fire is put out, and you're left with nothing but yourself.

Jacob swirled his straw around in his cup. "His loss," he said. "What kind of guy lets a girl like you go over something so minor?"

I looked into his brown eyes and quickly looked away. "I guess it wasn't so minor."

"It's crazy that your dad and his partner didn't notice such large withdrawals," he said.

"That doesn't surprise me. My dad doesn't notice a lot."

"Did they have many employees?" he asked.

"They had a few teenagers who came and went. But Mr. Ballinger practically ran the store himself."

Jacob nodded. "Nice guy?"

"The nicest." My chin hit my chest. "But I don't see him much anymore."

"Are you and your dad close?" Jacob asked.

"We've drifted apart, but I suppose we will always be close." I paused as my comment about my father reminded me of my feelings toward Dean. "Can you be both with a person? Distant and near?"

Jacob took a sip of his shake. "Set the scene."

174

"Okay." I accepted the challenge. "The scene is a love story. And the girl really likes the boy."

Jacob grinned. "Of course."

"Naturally," I agreed, opening my hands in front of me. "She believes they're meant for each other, making them near. But he doesn't want her, making them distant. And she knows it's crazy, because how can you feel both incredibly detached and locked in all at once? But she does. And she knows she shouldn't want him, but she doesn't know how to want anyone else. So there she sits . . . in nonsensical love with someone who isn't even there." I paused. "What would you say to that girl?"

Jacob stared at me with intensity before his eyes plummeted toward his chest. "Well, I don't know what I would say to her. But I think I would spend the rest of my life trying to become that guy." He looked up at me. "Because he sure is one lucky idiot."

My eyes bounced back and forth between the table and Jacob. He stared at me with uncertainty, as if he wasn't sure I would receive his comment well.

"I . . . ," I said softly, looking down at my lap as I grabbed the back of my neck with clammy hands. "I . . . um . . ."

Just then, my eyes landed on a more pressing matter, down the hallway of the club, toward the sunroom. It pulled my body out of the booth like a magnet.

"I have to go," I said as I stood up, my heart still racing from his comment.

Jacob placed his forearm on top of the booth and turned around. "Wait, where are you going?"

"I'm sorry," I replied. "I'll text you later." I walked down the club's main hallway, my mind still at the booth with Jacob. I let out a deep breath before casually walking into the sunroom.

"You alone?" I asked Kyle as he lay back against the long wicker couch. Sunlight streamed through several expansive windows and danced across his tanned skin.

He looked up at me in despair. "Not anymore." He lifted the pillow beside him and gestured for me to sit down.

"What are you doing here?" I asked.

"I just came to think," he said, gazing out the window at the miles of manicured golf courses. The grass was so uniformly cut and verdant that it looked like vast expanses of green carpet.

"And watching golf helps with that? It puts me straight to sleep." I looked around the room as I realized my jokes were going unappreciated. "Are you okay?"

"I don't know what to believe anymore, Sonny." Kyle exhaled. "I know you hate Cliff. I get it. But you don't know him like I do. Nobody does. When the video of Lana was leaked, he lost his mind. It undoubtedly turned him into a bone-chilling asshole, but before the personality switch, he cried in my arms about her. It broke him. That's why I know he couldn't be a complete sociopath."

"And Ari?" I said.

"She's been the love of my life for years." He stared down at his clasped hands. "I don't know who I am without her, Sonny." He paused. "I just don't think she would hook up with my best friend. I mean, how could anyone do that?"

I cleared my throat. "I guess the only way someone could do something like that is if they felt justified . . . in some strange way."

"Not Ari. She wouldn't do that to me. She knows how much I love her." He laughed. "Every broken, toxic part."

Kyle's logic was twisted. It's illogical to say you've fallen in love with a toxic person. Love is diametrically opposed to toxicity. But part of me understood his logic all too well. Part of me could relate, regardless of the contradictory statement. Because love isn't logical. *Love is twisted.*

"I'm not sure this is the right time to say this, but maybe you should figure out your feelings for Ari before you get in too deep with Casey. I know you two have been texting. A lot."

Kyle leaned his head back against the top of the couch and stared at the ceiling fan. "She's really sweet."

"And innocent," I said.

"And beautiful. And funny. And smart," he added. "Maybe even smarter than you."

"Don't get carried away."

Kyle dropped his chin to his chest. "I really like her, Sonny."

I could tell Kyle was torn between the two Cobalts—an unlikely battle for a powerful Violet like himself.

"I just don't want her to get hurt, okay?"

He rocked his head back and forth. "I'm not going to hurt her," he said. "I never could." He stood up and sauntered over to the sunroom's largest window, then pressed his fingers against the glass.

"I think you should know Piper likely leaked the video."

Kyle rested his forehead against the glass, then lazily rolled his head in my direction. "Piper?"

I knew Kyle was sober, but his depression made him look almost drunk.

"We think she's trying to distract us," I said.

Kyle looked back out the window. A man was taking a swing on a green hill, perfectly twisting his hips as if the act were orchestrated by a hidden puppet. "Or maybe you're wrong about this whole thing," said Kyle, opening his eyes to look at me. He pulled his head away from the window. "Maybe JC is lying." He ran his hand through his

178

hair repeatedly. "Maybe he's trying to piece together what's left of his reputation, and the only way to do so is by claiming he was framed. Other than a gut feeling from JC, and a riddle from Mr. Russell—what solid proof do we have?"

"Kyle . . ."

He followed my gaze across the golf course.

Some secrets are never supposed to be discovered. But if you're real lucky, when you're least expecting it, the most incriminating secrets will show themselves.

9
QUESTIONS

Questions. They come in many shapes and sizes. My dad once told me that smart people ask questions when they don't know the answer, but geniuses ask even when they do. That begs the question—how do we know what to ask? Or better yet—how do we know what not to?

"What is Piper doing here?" I asked.

Kyle put his hands over his forehead. "Maybe she's just playing a round."

I squinted, watching as Piper quickly walked across the green hills toward her golf cart. "Does she golf?"

"How am I supposed to know?"

Just then, we watched Piper stuff a manila envelope into her bag from across the way. She jumped into her golf cart, looked side to side, then drove off.

Kyle took a step back; he stared at me in a fog. "What do you think that was about?"

"I'm not sure," I replied, staring out the window. "But I'm going to find out."

The following day, we stood together in the hallway, where I shared the unusual story with the group.

JC punched the locker. "What the hell is she hiding? Why is she doing this to me?"

"Don't draw attention to yourself," I said through gritted teeth. "Nobody can find out about this. Not until we find out what's in that envelope."

"How do you presume we find out?" Buckets asked.

"We break into Piper's house on Saturday night," I replied. "While she's at the fall dance."

"The fall dance? You mean, the knockoff Halloween party?" Casey asked.

"Exactly," I said.

"Don't you think it will look suspicious if the six of us aren't there?" Winston asked. "Especially if Piper has her eyes on us."

"We'll go for half of it, and leave when we know she's distracted," I replied.

Casey stepped in front of me. "I don't know if we should do this, Sonny. I mean, breaking into our assistant principal's house? If we get caught, you and Kyle are both off the Chosen Ten and the rest of us are completely annihilated."

"Or killed." Winston scrolled through his cell phone. "I'm hoping this adventure takes me out."

"Look, we go in, we look for the envelope, and we get out. Piper's house is minutes from the school. We'll be back before anyone knows we're gone."

"And how exactly do you think we're going to get beyond their locked door?" Winston asked. "Or alarm?"

I looked around the group. "I guess I hadn't thought of that."

"Man in the yellow hat," Winston whispered to me.

"I know the code," JC said. "To the garage and alarm. It's four zeros and a one. Pretty easy to remember."

"How do you know that?" Kyle asked.

"I spent the weekend with Piper when Principal Clemmons went out of town last year," he replied. "It was the best and scariest weekend of my life. I was looking over my shoulder every second for Clemmons."

We all looked at one another in confusion. No one could believe he had the guts to enter the forbidden house.

"Well, I don't think you should come, JC," I said. "You have way more at risk than we do."

JC nodded and checked the time on his phone. "I have to get to first," he said. "Mr. Singleton wants to talk to me about one of my assignments."

I watched JC walk away, then turned my attention back toward the group. "So? What do you say?"

Buckets stepped forward. "I say this has gone too far. If we get caught, we could be kicked out of Westcott and possibly arrested."

"We aren't breaking in to steal anything," I said. "We're just breaking in to look at something."

"I don't think that's a justifiable excuse in the eyes of the police," Buckets said.

I tossed my hands in front of me to help drive my point home. "If we can prove Piper framed JC, we can get him back on the wrestling team."

"Why do you care so much?" Winston asked.

"Because I know what it feels like to have everyone shun you for something you didn't do." My mind flashed to Lana. "If JC didn't do this, he deserves for his name to be cleared." I glanced at Kyle. "He needs us, Ky."

Kyle exhaled, his eyes expressing concern. "Yeah. Okay."

"What if we get caught?" Casey asked.

"We won't," I said with a vast amount of uncertainty. "Trust me."

Kyle glanced at Casey. "I won't let anything happen to you. I promise."

"What about me?" I asked him.

"You're on your own," he replied.

I gently punched him in the arm, then looked at Buckets. "Are you in?"

"Fine," he said reluctantly as he shook his head. "I'm in."

"All right," I replied. "We'll meet outside the gym doors at seven. Everyone just lay low until then."

I nodded at the group, hoping to collect their approval. I wasn't exactly sure I fully got it.

"Casey"—Kyle pulled her to the side—"I wanted to ask you something."

"Uh-oh." Winston pretended to adjust his scarf while he eavesdropped.

I glanced at him and then turned my attention toward their conversation.

"What's up?" Casey tied the front of her oversized tie dye T-shirt into a knot, then pushed away strands of hair that had escaped from her messy ponytail. Tucked underneath her arm was a heavy book about tornadoes.

"What's that?" he asked.

She looked down at her book. "Oh, it's just something I'm reading."

"Do you just enjoy reading about everyone's worst nightmare or are you working on a project?"

"Both," she replied. "I sort of love tornadoes."

Kyle ran his finger over the edge of the book. "Really?"

"Really." Casey looked down and traced his finger with her eyes. "They're pretty fascinating."

"Yeah?" Kyle's finger left the spine of the book and gently grabbed a string of Casey's hair. "How so?" He twirled her hair around his fingers as he waited for her reply.

Casey's eyes dropped toward her hair and then shifted toward his. "You said you had a question."

He smiled and released her hair, breaking away from the tension between them. "Right." He stepped back. "Do you, uh, do you want to go to the dance with me?"

She took a deep breath as she hesitated, her mouth hanging open and her eyes wandering.

"I wanted to ask you on the phone last night, but I thought putting you on the spot might increase my chances."

Casey finally exhaled. "I don't know . . ."

"We don't necessarily have to go together in a date-type fashion. Maybe I could just pick you up?" he asked.

Casey tilted her head. "So you want to drive me to the dance?"

"That's exactly it. *To* the dance, specifically. You'll have to find your own way back."

"Well, when you put it that way . . . I'd love to."

Kyle looked her up and down, softly biting his lip. "Just text me your address, and I'll pick you up around six thirty."

"No!" Casey dropped her book.

Kyle leaned down to pick it up. "What's wrong?"

"Nothing," she replied. "I'll just meet you there, okay?"

Kyle's eyebrows drew together as he stood; he handed Casey her book. "Okay," he replied. "I'll take it."

Winston looked at them in disgust. "Ew. I can't watch this."

"Would you hush?" I tapped Winston on his stomach.

"Mark my words—she's going to get hurt. I'm never wrong."

"You're typically always wrong," I said.

"I wasn't wrong about him."

I followed Winston's eyes down the hallway as Dean approached us.

Dean Ballinger. *The lucky idiot.*

"Sonny, can we talk?" His voice was low. His head too.

I thought I'd be nervous when the time came for me and Dean to talk. I thought it would feel like we were estranged or too far gone. But in that moment, as I looked into his tortured eyes—those eyes I missed seeing—I realized we hadn't really gone anywhere.

"Sure," I said.

Winston tugged down on his distressed jean jacket, then lifted his chin. "Dean."

Dean pressed his lips together. "Winston."

"I'd shake your hand, but I'm allergic to Norah," Winston said.

Dean slowly nodded as he studied Winston's eyes. "Sounds good."

I broke through their awkward conversation and walked to the other end of the hall. Dean followed and we entered our history classroom. Scattered conversations of students trickling in filled the air, yet somehow the room was eerily silent.

Dean leaned against a desk, and I stood in front of him with crossed arms. The World War Two posters hung on the wall behind him; the irony was almost amusing—if it weren't for how sad the situation was.

"I got your note." Dean stared at the ground. "You didn't have to—"

"I wanted to," I interrupted.

I wanted to talk to Dean on the anniversary of his mom's passing. I had so many words for him—words I would only feel comfortable saying to him. And I wanted to face him—I did. But how do you look into the eyes of the person you love and accept that they love somebody else? You can't. So you write them a letter instead.

He looked down for what seemed like an eternity. "Well, thank you for the things you wrote about my mom." His blue eyes seemed sincere.

"Sure." I paused. "I really loved her."

"She loved you too." Dean nodded slowly. "Listen . . . Sonny . . . I've been wanting to tell you something. . . ."

I hugged my arms around myself, mentally preparing for what I knew was coming next.

"I'm . . . um . . . I'm sorry for the way I ended things with you," he said, his voice at an all-time low. "Things were getting so intense between our dads. I felt like I had to pick a side."

"And you picked one."

Dean dropped his chin to his chest. "Sonny . . . don't do this. You expected me to pick you over my own dad?"

"No," I replied. "But I wish you could understand the position my father was in. He didn't try to ruin you, as you suggested. Your dad did some shady things."

"You don't know that for sure."

"There was evidence, Dean."

"Hardly."

"There was."

"He could have been framed."

"By who?"

Dean tossed his hands into the air. "Anyone."

"I don't think so," I replied.

"Look, I didn't ask you to talk so we could fight about our dads." Dean took a deep breath. "Defending my dad to the death wasn't worth losing you. Especially not to that Jacob kid."

I nodded. "So that's what this is about? You're jealous of me and Jacob?"

"Of course I am." He shrugged.

"Big deal, Dean. I made a friend. Do you realize you dumped me for Norah?"

"I didn't dump you for her. You and I broke up and she was . . . there."

I placed my fingers on my forehead. "I never wanted to break up."

"I didn't either, Sonny. I made a mistake. I was hurt and so I hurt you. I've thought about it every day. I've thought about everything I should have done differently or could have said, but didn't. I want to make it right. Tell me what I can do."

My eyes locked in with Dean's. "How could you break up with me, Dean? It's me."

"I know." He searched for sympathy in my eyes. "Look, what else can I say? I was a coward. I should have never let what happened between our dads get in between us. It was the dumbest decision I've ever made, and I'm crazy sorry for it. Tell me what to do and I'll do it."

"I can't tell you that," I replied.

"Well, then give me a chance to figure it out. Give me until after the fall dance this Saturday."

"Why?"

"I'm Norah's date," he said. "But I plan to end things with her after the dance. Just give me until then. Please."

I paused. "Why should I trust you, Dean?"

I was strangely aware of feeling alone in that room with him; the scattered desks, the Smartboard screen, the clock on the wall all seemed to be watching us.

"You shouldn't," he replied. "But you know you already do." He looked me up and down, as if he missed every inch of me. "So? Will you give me that chance?"

I wasn't sure I wanted to say no. I wasn't sure my answer was yes. Part of me never wanted to see him again and part of me, perhaps the more hopeful part, urged me to risk it. And I guess that's the scary thing about risks—you never really know which are good ones to take.

"Five-minute warning!" Mr. Jones stood in front of his desk. "Find your seats!"

I quickly brushed by Dean and walked to the front of the room, my hand raised and my head down. "Restroom," I said as I walked toward the classroom door.

"Quickly, Ms. Carter," said Mr. Jones.

I walked back into the hallway and headed toward the restroom, unsure of who I was running from—Dean or myself. I looked down as I placed one foot in front of the other on the squeaky floor, stopping just shy of turning the corner, where I heard a familiar voice. I peeked my head around the edge of the wall.

"Can we talk?"

"Ari . . . To what do I owe this pleasure?" Cliff asked.

"I thought you said you'd shut down the rumor mill," she said, her hands on her hips. "It's still spinning strong."

"I did what I could do, Ziegler. People are going to believe what they want to believe."

"Look, I need this to go away. What do I have to do?"

"Why are you asking me?" Cliff rummaged through his locker. "Go talk to Piper. I heard she leaked the video."

"Wait, what? Piper leaked the video? My Piper?"

"Apparently. Look, what does it matter, Ari? So what if a few people think we kissed?" Cliff slid a pencil behind his ear. "As long as Kyle doesn't suspect anything, we're good."

"And how are you so sure he won't?"

"I'm not," Cliff said.

Ari gritted her teeth, splaying her hands and then relaxing them again. "Aren't you the least bit nervous about the fact that someone is messing with us? Why us? Why now? Especially after the SCC was changed. Whoever leaked this clearly has nothing to lose. That's a dangerous thing. They have us on video—"

"Shut . . . the hell . . . up." Cliff looked around the hallway. "Nobody knows about us. About any of it. Let me remind you of our deal. We deny everything. If this gets out, your relationship is done, and Kyle could turn on me. We plan to play football together at Cornell."

"Don't you think I know that?" Ari glared at him.

"Well, so help you God if you ruin our friendship." Cliff paused. "Stop trying to figure this out, Ari. Drop it."

"Are you threatening me?" she asked.

Cliff ran the back of his pointer finger over his top lip, exhaling slightly. "Despite what we had, and what we had was good, I'd turn on you faster than you could say 'Cobalt' if it meant my relationship with Kyle, or my future."

"You wouldn't do that to me," Ari said. "After everything we—"

"Jesus!" Cliff slammed his locker. "There is no *we*, Ari. Don't you get that by now?"

"There could have been," she replied.

Cliff raised his eyebrows and leaned down toward her. "Stop that."

"You're the one who came crawling back to me after you and Lana broke up." Ari crossed her arms. "If you didn't want me—"

"I never said I don't want you." Cliff paused. "I can't have you."

"All of a sudden you can't be with me?"

"All of a sudden?" A quick, nervous laugh escaped from Cliff's mouth. "Of course I can't be with you, Ari! Kyle's my best friend!"

"Right. You can only hook up with me behind his back."

"Look, do you think this has been easy for me? Watching you and Kyle? Dating Lana last year was the only good thing that's happened. It stopped us."

"Just until you broke up. Then you came back to me."

"You took me back! I'm a guy, Ari. What was I supposed to do?"

"Oh, so this is *my* fault?"

"It's *our* fault," Cliff said. "You're letting your emotions cloud your judgement. Just drop it, okay? You don't want to go to war with me, Ari. Believe me—you'll lose."

"Maybe you've underestimated how tough I am," Ari retorted, stepping toward Cliff.

He leaned in closer and lowered his voice, not breaking eye contact with her—not even to blink. "Tough? One video leak and you're crawling to my locker on shaking hands and knees. You're weak, Ari. You always have been. Which is likely why you thought hooking up with your boyfriend's best friend was a good idea."

"And what does that make you?" Ari asked.

"A Violet." Cliff rocked backward down the hall and smiled. "I'll always be a Violet, Ari. And despite who you curl up next to at night—you'll always be a Cobalt. Remember that."

I peeled myself away from the edge of the wall, my hand over my mouth. And with nowhere else to run, I ran back to history class.

Thankfully, Saturday morning arrived quickly. Impatience for the weekend was an emotion most students felt—but doubly so for Westcott students.

"I hope you said no." Jacob leaned against his kitchen counter, his hands in his jean pockets.

I mindlessly stirred my spoon around in my hot herbal tea, shoveling the honey from side to side at the bottom of the mug as I waited for my meeting with Ron. And while I thought I was paying attention to Jacob, I couldn't be sure. My mind hadn't quite allowed me to stop thinking about what I'd overheard in the hallway earlier in the week. I wanted to tell Kyle, or at least someone, but I couldn't find the courage—no matter how hard I looked for it.

"Sonny?" Jacob tried again to get my attention.

I looked up. "Sorry."

"So? Are you going to give Dean another chance?"

"It's complicated," I said.

"It's actually simple." Jacob clutched the counter with his hands and hopped backward onto it. "He's dating Norah."

"Just until the dance tonight. Then he's breaking up with her."

Confusion filled his eyes. "For you or for him?"

"Can't it be both?" I licked the honey off my spoon in a daze.

"Is he at all concerned with your happiness?" Jacob asked, tapping his fingers on the marble countertops.

I took a sip of my tea. "Well, I'm assuming that's why he's breaking up with Norah."

"No, Sonny. If he cared about you at all, he'd do what's best for you. And what's best for you is not dating someone who thinks it's okay to bounce back and forth between girls."

The urge to defend Dean suddenly kicked in. "And how would you know what's best for me?"

"Maybe I don't," he replied. "But I know how good guys act. And that's not it. Dumping her at her own dance? Who does that?"

"Technically he's waiting until after the dance." I looked down into my mug, continuing to stir. "Besides, like Norah will care."

"That's not the point, Sonny. Dean should. It's an integrity thing."

"Why are you getting so heated, Jacob? Isn't this good news for you?"

"How so?"

"If Dean breaks up with Norah, it means she's up for grabs. Wasn't that what you wanted? Norah?"

Jacob paused for an uncomfortable amount of time. "Look, I just don't want to see him hurt you again. That's all."

"Well, you didn't see it the first time."

"Lucky him." Jacob stared through me.

"Look, Dean and I are just working on our friendship."

"Is that what he told you?" Jacob hopped down off the counter, becoming antsy.

"He's special to me, Jacob." I tapped the top of my mug with my spoon. "That's never going away."

"Okay," Jacob said as he leaned over the island in front of me. His strong arms rested just shy of the stove. "Just go to the dance with me tonight."

"Uh, no. I don't dance," I said.

Jacob pushed himself off the island and back toward the countertop behind him. "Perfect," he said. "I don't either."

"No, really, I can't."

"Go with me or dance?" he asked.

"Both."

"I might believe you have zero rhythm, but in no way do I believe you can't go with me."

"Believe it." I took another sip of tea. "And I sort of have something to do when I get there."

"Please," he pleaded. "It's just one night."

Suddenly, Ron shouted from the upstairs hallway. "Come on in, Sonny! Sorry for the delay!"

I looked toward the steps and then back at Jacob.

"Fine." I reluctantly agreed. "But this is not a date."

"This is most definitely a date," he replied.

"Not a date," I said as I hopped down from the barstool, taking one last sip of tea before walking away.

"Definitely is!" Jacob shouted as I approached the stairs. "I'll pick you up at six thirty!"

"I'll meet you there!" I yelled, taking back some control.

For the next two hours, Ron and I went over the Farrah Klein case as I continually beat my pencil against numerous parts of my body. I did my absolute best to pay attention to the intricate details of the trial, but the only thing on my mind was asking him one question.

"Thanks so much for today," I said as I packed up my notepads. "I think I have enough information to begin my paper."

"Oh, of course." Ron came to the other side of his desk and leaned against it. "I love talking about the Klein story. It was the highlight of my career."

"So far, I'm sure."

"Well, I'm always working on things." He looked around his desk at the scattered paperwork.

"Really?" I asked, intrigued by his project.

"It's hush-hush," he said.

I nodded. "Mr. Harrison, can I ask you something a bit more personal?"

"Certainly," he replied.

"If I had incriminating information on someone at my school—or rather, suspicions—what should I do?"

"Well, that depends. Are you in any danger?"

"No," I replied. "This is all hypothetical."

He coughed into his closed fist. "Well then, hypothetically speaking, you should bring your suspicions to your principal."

"What if I didn't want to get my principals involved?"

"Then I suppose you'd need to bring your suspicions to someone else."

"Someone . . . like . . ."

"Me," he said.

His sentence shot right through me.

"Those are interesting questions, Sonny. Is there anything you'd like to share with me?"

"Possibly," I replied. "But there's something I need to do first."

Questions. Some are silly and harmless. Others are powerful and meaningful. Perhaps the most powerful one of them all is this: Are we ever really ready for the answers?

10
MASKS

Masks—those dangerous things we slip on when we're tired of being our true, authentic selves. We will all wear one at some point in life. Sometimes we wear them to hide, other times to escape. If you're one of the lucky ones, you'll always be able to differentiate between you and the charade. And if you aren't so lucky, in the most unfortunate way, the charade will become you.

"Where the hell is she? It's seven thirty." Buckets's eyes roamed the dark courtyard with intention.

I tucked my black blouse into my high-waisted black jeans. "She'll be here, Buckets. She probably got caught in traffic."

"It definitely doesn't feel like Halloween." Kyle checked the time on his cell phone, then skimmed the parking lot with anxious eyes.

"That's because it isn't," Buckets said as we watched students flood through the gymnasium doors—some in costume, some not.

At Westcott, we had exams over the week of Halloween. It was more or less standardized testing to determine our academic rankings, but nonetheless, we had our Halloween dance a few weeks early so we could all use that week to study. The current theme was masquerade. And wearing masks seemed to be quite fitting on a home-invasion night such as the one we were planning.

"Hey, guys." Casey approached the circle wearing a white long-sleeved lace shirt and tight white skinny jeans, her straight blonde hair falling against her shoulder blades. Her outfit hugged her body tight, and everyone took notice —especially Kyle.

Winston tossed his hands up in the air. "When did you two plan to dress in solid colors and why didn't you tell me? What a missed opportunity for my red corduroy pants." He looked down at his red button-up shirt.

"And I could have been the yellow ranger." Buckets mocked his idea.

I looked over at Kyle, who was losing himself in the act of staring Casey up and down.

"Where were you?" Buckets asked her as he begrudgingly put on his yellow mask.

"I parked in parking lot C."

Kyle looked out into the parking lot. "Why did you do that? There has to be fifty parking spots open right here."

I often wondered what it must feel like to not have a wealthy father and mansion to run to when you got tired of living at your middle-class mother's house. And how it must have felt to be Casey—who had neither.

Casey glanced over at the rows of luxury vehicles as she tucked the keys to her ten-year-old beater car into her back pocket. "Oh," she replied. "I must have missed them."

I felt bad knowing that Kyle was becoming increasingly and genuinely confused by Casey. I also knew he liked that in a girl.

"Well, you look pretty." Kyle tapped Casey's arm.

She ran her fingers through her hair, grabbing her neck on the way down. "Thank you," she said.

At that moment, I felt two strong hands grab my waist as a very recognizable scent swept in from behind me.

"What's up?" Jacob said.

I turned around and instantaneously scouted his body, thankful my black mask gave shield to my blushing cheeks. He wore fitted navy-blue slacks with a tight burgundy V-neck sweater, the collar on his navy-blue button-up hanging out. He tucked his hands into his pockets and took a step back.

"You clean up nicely," I said, still scouting.

He took a moment, then swallowed and spoke. "So do you."

Suddenly, Buckets coughed and glared at me. I read his expression.

"Um, can you wait for me inside, Jacob?" I asked him. "I have to talk to the group for a minute."

"Sure." He looked down and dragged his dress shoe across the concrete, his hands still in his pockets. "I'll be right inside the door."

I watched him walk away—for longer than necessary.

"You didn't tell him about our plan, did you?" Buckets asked.

"No, of course not," I said, focusing my gaze on the clusters of our fellow classmates passing by.

"So, when are we doing this?" Kyle asked.

"I need to buy thirty minutes with Jacob," I replied.

"What? You didn't inform us you'd come bearing a date. We're supposed to have back sweat from anxiety for half an hour while you dance with Zorro?" Buckets looked at me while tapping his foot.

"Would you relax?" I said. "We can't disappear the second we walk inside. That's too suspicious. We wait it out for thirty."

"You better hope you've thought this through," Winston told me. "Your seat on the Chosen Ten is on the line."

Kyle rubbed his temples. "We're all on the line. This could cost us everything."

I looked around the circle, into the faces of my friends, wondering if even I knew what I had gotten us all into.

"Let's move it." Buckets shoveled us toward the gym's double doors. "We all look suspicious."

The dances at Westcott High were unlike those at most schools, or so I'd heard. An established and reputable event planner came in to throw us the most decadent of parties. School dances were perhaps the only time we WH students felt like normal high schoolers. It was a time when we could loosen up and have some actual fun with one another —outside of double-crossing each other to climb the social and academic ladders.

"Wow, I see they didn't hold back this year," Casey said, her voice barely audible over the thundering music.

Our eyes slowly floated around the room. Blue-and-white balloon bunches covered the high ceiling, and cocktail tables—stacked with gourmet appetizers and desserts—surrounded us. Even the cupcakes looked rich.

Winston slapped a massive cluster of shiny balloons out of his face. "Do they ever?"

"You wanna go sit?" Jacob once again came from behind and grabbed my waist.

I looked down at his hands, unsure of whether or not to move them or be moved.

"Meet at the stairs in thirty," I said to the group as Jacob led me away toward the lounge area.

"I can't thank you enough for being my date," he said.

I grabbed a drink off a waiter's tray and rolled my eyes. "Happy to be here."

"I know I practically begged you to come with me," said Jacob, "but just so you know, I hate school dances."

I scrunched my nose, attempting to digest the potent punch. "Then why did you want to come?"

He leaned in toward the side of my face. "To spend time with you."

"Well, we could have done that anywhere," I replied.

"You're right. Let's blow this Popsicle stand and go back to my place."

"Wow." I nodded. "You just keep getting cringier."

Jacob dropped his chin to his chest and laughed. "I'm the new kid. I can still be cringy until a clique decides to adopt me. Then I'll need to adapt to my surroundings and become a replica of my new friends. Whoever they will be."

"Well, hopefully it's not the brocks," I replied, staring back and forth between Jacob and the room full of dancers.

Jacob's eyes slowly skimmed my body.

I took notice.

"What?" I tucked my hair behind my ear with my left hand, the glass of punch still in the right one.

He skimmed some more and grinned. "Nothing."

"What is it?" I asked again.

Jacob took a step back and stared down at the gym floor, then looked at me. "You're just so beautiful."

I wasn't sure why I could never respond to Jacob's sweet comments, and why I always chose to stare at him in silence. Perhaps they always took me off guard. Or maybe they just always took the breath out of me.

"Hi, Sonny," Dean said as he drew near, interrupting Jacob's and my mutual gaze. He wore a fitted black T-shirt and dark jeans, with his faded black bomber jacket.

Something about him caught my eye in a way it never had before. He looked refreshed. Like he'd taken a long, meaningful shower and washed away all that life had thrown at him.

"We match," I said.

Dean grabbed his jacket and opened it; he looked down at his shirt. "So we do." He nodded. "Great minds."

"You know, I heard that's a myth," I replied.

He pulled his head back. "Really?"

"I think it just stems from society's need to find consensus. There's no way two totally separate minds could think the same thing, the same way."

"Unless they're twins," Dean replied. "I hear most twins are telepathic."

"What about conjoined twins?" I asked. "That share the same brain?"

Dean's eyes danced across my face. "Is that a thing?"

"I think it's a thing." I nodded. "*They* must be able to think alike."

"I don't think I'd want to know what my conjoined twin was thinking all the time," Dean said.

"Or would it be you thinking it?"

We stared into each other's eyes as smiles slowly emerged on our faces.

Jacob's eyes bounced back and forth between Dean and me. "I'm Jacob." He went in for a handshake. "I saw you at tryouts."

"Dean," he replied, his hands remaining tucked into his bomber-jacket pockets.

I caught a glimpse of their egoistic power struggle over the side of my cup as I tried to wash down my uneasiness.

"You getting ready for the big scrimmage?" asked Dean, swaying back and forth before finding a stance.

Jacob put his hand back into his pocket. "I have to make the team first."

"Think you'll make it?" Dean looked Jacob up and down, folding his arms in front of him.

"I think so," Jacob replied.

Dean nodded. "I think it's too early to tell."

Jacob ran his thumb over his bottom lip before crossing his arms. "I think I'll worry about me, and you can worry about you."

"That might be difficult," Dean said. "Considering I'm the captain."

"I'm sure we can make it work." Jacob widened his stance.

"What do you need, Dean?" I asked, hoping to bring an end to the heated exchange.

"I just came over to say hi." Dean grabbed my arm and pulled me in toward him. He gently removed my black mask from my face and placed it in my hands. "I miss you," he said, wiping the loose glitter off my cheeks.

Our eyes met, and although I knew it wasn't true, I was somehow convinced we were the only two in the room. It was the first time I'd felt his touch in months. I almost forgot how much I needed it.

"Where's your date?" Jacob asked Dean, his voice competing with the music.

Dean kept eye contact with me, dismissing Jacob's question entirely. "I'll catch up with you later, okay?"

My heart skipped a beat, or twenty, as I watched him walk away.

Jacob suddenly turned toward me, cutting my gaze short. "What are you doing with this guy, Sonny? Just tell me what it is about him. I don't get it."

"He's a good person," I said.

He tugged at his sweater and shifted his weight from leg to leg. "He's a cocky little shit."

"Jacob—"

"No, Sonny! You can do better than him."

"You don't know him, Jacob."

"I know he doesn't deserve you." Jacob's forehead glistened in the light of the mirrored disco ball spinning from the gymnasium's ceiling.

I gave him a sad, shameful stare—one that implied he was wrong, and in the same breath, one that suggested he may be right.

Just then, I spotted JC on the other side of the room. He was sitting alone on a sizable white couch. His elbows dug into his knees, and his hands cupped around his mouth.

I wrapped my fingers around Jacob's bicep and gave it a tiny squeeze. "I'll be right back," I said.

"Where are you going now?" he asked.

"I'll be back. I promise."

"Who am I supposed to dance with?"

"I told you—I don't dance." I took a few steps in the opposite direction, then turned back around to face Jacob. "Try Norah!"

He dropped his head and sighed. "I don't—"

My eyes narrowed.

"Yeah." He paused. "I'll do that."

I could feel Jacob's eyes on my back as I walked toward JC. I eventually plopped down on the sofa—accepting defeat.

"I didn't take you for a wallflower kind of guy." I stared out into the crowd with JC, offering him my company—if not much more.

JC laughed under his breath, but I could tell he was in no mood for my jokes.

"She looks happy." JC watched Piper engage in casual conversations from across the way. "At least more so than usual."

"Doesn't everyone? Look happy?" I sighed, inconvenienced by my own polemicist ways.

JC shook his head and let out a short breath. "Why do you always do that? Come up with these alternative options as to what things could be or might mean?"

"That's what good writers do," I replied.

"Yeah." JC bowed his head and nodded. "I guess you have always been that—a good writer."

"She'll come around and come clean." I tilted my head toward him. "I don't know why Piper did this, but I know she loves you."

"And how would you know that?"

"Because I know love." I paused. "Sure, love can do a lot of things to throw you off. But I know what it looks like, and what it doesn't. I know when it's dead, and I know when it's not."

JC dropped his face into his cupped hands and rubbed his fingers up and down. I couldn't begin to understand the torture that comes with despising the person you're despondently in love with. Perhaps not even Jeremy Coleman could wrestle with those kinds of demons.

"You seem to know a whole lot about love for someone who can't see it when it's slapping them in the face," he said, still rubbing his head all over.

I looked over at JC, my eyes expressing confusion.

"Jacob likes you, Carter."

"You don't know that," I said.

"I know that," JC replied swiftly. "He's been practically undressing you with his eyes since you walked in."

"Jacob likes Norah," I countered.

"I can tell by the way he asks me questions about *you* when we shoot hoops together."

"We're friends," I said.

"Friends." JC leaned back, resting his forearms on the back of the couch. He grinned at me and nodded. "Okay, Carter."

I quickly looked away. My eyes locked in with Casey's as she motioned me to come over. My heart sank, knowing the evening's adventure was ready to meet me. "Looks like it's time." I reluctantly pushed myself off the couch and stood to my feet.

"Sonny . . ." JC stopped me before I could walk off.

I stood in front of him and stared, my arms dropped by my side.

"Be careful with Ballinger," he said. "Love can lie too."

Suddenly, Casey walked up behind me and pulled me away.

I gazed at JC until I could no longer see him, unable to break away from his haunting statement.

"We have to come up with a plan B," Casey said as we walked toward the others. "Piper's been eyeing us since we walked in. She's definitely on to us."

My feet were moving, but my mind was still on the couch with JC, and my heart was still bouncing back and forth between Dean and Jacob. Beautiful dresses and colorful masks swirled around me as I pushed through the crowded gymnasium.

"We can't all leave at once," Buckets said as Casey and I approached the stairs. "It'll be too obvious."

I put my mask back on. "Then I'll go alone."

"No way in hell," Kyle interjected. "I'm going with you."

"Then go now," Winston said, glancing behind him toward Piper. "Before she realizes something's up."

"Come on." Kyle grabbed my arm and pulled me toward the exit.

"Clemmons is standing at the doors," Buckets said. "You'll have to go around the back."

We stopped in our tracks and took a sharp right turn.

"Keep your phones on in case I text you," Kyle shouted as he looked at the group.

"Man! I was just about to turn mine off!" Winston's sarcasm sliced through the thick air.

We turned the corner toward the back of the school where the classrooms were and immediately slowed our pace. I had never seen the hallway so dark, and metaphorically speaking, that was saying something. I placed my hand out in front of me, moving it from side to side in a futile attempt to push the heavy shadows out of my path. The stillness was uncanny.

"Did you feel the temperature drop?" I grabbed my arms.

Kyle took off his expensive jean jacket and placed it around my shoulders, giving them a quick rub before letting go. "Here."

"They must keep the air on over the weekend," I said.

"No, I don't think they do," he replied, adding to the bone-chilling feeling jolting through my body.

"Why aren't you wearing a mask?" I asked him.

Kyle rolled his eyes to the right, silently answering my question.

Suddenly, a shadow appeared just before we reached Mrs. Penn's classroom door. "What are you up to?"

We jumped back in horror. "Jesus!" we yelled in sync.

"I hope you're praying," Principal Winchester said, his arms crossed.

"What the hell are you doing lurking in the dark hallway?" Kyle shined his cell phone light in his dad's face.

Principal Winchester's eyes nearly closed as he held up his hands to block the brightness. "Language, please," he said. "And I could ask you two the same question." He stepped forward, squinting. "Kyle?"

"I, uh, I forgot something in Mrs. Penn's room."

"What did you forget?"

"My gym bag. I left it in there by accident."

I was impressed by Kyle's ability to lie on cue.

"And you?" Principal Winchester said, pointing at me.

I slowly removed my mask, placing it on the top of my head like sunglasses.

"I'm just tagging along, sir," I said.

He gave us a stern look.

Mr. Winchester's presence was intimidating. He was tall, powerful, and stone cold—not the type of man to stand around listening to teenagers offer nonsensical explanations.

Principal Winchester turned around. "You have one minute," he said as he took out his keys.

The gold key ring caught my eye as he shoved the master key into the lock on Mrs. Penn's classroom door. The sound it made was deafening.

We waited until he was out of sight before attempting to move.

"Let's get out of here," I said, running toward the exit door and into the parking lot. Kyle followed closely behind me.

"We'll take my car," he said as we walked quickly toward his white Range Rover.

He opened the passenger-side door for me, and I crawled inside. The moonlight beamed through the windows and bounced off the dashboard, barely providing enough brightness to see. Kyle opened the driver's side door and jumped in, then cranked the car and backed out of his parking spot with intention.

"I can't believe we're doing this," I said.

"Really? I swear it was your idea." Kyle's sarcasm rolled off my shoulders as we pulled onto the main road.

"Just hurry," I said, checking my cell phone every second for a text from the others.

Kyle ran a red light.

"This is illegal, right?" My sweaty palms reached for my seat belt.

"Very," he said, making a sharp left turn.

"Kind of like that time we broke into your neighborhood pool after closing?" I asked.

"Kind of," he replied. "Except not at all. Besides, you broke in. All I did was hold your foot and propel you over the gate so you could unlock it for me."

"Nice." I nodded. "Is that how you plan to respond if we're caught tonight?"

Kyle reached into his cup holder. "Gum?" he asked, holding a pack of chewing gum toward my face.

I grabbed a stick, unwrapped it, and tossed the crumpled-up wrapper at Kyle's head.

We drove for another minute before approaching the entrance to Piper's neighborhood. As we passed by the looming mansions, I was nearly gasping for breath.

"On second thought, maybe this isn't such a good idea," I said.

Kyle cautiously approached Piper's home. He parked along the curb and unbuckled his seat belt. "Too late," he said as he unbuckled mine too. "Let's go."

I reluctantly got out of the car, and Kyle met me on the curb. We walked toward the house, looking around on the dark street with every step we took. I could almost hear Kyle's heart beating. Or perhaps it was my own.

Piper's home resembled a castle. The taupe brick went higher than my eyes could see. There were arched windows upon nearly every foot of the home, and the white columns stretched twenty feet high. The striped grass was perfectly executed, and yard lanterns lit the way as we walked along the stone driveway toward the garage.

"I didn't know Piper lived at Hogwarts," I whispered.

Kyle looked up toward the sky. "Even the trees seem taller than normal."

We approached the garage door.

"Are you sure they don't have cameras?" he asked. "This would seem like the type of house to have them. We definitely do."

"JC said they don't," I replied, reaching for the keypad. I slowly punched the numbers, and the garage door rolled up.

We both looked at each other, unquestionably more terrified than we were while breaking and entering at the pool.

"Let's go," he said as he walked inside.

I followed.

We opened the side door to the house, and I punched the alarm code in. The wealth met us at the door. Perhaps Kyle was used to a home so beautiful, but I was taken aback. My father did well for himself—but not this well. And my mother? Not even close.

We walked through the kitchen and then into the living room toward the staircase, which curved upward toward the second story. The room's modern furniture sat on a polished wood floor. The walls were off-white, and the white-and-gray chevron area rugs had vacuum marks across them. The matching white drapes framed the windows, and the moonlight reflected off the glass furniture.

"Wow." Kyle looked around the room. "Cozy."

I was too nervous to laugh. "Come on!"

We walked up the stairs; each creak I heard sent a rush through my blood.

"JC said Piper's room is the first one on the right." I pulled up a text from Winston. "And Piper's still at the dance. Winston has his eye on her. And Clemmons."

We got to the top of the landing, which could accommodate a herd of elephants. The walls were covered in photos of Piper, some of her dad, and none of her mom. Apparently, the divorce was worse than anyone knew. We made a right turn and entered Piper's room.

"I could've sworn we just came from here," Kyle said.

I looked around. The décor was the same off-white walls, chevron-patterned rugs, and glass furniture from before. The only color in sight came from the rows of books lining the two tall bookshelves.

"At least they're consistent," I said. "Let's just look for the envelope and get out of here."

I rushed into the dark room, turned on a glass desk lamp, and began searching through Piper's desk drawers. Stacks of sheet music and homework were piled everywhere. A Princeton mug sat center of the desk, with color-coordinated ink pens stuffed inside. One of her many violins sat in the corner of her room next to a wooden stool, and on top of the stool sat a black folder. I walked over and picked it up.

"Look at this," I said as I lifted the folder toward my face. "It says Westcott Awards. This must be her piece."

Kyle walked up behind me as I opened it.

" 'Puppet,' " he read aloud. "Random title."

I ran my fingers over the sheet music. The pen marks, scribbles, and music notes meshed together to create a whole lot of gibberish. I couldn't understand it if I wanted to. Perhaps her musical piece wasn't the only thing I couldn't begin to understand.

"Maybe that title is not so random," I mumbled as I looked around Piper's lifeless room.

"Can I ask you something?" Kyle said.

"I don't know." I walked back to Piper's desk and began searching through the stacks of papers. "Can you?"

Kyle tipped a book off the shelf and mindlessly flipped through the pages. "Do you have to correct everyone's grammar?"

"Do you have to fight it?" I asked, squinting at each paper. "What's your question?"

"What's the deal with Casey?" he asked.

My frantic search became slower as his question took me aback. "What do you mean?"

"I mean—it seems like she's hiding something."

"Like what?" I asked.

"I don't know. Okay, for example, she didn't want me to pick her up tonight, which was super weird."

"Not weird," I replied. "I didn't let Jacob pick me up."

"That's because you play hard to get."

"Maybe I am hard to get."

"Or maybe you're a control freak."

"Or maybe both," I said.

"But then Casey parks on the opposite end of the school. Parking lot C is almost a quarter of a mile away from where we were supposed to meet."

"Maybe she wanted the exercise." I skimmed through a third stack of papers.

Kyle closed the book and picked up another one. "You do know I can tell when you're lying."

"I'm not lying. I'm just passively responding to your statements."

"Come on, Sonny. What gives?"

I slammed a drawer closed and looked up. "Look— Casey's just—she's just not like the rest of us."

"What? She's a Cobalt?" He shrugged his shoulders. "I already knew that."

"She's more than a Cobalt. Or less, rather. She's—"

"What are you trying to say?"

I dropped my head. "Casey's dad is in prison."

Kyle's eyes descended toward the chevron rug.

"He was arrested for drug trafficking, amongst a list of other charges. Her mom is also a user. And an alcoholic. She sent Casey and her brothers to Westcott to live with their aunt."

"So she doesn't want anyone to know about her parents?" he asked.

"Or the fact that they're broke. Her aunt works tirelessly but can hardly afford to take care of the three of them. They struggle—to say the least."

Kyle stayed quiet, looking lost in his own thoughts.

"She parked in parking lot C because that's where she always parks," I said. "So nobody will ever have to see her beat-up car. And she didn't want you to pick her up because she probably didn't want you to see her house."

I watched Kyle as he tried to understand something he never could.

"Why didn't she just tell me?" he asked. "We've been talking every night. That wouldn't have come up?"

"That definitely wouldn't have come up," I replied. "Besides, did you tell her everything about your parents?"

Kyle ran his hand through his hair, brushing off my question. "I heard you reached out to Dean," he said.

I opened Piper's bottom left desk drawer. "Who told you that?"

"Dean," he replied. "I caught him crying in the bathroom."

"Caught him? Well, thank God you were there to stop it."

"He showed me your letter."

"He showed it to you?" I asked.

"I didn't read it," Kyle said, lifting his hands in the air. "But it looked like you pulled out the big guns. He was pretty torn up."

"Well, I really cared about his mom."

Kyle nodded. "And Dean too, right?"

I peered at a stack of papers. "I don't want to hear another lecture about Dean."

"Who gave you the first one?"

"First . . ." I smiled. "If only I were so lucky."

"Shouldn't that be a sign? That multiple people are expressing concern?" Kyle asked.

"Look, I know he made some mistakes. And he regrets them. But Dean . . . well, Dean is my soulmate."

"I thought I was your soulmate," Kyle replied.

I reached into the drawer and grabbed another stack of papers. "I only agreed to marry you if I was still single at thirty."

Kyle lifted up his fingers and pretended to count. "Fourteen more years."

"That's it?" I pretended to look horrified.

"Very funny," said Kyle. "Look, Sonny, I support you. Just like you support me and my dumb decisions, but—"

"Dean is a dumb decision?"

"Oh, yeah," he replied. "The dumbest. But I still support you, as long as you promise to always be mindful. And I'm not so sure falling for two guys at once is a good idea."

I smirked. "That's rich coming from you."

"I'm serious, Sonny. I don't want you to get hurt."

"Why does everyone think Jacob and I are anything more than friends?" I asked.

"Jacob might be your friend . . . but you're not just a friend to him."

"And what makes you so sure that he likes me?" I opened another drawer.

"He asked you to the dance, didn't he?"

"So? You asked Casey."

"I like Casey. Point proven."

"You also like Ari," I said.

"And you also like Dean. Looks like we're in the same boat."

"The same *unmindful* boat?"

Kyle let out a deep breath and looked toward the ceiling. "Just be careful."

Just then, I reached into my back pocket and pulled out my buzzing cell phone. "You have nothing to worry about." I opened my text messages. "I'm always careful."

Kyle tossed a book into the air like a football. "Sure."

"Oh no," I whispered, staring at Winston's text. "He's lost eyes on Piper."

Kyle ran over to help me, ransacking through Piper's mountains of papers.

"We have to find the envelope," I said.

"It's not here," Kyle replied, panic rising in his voice.

"It has to be! Keep looking."

"Maybe she hid it somewhere," Kyle suggested.

"Like where?"

"I don't know," he said, tossing his hands behind his head.

I made my way over to Piper's nightstand and searched the drawer, where I found an array of prescription medications. "What is all of this?"

Kyle peeked over my shoulder. "Whoa . . ."

We stared down at the plastic orange bottles in a daze.

"Where, uh, where would you hide something in your room?" Kyle asked me, attempting to look away from the drawer full of pills.

"What am I hiding?" I closed the drawer.

"Anything," Kyle said. "A love letter? A magazine?"

"Do you think I'm twelve years old?" My eyes skimmed the room. "I guess if I needed a good hiding spot I'd pick under my mattress."

We stared at one another until the light bulb went off in both of our heads. I fell to my knees and shoved my hands underneath her mattress, frantically moving them around in circles.

"Oh my God!" My hands came to a stop.

All the way in the middle of the box spring was the item in question—the manila envelope.

"I found it."

Kyle kneeled down beside me, placing his hand on my back. "Open it. Quick!"

I pulled the envelope toward me as sweat began to emerge on my forehead.

"What's inside?" Kyle asked as he tapped my back and glanced at the bedroom door every five seconds.

I brought the envelope to my lap and carefully opened it. My hand slipped inside, and I pulled out a catalog.

"A Princeton catalog," I said, dropping the envelope to my lap.

"That's it?" Kyle grabbed it from my hands, flipping through the pages.

I dropped my shoulders in defeat. "You've got to be kidding me."

"Hand me my cell phone," Kyle said. "I want to take some photos just in case."

I stood, grabbed Kyle's phone out of his back pocket, and tossed it to him. He began snapping pictures at a speed that Buckets himself would envy.

"Are we sure that's the right envelope?" My eyes floated around the room.

"I'm guessing so," Kyle replied.

"But why would Piper need to hide a Princeton catalog underneath her mattress?"

He glanced at me. "Good question."

I shook my head and exhaled. "Let's just get out of here."

Kyle dropped the catalog back inside the envelope and shoved it under the mattress.

Without much thought or words, we both walked to the door, stopping in our tracks when we heard a noise from downstairs.

"What was that?" Kyle whispered.

We stared at one another with wide eyes as we heard another loud noise.

"Shit," he whispered. "She's here."

"Or he," I said, looking around the room.

"Let's jump out the window," Kyle said.

I knew the suggestion was idiotic, but I peeked through the blinds just to check. "We can't," I whispered. "We're too high up!"

All of a sudden, we heard the sound of high heels slowly clicking against the stairs. The sound echoed—each step sounding louder and more final than the last.

"What do we do?" Kyle asked.

My breathing became heavy. It wasn't an option for us to get caught, to get written up before we proved JC's innocence. But with nowhere to go besides through a window, and nowhere to hide besides underneath glass nightstands, we waited in the middle of the room to meet our fate. I tightened my mask, hoping to offset my loosened standards.

Kyle placed his fingertips on my thigh as he stepped in front of me.

Suddenly, the bedroom door creaked open.

"I think you have the wrong house." Norah peeled back her hot-pink masquerade mask, revealing her smudged makeup and puffy eyes.

"Jesus, Norah!" Kyle exhaled, turning his head toward the window in disbelief.

I stepped forward. "What are you doing here?" I whispered sternly.

"Really, Carter?" Norah's crossed arms wrapped around the waist of her tight pink dress. "You're asking *me* that?"

"How did you get in here?" Kyle asked.

"You left the garage door open," she replied. "Seriously, Winchester, if you're going to go breaking into people's houses—at least cover your tracks."

Norah walked to Piper's desk and ran her finger over the glass surface.

"How'd you know we were here?" I asked.

"I saw you two rushing into the parking lot toward Kyle's car," Norah replied. "Looked like you were up to something. So I followed you."

"What were you doing in the parking lot?" Kyle looked through the blinds.

"I was dumped." Norah sat down on Piper's desk chair and glared at me; her eyebrow was raised to the ceiling. "Had nothing else to do."

I looked at Norah's streaky face and couldn't help seeing myself in her.

"So you decided to follow us here?" Kyle asked.

Norah crossed her legs, her nude high heel pointing back at us. "I don't know why I'm on the stand," she said. "The real question is what are you two doing in my friend's bedroom?"

"Let's go." I looked at Kyle before walking toward the door.

Kyle followed.

"You can either tell me"—Norah held her phone in the air—"or you can tell Piper."

I stopped in my tracks and clenched my fists; then I jerked my body back around and stood in front of Norah. "You really are a cold little Violet."

Norah smirked, twisting herself around in the desk chair. "The coldest."

"We aren't going to stay here like sitting ducks," Kyle said. "We're leaving."

"Don't worry," Norah replied. "Piper went to the music room to practice for the Westcott Awards, and Clemmons is a chaperone, so he can't leave the dance quite yet." She looked at her fingernails. "We have time."

I exhaled in frustration. "You have to promise you won't tell."

"I don't make promises," Norah replied.

"Piper set JC up," Kyle blurted out.

"Kyle!" I shouted.

Norah's eyes narrowed. "What for?"

I sighed, knowing it was too late to turn back. "We don't know. That's what we're trying to figure out."

"And you thought snooping around Piper's room would give you your answers?"

"We thought this would." I reached back under the mattress and pulled the manila envelope toward me, then handed it to Norah.

She removed the contents. "And this is?"

"It appears to be a Princeton catalog," I replied, glancing back at Kyle.

Norah flipped through the pages. "Have you called the police?" She smirked, handing it back to me.

"Real funny," Kyle said.

"Oh, come on Winchester," Norah continued. "You think Piper had access to the answer key and planted it in her own boyfriend's wrestling bag?"

"JC also thinks Mr. Russell dropped this on his doorstep over the summer." I reached into my back pocket and handed Norah the riddle.

With narrowed irritated eyes, she unfolded the paper.

"We thought Mr. Russell was trying to suggest that there's something at Geraldine's," Kyle said.

Norah's eyes left the paper and shifted toward his. "Like?"

"Like evidence that would link Piper to the setup." He shrugged. "But we found nothing."

"We did, however, see Piper there. Which further confirms our suspicions."

"How so?" Norah asked.

I ran my fingers through my hair. "Not only did she warn me not to get involved, she saw me talking to Cliff at Geraldine's. The following Monday morning—his video was leaked."

"You think Piper leaked it?" Norah asked.

"To distract us," Kyle said. "She doesn't want us looking into it, because if we figure out she framed him, she goes down."

Norah took out a compact mirror from her purse and began wiping underneath her eyes. She then slowly uncrossed her legs, stood, and walked toward me. "I should have you ripped from the Chosen Ten for this, Sonny. One meeting with Winchester and—"

"No!" Kyle stepped forward. "Don't do that!"

"Don't worry, Kyle," Norah said. "You're safe."

"God!" Kyle ran his hand through his hair with force. "Why does everyone think my dad shows me favoritism?"

Norah crossed her arms. "Doesn't he?"

"Not at all! He left when I was ten. The only time I see him is every other weekend when he leaves me his black card, pats me on the shoulder, and goes to play golf. He can hardly look me in the eye because I took my mom's side after the divorce. We have no relationship."

Kyle and I stood in front of Norah. The silence in the room was heavy enough to shatter the glass furniture.

"I'm no enigmatologist." Norah cleared her throat. "But I think the riddle wants you to go through the school's safe."

The school's safe—a paragon of all things secretive. No student has ever seen it, and if I had to guess, no student ever thought to try.

"See yourself out," she said as she walked through the doorway and toward the staircase. "Before I change my mind and rat."

Kyle and I exchanged a look of confusion and followed.

"Norah, wait!" My voice commanded her attention. "Why are you helping us?"

She slowly turned around, her heel resting on the top step. "Because I love puzzles." She paused and glanced at Kyle. "And I really hate shitty fathers."

Sometimes we become our masks, slowly suffocating behind their hard plastic exteriors. But when the masks come off, because they always do, we learn that some of the faces underneath were never worth our fear.

11

THE PLAN

The early bird gets the worm. It's a popular concept, but far too often, the lazy birds who slept in are overlooked. If all the birds got up at the same time to get the worms, there wouldn't be enough to go around. So isn't the success of the early bird, in a way, due to the laziness of the birds that are still sleeping?

By the same token, would anyone be considered a winner without people who were okay with losing? Can a group be rich and powerful without a class of the poor and powerless? And in the same breath, can moralists stay perched on their moral high ground without the disgraced embroiled in scandals?

"A Princeton catalog?" JC held Kyle's phone in front of his face as he scrolled through the photos. "That's what was inside of the envelope?"

"We were just as shocked as you," I said as I scooted into our usual booth in the corner of the club's café the following Monday.

Casey followed closely behind. Then Kyle.

"I can't believe Norah agreed to stay quiet," Buckets said, still flipping through the photos with JC on the opposite side of the table.

"So she says," I added.

JC slammed Kyle's phone on top of the table.

"Whoa, JC, calm down," Kyle said.

"Calm down? Piper is hiding something and we have absolutely no idea what it is. Everywhere we turn is a dead end."

"We?" Buckets raised a brow.

"Quit being such an asshole," Kyle said. "We're trying to help you."

"The food will be five more minutes," Winston said, plopping down beside Buckets.

We all stared at him, and each other, in silence.

Winston looked around the table. "What'd I miss?"

I shook my head, exhaling loudly.

"So what do we do?" Buckets sipped on his energy drink. "What's your plan this time, Sonny?"

"I think we should bring our suspicions to Ron Harrison," I said. "He does PI work, and he's the best of the best. Maybe he'd be willing to look into things. We can tell him Piper framed JC, and we can show him Mr. Russell's paper."

"Jacob's dad?" Casey asked.

I nodded.

Buckets slammed his flat hand down on the table. "Take this to Ron? What evidence do we have? Photos of a catalog and a riddle?"

"Okay, could everyone stop beating the table?" Casey asked. "People are staring."

"We'll have more evidence than that," I said. "If you're all willing to help me get it."

"What are you saying?" Kyle questioned.

"We need to get into the safe," I replied.

"Jesus, Sonny!" Buckets looked side to side. "Absolutely not!"

"Why would Mr. Russell want us to go through the safe?" Casey asked.

"Let's find out," I replied.

"I'm drawing the line," said Winston. "Sounds moronic, since I probably should have drawn it while you attempted to convince us to break into Piper's house. But this? The safe? No way."

"I'm in," JC said. "I want in."

I looked up. "JC—"

"No, Sonny, I'm not letting you five do all of my dirty work," he said. "I want to help."

"When do you suppose we do this?" Kyle asked.

"Saturday night before the scrimmage," I replied. "It's the only time we know the office will be vacant."

Winston slammed his fist down on top of the table. "What is it with you and Saturday-night break-ins?"

"Winston!" Casey yelled.

"What?"

"The table," we all said in unison.

"Look, how are we going to pull this off?" Buckets asked. "There are cameras."

"You're going to freeze the frames," I replied.

"Really? That sounds a whole lot like something I'm *not* going to do," Buckets replied.

"Come on, Buckets! I know you can easily figure out how to hack into the security system. You're a technology genius."

"Sonny, I work with teenagers, not the government."

"So you can't do it?" Casey asked.

"I can," he replied. "I can't, however, break into the office. They keep it locked. How are we going to get in?"

"With Principal Winchester's keys . . ." I glanced at Kyle.

"No way," Kyle told me. "If he notices they're missing —I'm dead."

"He won't notice. You can put them back after the game."

Kyle rolled his head in circles. I could see he was tormented by the idea.

I leaned in closer to him. "Kyle . . . I wouldn't be asking you to do this if it wasn't necessary. We go in, we get into the safe, and we finally put this riddle to rest. Whatever's inside might give us our proof."

He shook his head. "I don't know."

"Please, Ky?" I stared into his hesitant eyes. "I need you."

"Don't do that."

"Do what?" I asked him.

"That thing. That needy thing you do with your eyes."

"Did it work?" I asked.

Kyle exhaled loudly. "You guys need to understand that if we get caught . . . we're done."

We all looked around the table at one another, lost in our own thoughts. Nobody talked, because in a situation so intense, *words fall short.*

"Are you decent?" Dean slowly opened my bedroom door.

I looked up at him from my bed, papers sprawled all around. "What if I wasn't?" I asked as I pulled my crop-top sweater down.

"Your mom let me in."

I tossed my pencil down and tightened my messy bun. "She doesn't do that for everyone."

"Yeah? Well, we do share a common dislike for her ex-husband. I plan to milk that." Dean sat down at my distressed orange desk.

"You know, I hear there's no greater bond than that of mutual hatred for another person."

"It works well for us." Dean smiled. "I also come bearing shakes." He held up two covered Styrofoam cups.

"Oh. Yum." I leaned over and took one of the cups from his hand.

"You don't have to pretend to like them. I know you don't."

"Thank God," I replied, tossing it into the trash can.

Dean's jaw dropped. "That was my peace offering!"

"That's a crappy peace offering," I said, curling back up to work on my paper.

"Noted for next time," he said. "Where were you today? I stopped by after school and you weren't here."

"I was at the club with some friends."

"What are you working on?" He took his jacket off.

"Just trying to put this paper together," I replied as I watched.

"For the Westcott Awards?" he asked.

"That's the one." I stared down at my interview notes. "By the way—how are you feeling after your big breakup? I hear you took a strong one to the cheek."

"She got me pretty hard." Dean rubbed his face.

"I also heard she was pretty rattled," I said as Norah's streaky face flashed across my mind.

"I noticed." He spun one of my pens around on my desk. "It was the right thing to do. Probably not the best place to do it, but definitely the right decision."

"I thought you said you were going to break up with her *after* the dance."

"That was the plan." He paused. "But she picked a fight with me, so I took that as my opportunity."

"What was your fight about?" I asked.

"I think she may have seen me talking to you," he replied.

I curled my fists up into my sweater. "That'll do it."

"Yep." Dean looked around my room. "It seems like it's been years since I've been here."

"It certainly does," I replied.

We paused, the silence hanging between us like a curtain.

"How's your dad doing?" I asked.

"He's finally bouncing back."

"Good," I replied.

Dean looked down at his shake. "It's been rough . . . for both of us." He sighed, spinning the pen some more. "I just don't know what he could have done with all of that money."

"What do you mean?" I asked.

"Well, it's not like he bought a boat. There was nothing to show for the amount of money that was withdrawn. He showed your dad his bank statements. He never deposited a dime. So if he didn't spend it on materialistic items, and he didn't put it into savings, where did it go?"

I stared at my low ceiling. "That's a good question."

"It doesn't matter anymore," he said. "I'm just happy I finally fixed things with you."

I looked down at the colorful blocks on my quilt. "Well, to add to the bright side of things, now that you're not with Norah you can save your money. I heard she's quite the expense."

Dean shook his head. "Would one fifty for a birthday dinner qualify as expensive?"

"And all you ever gave me was strawberry shakes and heartache."

Dean threw the pen at my legs. "You're not high maintenance."

"You know, I'm not sure you mean that as a compliment, but I'll take it."

"Good," Dean replied, smiling a little. "Speaking of Norah . . . what's up with her and Jacob?"

"What do you mean?"

Dean placed his hands behind his head and leaned back in the chair. "I saw them hugging in the hallway this morning."

"Hugging?" Although I wasn't sure why, my heart nearly shattered at the thought. "Norah and Jacob?"

"Yep."

"Are you sure it was them?" I asked.

"I'm positive," he replied.

"I don't know," I said. "I know he likes her. Maybe he's making his move now that she's single."

Dean gave me a dry smile. "Norah isn't who Jacob likes."

If looks could chastise.

He coughed. "I, uh, I should go. I have practice tomorrow. Better rest up."

"You made the team?" I pretended to be surprised.

"Funny." Dean stood up and put his jacket on. "Your friend made it too."

"Really?" My heart smiled for Jacob, although I tried to hide my excitement. "That's . . . cool."

"Very." He grabbed his shake. "You should put your paper away and get some sleep."

I watched Dean as he tugged down on his jacket and walked toward my bedroom door. His body language exuded loneliness. The kind that makes you wish you'd never met a person—so you didn't have to feel what loving them and losing them is like. The kind that has a certain type of potency, persuading you to draw near. And that's the unfortunate thing about loneliness—*it makes you believe you can be lonely together.*

"Dean . . ." I closed my notebook and jumped off my bed.

He spun back around to face me, his heavy eyes barely making the turn.

"Will you stay?"

Winston and I walked toward our cars the following day after school. The sky was dreadfully cloudy, and the air felt thick. I dragged my feet against the pavement as we drifted in between the rows of cars.

"I overheard Ari and Cliff talking in the hallway the other day," I said. "They've been hooking up ever since he and Lana broke up."

Winston scrolled through his cell phone. "Mm-hmm."

"He also admitted it was he and Ari in the video, not Lana. Which we already knew."

I was met with silence.

"Are you listening to me?" I asked.

He looked up. "Oh, come on, Sonny. You're not shocked, are you?"

"I'm not, but Kyle would be. He doesn't know it's her in the video. And they plan to keep it from him."

"Kyle knows, we know, the middle schoolers know. He just refuses to face it." Winston yawned. "So, when are you going to tell him?"

I continued dragging my shoes against the concrete, not looking up and not answering his question.

"Oh, no. No, no, no. No. You have to tell him!"

"I—can't." My eyes sunk.

"If you didn't plan to tell him, why did you tell me?" Winston stomped his foot. "Now I know about it too! I don't want to know secrets that I won't enjoy keeping. You know this."

"I had to tell someone! I just can't bring myself to tell Kyle. He's so . . . good. Maybe it's better if he doesn't know. Maybe he'd rather turn a blind eye."

"This is Westcott." Winston sighed as he looked side to side. "You don't get to turn a blind eye. It's going to come out on its own—eventually."

We continued walking and passed directly by Jacob's black Jeep. I dragged my finger against the hot hood.

"One more thing—I heard that Jacob and Norah hugged in the hallway yesterday."

"So?" Winston said.

"So—don't you think that's a little strange?"

"Doesn't he like her?"

I tilted my head. "So he says."

"Then what's the big deal?" he asked.

"It was the way Dean said it . . . as if he were implying that it must have meant something."

"Dean? So Dean told you this? Did you ever consider he's trying to come in between whatever it is you and Jacob have going on?"

"Which is what?" I asked.

"You tell me. You're the one riding two horses with one ass."

I glared at him, dismissing his insensitive claim. "I don't know. I'm just not so sure Jacob likes her. Which is why I'm wondering why they were hugging."

"You're not sure Jacob likes her because it's obvious he likes you," Winston said.

"It's more than that," I continued. "When I told him Dean was going to break up with Norah, he took it as an opportunity to scrutinize Dean."

"Yeah, so?"

"If he really liked Norah—wouldn't that have made him happy? It's like every time I mention Norah, he seems completely uninterested."

"You have a point." Winston opened his trunk. "But why would Jacob lie about liking Norah?"

"Why would he need to lie about seeing her the night of Dustin Coleman's summer party?" I asked back. "I have no clue."

"If you're so worried about it—why don't you go through Jacob's phone? Maybe we can find out what he's hiding," Winston suggested, tossing his book bag into his trunk.

"Are you insane?"

"You know, coming from you and your recent history of breaking and entering, I find that question pretty hypocritical."

"I can't go through Jacob's phone! We aren't even dating."

"Maybe you can't"—he closed his trunk—"but I can." He began walking back toward the school. "You coming?"

"Where are you going?" I yelled, tossing my hands into the air.

Before I knew it, we approached the door to the men's locker room. "You cannot do this," I whispered solidly from the door frame.

"Jacob's in practice," Winston argued, pulling me into the muggy room. "He'll never know."

I pulled my arm back. "No, Wins! This is an invasion of privacy." I stared at the rows and rows of blue lockers. The room reeked of sweat and cologne.

"Oh, please. He waived that right when he came to Westcott." Winston kicked a gym bag with his foot.

"Just hurry up!" I whispered. I dug my fingers into my temples and fell against a row of lockers, dropping to the floor in defeat.

Winston began confidently looking through the adjacent lockers, searching for Jacob's belongings. "I came by your house last night," he said with a suggestive tone of voice. "Apparently I wasn't the only one."

"Dean came by, if that's what you're alluding to."

"Dean didn't leave either." Winston paused. "I also drove by this morning."

I closed my eyes and rubbed my temples in a quick circular motion. "What happened to not meddling?"

"What happened to your convincing 'firm stance' on being done with Dean? Now you're spending the night together?"

"We fell asleep watching a movie," I said.

"You know I don't care what you do—just who you do it with." Winston picked up a dirty T-shirt and threw it on the floor.

"We're just friends."

"Until someone catches feelings again," he replied. "Then you're both screwed."

"That's not how that works."

"It is if your feelings are for Dean Ballinger. He's unpredictable, Sonny. Ever since his mom died—he just hasn't been the same."

"Would you be the same if that happened to you?" I asked. "She had an unexpected heart attack."

"I don't think there's an expected kind."

I rolled my eyes. "Not everything's a joke, Winston."

"I think Dean's a little dangerous—that's all."

"Look, I've known Dean for years. We were best friends before we ever started dating. He's not dangerous— I know him. I know him, and he knows me."

"Oh, you walked right into this one. Did you know that he'd dump you? Or how about when he asked Norah out? Did you know him then too?"

"He made a mistake," I countered.

"You're making excuses."

"He's been through a lot, Winston."

"Have you forgotten he's been a rich kid his entire life? He used to be neighbors with Cliff, for God's sake. I'd hardly call his story a sob. They had to count pennies for a while—big deal. Welcome to the harsh reality of being a Cobalt."

"Give him a break, Wins. He's had everything taken away from him."

"Oh, please. Losing your Lambos and moving into a sizable home in the valleys isn't exactly walking through the trenches. He's a privileged kid to his core. They will bounce back and move back to the hillside, and when they do, his victim act isn't going to hold up."

"Isn't he, though? A victim?"

"Who cares? He's not your project, Sonny. You can't fix him."

"I can love him," I said loudly, jerking my hands down toward the ground.

Winston nodded. "Can he love you?"

Suddenly, the locker-room door swung open and distant chatter began filling the empty space. "Take five," Coach T shouted as the basketball players piled in.

I jumped to my feet. "What do we do?" I asked, bouncing on my sneakers and looking side to side.

Winston grabbed my hands and did the same. "You're the smart one!"

I grabbed Winston's arm and pulled him around the corner, into one of the dewy showers.

"Remind me to burn these entirely," Winston whispered as he looked at his shoes in disgust.

"You are always getting us into these situations," I hissed under my breath as I slapped his chest. "If it weren't

250

for you insisting we go through Jacob's phone—we wouldn't even be in here!"

Winston's mouth opened. "Oh, really, manila-envelope girl?"

"Harrison! Got a minute?" Dean asked.

I placed my pointer finger over my mouth as I looked into Winston's eyes, my nerves filling the shower like steam.

"I saw you and Norah hugging in the hallway yesterday. What was that all about?"

"You spying on me, Ballinger?" Jacob asked.

"Just wondering what you're doing hugging a girl you hardly know," said Dean. "Seems a little odd."

"I hug a lot of people," Jacob said.

"That didn't seem like your average, everyday hug. It looked more like an embrace."

"You aren't jealous, are you, Dean?" said Jacob. "I mean, after all, you did dump her like a bad habit in front of everyone at the dance. You couldn't possibly be threatened by a little physical contact between Norah and I."

"Not threatened. Just suspicious. Seems to me like you and Norah are hiding something."

"And what exactly do you think we're hiding?"

"You tell me," Dean replied.

251

"Cut the shit, Ballinger. You don't like me because I'm getting to know Sonny. It has nothing to do with Norah. Leave her out of it."

"You don't know Sonny."

"I know you broke her," Jacob replied. "I know that she can do far better than a guy like you."

"There is no one better for Sonny than me," Dean said. "Yet."

"Look, what do you want from me? I'll make sure you start if you stay away from her. I can do that for you," Dean said. "I'll do that for you if you do that for me."

There was a long moment of silence as I held my breath.

"I can't do that," Jacob replied. "And I'll earn that on my own, captain."

Winston looked over at me, his eyes wide. If there was one thing Dean didn't like, just one thing, it was someone not respecting his home-court advantage.

"Ouch!" Jacob yelled as he lay sprawled across his couch.

I placed a bag of frozen peas on Jacob's ankle. "Sorry."

"Had I known you planned on coming over to torture me—I wouldn't have opened the door." Jacob shifted his body, wincing.

"There was no way I wasn't going to come check on you after practice today."

He propped himself up against the arm of the couch and sighed. "It wasn't that bad."

"Really?" I reached into my back pocket and opened our text thread. "Do I need to read these? You told me you were dying."

"They worked," he said, rubbing his calf. "You came."

I nodded. "Well, I'm sorry you didn't have a good experience."

"Dean's pretty skilled," he replied. "I couldn't guard him for shit."

"Maybe he didn't get the brotherhood memo," I said.

Jacob crossed his arms. "I don't think he did." He paused. "You two still working on your friendship?"

"I guess so."

"I see," he replied.

"I know you don't like him."

Jacob repositioned the peas. "I don't necessarily dislike him. I just think you deserve better."

"And what makes you so sure I deserve better?" I asked. "Maybe I don't. Maybe I deserve nothing more than everything I already have."

"That's not fair to say," he replied.

"And why's that?"

"Because if you paint that picture, then no guy would be able to come along and give you the world. That's simply cruel to deprive said man of such a thing."

"Well, maybe I don't want the world."

"I'm almost positive you don't have a choice," he said. "Girls like you get it."

My eyes became heavy as I stared into his. "Does it, um, does it still hurt?" I asked, attempting to break eye contact. I moved the peas and pressed down on his swollen ankle.

"A little."

"If it's still swollen like this tomorrow, then you should have the athletic trainer look at it again," I said, still mindlessly poking around on his foot.

"I will." He reached down to touch it, grazing my hand along the way. He slowly ran his fingers up and down on my fingers. I watched for a moment and then glanced up at him.

"So . . . have you and Norah had a chance to hit things off?" I asked.

Jacob slowly removed his hand and leaned back. "Uh . . . yeah. She's . . . sweet."

I planned to ask him about the hug. About his inconsistencies and wavering story. I wanted to know why he claimed to like Norah, yet chose to spend all his time with me. But something about the way he looked at me made me believe he wasn't capable of lying, even though I knew he was. And that's the scary thing about those guys—*they make you forget what you know and do as you feel.*

"I should go," I told him. "It's getting late."

"Or," he said, clearing his throat. "Or you could stay and watch Netflix with me."

I looked at my watch. "No. I should probably go work on this paper. I'm a little behind."

"Behind?" Jacob leaned over and grabbed the remote control from a beautifully carved end table. "Come on. You have months to work on that paper. Take a little break."

I took a deep breath and exhaled.

"I'll even let you pick the movie. And if you knew how much I love movies, you'd understand how big of an offer that actually is."

I jerked the remote from his hands. "If we're going to watch Netflix, we're going to start a new series, not watch a movie."

"No way." Jacob held up his hands. "I can't commit to one more series right now. I'm still midway through three other shows."

"You know—it should be illegal to casually watch a series. If you aren't a binger, you aren't a true Netflixer."

"Fine," he said. "Make it a good one."

I began scrolling through the numerous options on Jacob's enormous TV screen. Finally, I landed on a series, and we lay down on opposite ends of the couch. Jacob tossed me a throw blanket, and I cuddled up into a ball.

"Thanks."

"Sure," he said with a tired smile.

Perhaps the disgraced are embroiled in scandals because it's all they know. And maybe that's how all scandals begin. Or maybe, in more regrettable situations, because the innocent forget to close their blinds.

12

SONNY'S SCANDAL

How can you tell when someone's fallen in love? Is it a physical change? Do they wear it on their sleeve or carry it in their smile? Maybe it's in the way they walk? I imagine you'd carry yourself quite differently if you had a reason to. I like to think it's all in the hints. The subtle laughs. The good-smelling cologne. The new dress. Perhaps everyone has their ways of showing they've fallen. Some lay it on you a little at a time, while others lay behind you.

I slowly opened my eyes to the sound of an alarm so soothing it could put anyone to sleep. As I attempted to become aware of my whereabouts, I noticed an arm hanging over my left shoulder. I carefully turned my head around, not yet able to shake off the grogginess.

Somehow Jacob managed to maneuver his way behind me on the couch. His hoodie was off. The throw blankets were bundled up in wads, the Netflix screen was asking if we were still watching, and Jacob's scent was overpowering.

My heart began to race as I realized where I was. I abruptly jumped up from the sofa. "Oh my God!" I grabbed my cell phone from the coffee table.

Jacob jumped up shortly thereafter.

"My mom has called me seventeen times," I said in a hoarse voice.

"What time is it?" Jacob looked around the living room in a fog.

"Eight forty-five," I struggled to say. My heart sunk underneath the couch cushions.

We exchanged a look of shock. At Westcott, being late —or missing a day of school and breaking your perfect-attendance record—was more frowned upon than receiving a B on an assignment.

"Can you turn off my alarm?" Jacob scuffled to gather himself; his eyes struggled to stay open.

"Oh, and by alarm, I'm assuming you're referring to this lullaby?" I slammed his cell phone onto the couch. "What kind of alarm is this?"

"Whoa, take it easy." He put his hoodie back on.

"Why is your alarm set so late?" I asked.

"I must have hit the wrong numbers," he replied. "Calm down."

"Hit the wrong numbers?" I tossed blankets all around the room in search of my shoes.

Jacob kneeled down beside me and grabbed me by my shoulders with an unyielding hold. "Sonny, take a deep breath," he said. "Let's just get to school. You can call your mom back on the way." He glanced down at my shirt. "But first you need to change."

"I don't have time!"

"Sonny, you can't walk into school late wearing the same clothes you wore yesterday."

I combed my fingers through my messy hair. "I've never been late to school before."

"Well, you're already late," he said. "What's ten more minutes?" He led me upstairs into his parents' room. As the door creaked open, a gust of cold air brushed by my feet. I slowly walked inside, unsure I belonged in such a grandiose space. The walls were the prettiest shade of green. The California king bed sat on top of a fluffy white rug, and the all-white bedding paired nicely with the rustic white furniture. Above the bed hung a crystal chandelier.

Jacob opened the closet door, and the Chanel slapped me in the face. "Pick something."

I walked into the massive closet, nonchalantly brushing my fingers against the rows of expensive designer garments. It was a far cry from my mother's collection of workday attire. I turned my head to the right, noticing a mass collection of brooches sitting on a shelf. "These are beautiful," I said, admiring each one. Suddenly, I wasn't in such a rush.

"Her pins?" he asked.

I twisted them in the air, giving each a good look before carefully putting them back into their place on the shelf. "Did you know that brooches weren't always used for a fashion statement? They were originally made out of thorns and were used for practical reasons—like to secure loincloths. But they were eventually made from metals. Usually they were worn to show status and wealth . . . so every time I see someone wearing one, which isn't often, I assume they are wildly privileged. They're so—eclectic and cool," I rambled on.

"Fascinating." Jacob checked the time. "Hurry up and pick something!"

"Your mom won't mind?" I asked.

"She won't notice. She travels for work fifty percent of the year. We'll put it back."

I nodded, quickly grabbing the cheapest shirt I saw.

Jacob stood in the doorway.

"Do I have to ask?" I glared at him.

He pursed his lips and turned around to face the bedroom. "Just hurry."

I finished getting dressed, and we headed toward the steps, briefly stopping by Jacob's room for a fresh hoodie. He took last night's off and changed into the new sweatshirt as we raced down the stairs. I couldn't help but feel overwhelmed with hypocrisy as I watched. His back muscles bulged as he put his arms inside.

"I'll drive us," he said. "You can grab your car later."

We hopped into Jacob's Jeep and sped toward school.

"How did this happen?" I asked in agony, attempting to fix my smudged makeup.

"Somewhere between episode three and seven we must have fallen asleep."

"Not before you managed to cuddle up behind me?" I looked at him pointedly.

"No idea how that happened," he replied. "I planned on waking you around ten last night. I didn't plan on falling asleep myself. I'm sorry."

I glanced down at my phone.

"What are you doing?" he asked.

"I'm texting my mom to tell her I'm all right."

"I'll explain everything to her," he said. "I'll take full responsibility."

"My mom doesn't need an explanation. She's been through much worse than her daughter falling asleep at a guy's house." I paused. "I'm more worried about my dad finding out I'm not at school."

"Has he texted you?"

"Not yet," I replied, staring down at the multiple missed calls from Dean. "Where is your dad?"

"He's out of town until Saturday." Jacob sped through a yellow light.

I locked my phone, then shifted my weight around in my seat as we pulled into the school parking lot.

Jacob put the car in park and faced his body toward me. "Hey," he said. "It's just a tardy."

"A tardy is unacceptable at Westcott, Jacob. I had to suffer through the flu last year during exams just so I didn't miss any days. My only comfort came from Mr. Foster sliding the trash can beside my desk. Oh, and Paul rubbing my back from the desk behind me, though I'm pretty positive he was just trying to unsnap my bra."

"Paul? That creepy, touchy-feely kid that sweats a lot?

"Yeah," I replied. "And I let him. That's how sick I was."

"Brutal." Jacob rubbed his eyes. "Look, just say you had an emergency. I'll say I overslept. Stick to that. Everything's fine."

Jacob and I jumped out of the car and ran toward the side entrance to the school. As we approached the steps, my knees began to shake, and I barely made it down each one.

We approached the double doors, and Jacob held one open for me. "You go first," he said, pushing against the top of the glass.

I looked up at him, unsure of the last time I'd felt so terrified and good at once. "I'll see you later."

I took a step forward, preparing to sign in at the office and then plow down the hallways in record speed.

"Sonny," Jacob said, grabbing me by my arm and yanking me back in front of him.

He pulled me closer and wrapped his hands around my neck, his thumbs on my cheeks. He stared into my eyes, leaned down, and kissed me.

Suddenly, everything changed. The daunting tardy that hung over my head seemed to disappear, my shaky knees buckled for entirely new reasons, and all of the suspicions I had about Jacob floated away. In that moment, everything felt perfect.

Jacob pulled back, his lips slowly leaving mine. He put his forehead against my forehead and looked down at my face. "See you later."

"Where were you?" JC sat down across from me in the cafeteria. "I didn't see you in first. Did something happen?"

Winston joined in.

"I had an emergency," I recited, rubbing my lips with my fingers in a daze.

"What is up with you?" JC asked.

"Nothing," I said, hoping to bury the topic. "I'm fine."

"You might be able to pull the cashmere sweater over JC's eyes," said Winston, "but you're not going to have much luck with me. I recognize those jeans from a mile away. They're your only pair of dark-washed, slightly faded designer jeans. You wore them yesterday, and I know you aren't a repeat offender. You didn't go home last night, did you?" Winston stopped midway through opening a bag of M&M's and waited for my reply.

"You know, maybe you should pursue fashion instead of music," I said.

JC leaned in. "Don't tell me it was Dean."

"No," Winston said, staring into my eyes. "I know the 'I spent the night with Dean' look. It's a little bit more shameful."

"Jacob?" JC asked.

I ignored his question and arranged the items on my lunch tray.

"Seriously, Sonny?" JC said. "You got your first tardy over Harrison? You know if you get more than one tardy you'll be written up, right?"

"Yes, I'm aware, thank you." I quickly tucked my hair behind my ears. "It wasn't on purpose, okay? Jacob and I were watching Netflix, and we both fell asleep. I've been so exhausted from all of this extracurricular drama. Plus, my schoolwork and paper have been relentless. The second I allowed myself to relax I just conked out."

They gave me blank stares.

"Nothing else happened," I said, emphasizing each word individually.

"Damn." Winston continued eating.

I took out my notebook. "Just drop it, okay? I don't need word getting around that we showed up late together."

"Don't you think you've tackled bigger rumors than sleeping with the new guy?" JC asked.

"Would you shut up?" I looked side to side to see if anyone was listening. "Nobody slept with anyone."

The vibe in the lunchroom was particularly tense on that day. Or perhaps it was just me. But everyone's shadow became a specter, and everything seemed to be moving in slow motion.

We changed the subject and tried to lighten the mood, but discussing the weather and cracking jokes didn't get me too far—because little did I know, the entire lunchroom was about to turn the joke on me.

"Carter," a voice said from behind.

Suddenly Cliff leaned down beside me and brought his lips to my ear. His presence felt heavy.

"I didn't know you had it in you," he whispered.

I looked out into the lunchroom as Winston and JC watched Cliff walk away.

"What was that all about?" JC brought his attention back to me, tugging on the strings of his orange headphones.

"I don't know." My eyes slowly made their rounds around the crowded cafeteria, where scattered whispers were brewing.

"What is going on?" Winston asked, pulling out his cell phone.

JC did the same.

I, too, followed suit.

I opened my phone. "Oh . . . my . . . God . . . ," I let out, breathless.

In that moment, although I'm not sure how, I managed to stand to my feet. The room began spinning, and the small talk rang in my ears. It was almost deafening. The sound of phones buzzing all around me felt like repeated punches to the gut. Everything became confusing, and everything became a blur. I was suddenly bum-rushed from behind as someone scooped me into their arms and walked me out of the cafeteria. I didn't look up—but I knew who it was. And although he didn't say a word—I heard him loud and clear.

Dean grabbed my cell phone from my hands and gently pushed me into a vacant classroom.

"Dean—"

"What the hell is this, Sonny?"

"Look, I don't know, okay? I don't know who took these pictures or how."

Dean looked down at the leaked photos. "Is this why you were tardy? You spent the night with Harrison?"

"I—"

"One night after you and I—"

"Dean—"

"Do you have any idea how this makes me feel?" Dean raised his voice. It wasn't something he usually did, so I knew the occasion was a serious one. "Seeing you put out there like this? Seeing you and Jacob together like this?"

"Yeah, Dean. I happen to know exactly how it makes you feel. Probably similar to how I felt watching you suck face with Norah for all these months."

"Don't bring her into this, Sonny. This has nothing to do with that."

"It doesn't?" I asked. "How is it different?"

Dean leaned in. "I apologized, okay? You said you forgave me. I'm trying to make it up to you, and you said you'd allow me to do that, but I can't do that if you're with this guy."

"I said I forgave you. I never said I was over it. And shouldn't you be the one comforting me?" I asked. "You're not the one in these photos." I pressed my clammy hand against my forehead. "Do you know what this looks like?"

The photos were innocent, as they almost always are. Jacob lay shirtless behind me, and I was covered underneath a throw blanket. But sometimes in high school, doing nothing wrong doesn't mean you did nothing wrong in the eyes of others. And just because you're innocent doesn't mean you'll always look that way. Not if you're in a high school where the truth isn't popular and where kids will do anything but ask for it. I knew the photos would paint me in a bad light because, after all, *rumors almost always do*.

"Yeah," Dean replied. "It looks a whole lot like Lana's video."

"That's a stretch," I said.

"I'm serious, Sonny. It looks like you slept with the new kid." He paused. "After you saw how Lana was treated for doing what she did . . . I would think you'd be more careful."

"You aren't helping." I paced the classroom floor.

Dean grabbed the back of his neck. "Look, I need to know that I'm not competing for you."

"Competing?"

"With Jacob," he replied. "I'll do anything for you, Sonny. But not that. I'm not competing with a guy you've known for a month."

"It's not a competition, Dean."

"Well, then stop speaking to him."

"Why?" I asked.

"Because he's no good," Dean said, "and that's not me being jealous; that's me recognizing there's something off about him."

My face expressed confusion. "You can't tell me who to be friends with."

Dean nodded, grabbing his chin and letting out a dry laugh. "Who took these?" he asked, emphasizing each word. "Who took these photos?"

"I don't know that either," I replied, my mind flashing to Piper.

"I think you do," Dean said. "You've been acting weird for weeks. Running around the school with your friends, acting crazed and stressed out, and now this? What is going on, Sonny? Tell me."

"Nothing is going on, okay? I'm just helping a friend figure something out."

"Who? What?"

"It's nothing," I replied, unwilling to drag him into this mess.

He grabbed his head in frustration. "Would you talk to me, please? If something is going on, I want to help you. But you have to tell me what's going on. You have to talk to me."

I stared into Dean's eyes as tears began filling mine. Up until that point, I had never been the subject of a scandalous photo leak before, and I never knew what it felt like to be *that girl*. The sudden fear of losing everything hit me like a freight train, and I needed to be anywhere other than in that classroom with Dean.

"I have to go." I brushed past Dean's shoulder and ran out of the classroom.

Dean followed quickly behind. "Sonny, wait!" he shouted from the door frame.

I turned around to face him, tears filling my eyes.

"Did anything happen?" he asked. "Between you and Jacob?"

The distance between us provided a barrier between what I once knew and what I was being pulled toward. Part of me wanted to run back, and part of me wanted to run to Jacob—and the other part of me, the more mindful part, wished I had listened to Kyle.

I turned around and walked away, charging into the women's restroom and collapsing into the furthest stall. I closed the door and locked myself in. It wasn't exactly how I thought I'd be spending my lunch hour, but there I was. I dropped to the floor and curled up into a ball—my knees to my chest. It was then when I realized, *my day* had come to meet me.

Suddenly, the bathroom door swung open, and I heard a familiar cry. I jumped up and tiptoed to the stall door, peeking quietly through the crack. I saw Casey's blonde hair. She was hunched over the porcelain sink—her home away from home—her safe haven of sorts. A place that wouldn't judge her for her hysterics. I placed my fingers on the lock, and just as I went to open the stall's metal door, the one beside me flung open.

"Ew," Norah said, walking out from the adjacent stall.

Casey grabbed both sides of the sink. "Hi to you too."

Norah walked up to the faucet, pumping soap onto her hands as she watched tears quietly fall from Casey's eyes. "Fine," she said. "What's wrong?"

"Like you care," Casey replied.

"I didn't say that I cared. I asked you what's wrong."

Casey's grip tightened. "Nothing."

"This wouldn't have anything to do with Kyle and Ari getting back together, would it?"

My mouth dropped as I hadn't yet heard the news.

Norah swayed her fingers under the water. "Look, Langdon, anyone could have told you they'd get back together. It's what they do. They break up, they make up, they break up harder, and they make up harder." Norah paused. "You shouldn't have gotten involved with Winchester."

"What are you talking about, Norah?"

"Oh, please," she replied. "You and Kyle have a thing. The blind can see it. Ari sees it too. Which is exactly why she's trying to lock him down again."

"Good for them," Casey said. "I'm glad they're happy."

"Saying you're happy for people does nothing for you." Norah turned the water off. "Be pissed and petty. That gets you places."

"Thanks, Norah. But I'm pretty sure I'm not interested in taking advice from someone who's so broken she lies about her own father's death."

Norah flung her fingers down beside her to shake off the excess water. "I'm not broken," she said. "I'm bitter. And you should be too. Kyle's been dragging you along for weeks now."

"Why are you trying to help me?" Casey asked. "Aren't you Ari's friend?"

"Of course I'm not trying to help you." Norah reached for a paper towel. "Don't flatter yourself."

"I won't." Casey began sobbing some more.

Norah sighed. "Kyle likes you. I may not like him, and I may not particularly care for you, but it's as obvious as the sky is black over this school."

"Yeah," Casey replied. "I can tell by the way he got back together with Ari."

"If you act like it's affecting you, then he'll know you care."

"I do care," Casey said.

Norah wadded up a paper towel and threw it into the trash can with force. "No, you don't," she said. "If Kyle thinks you care about him, or that you care that he and Ari got back together, he'll know he has you exactly where he wants you."

"I'm not like you, Norah." Casey wiped her face. "I'm not a heartless Violet."

Norah crossed her arms. "Oh, Casey. You have no idea how much heart us purple girls have to embody to withstand being Violets. I envy girls on the bottom. When you fall, you have a shorter drop and a softer landing."

"Is that before or after you kick them down with your stilettos?" Casey splashed water on her face.

"Maybe I'm not as heartless as you think," Norah replied.

"Or maybe you should stop pretending like you care about me," Casey said, tears still falling. "It doesn't pair well with your narcissism."

"Look, Langdon. I know a thing or two about guys. Narcissistic or not, I can help you."

"Yeah? How so?"

"When Kyle texts you tonight—because knowing Kyle, he will—don't text him back. And when he realizes something is wrong, apologizes, and asks if the two of you can be friends, you say no. Without a reason. Without a lame explanation."

"And how does this help me?"

"Just do it. Okay?"

Casey shook her head, tears still falling down from her cheeks.

"Casey?"

"Okay," she replied. "I'll do it."

"Good." Norah yanked a paper towel from the roll and pushed it toward Casey's chest. "Now wipe your face. Your desperation is leaking all over the sink."

Before I knew it, the bathroom cleared out. There was no more sign of Norah or Casey. I sat down on the toilet seat and stared out of the oval-shaped frosted window in my stall, allowing the sun to hit my face. It was the first time I'd spent my lunch hour in the bathroom, but it was surprisingly more peaceful than the cafeteria. I gazed at the sunlight, giving thought to what my junior year had become.

After picking myself up and pacing around the tiny stall for a few more minutes, I opened the bathroom door and walked back into the hallway. The lunchroom down the hall was filled with hundreds of students, including the person responsible for the leak—and the many others who were responsible for much more than that. Because once a rumor leaves the hands of the offender, it can only grow if others nurture and carry it the rest of the way.

"Sonny!"

I turned around to find Jacob walking toward me. He was out of breath, like he'd been running around the school looking for someone. I assumed that someone was me.

I fell against the wall of lockers and dropped to the floor in defeat.

Jacob sat down beside me, scooting closely by my side. "Look," he said, "I swear I had nothing to do with this."

I glanced toward the ceiling and let out a short breath, my eyes filling with tears. "I know."

"Are you being followed?" he asked.

I grabbed the back of my neck. "Maybe."

"Maybe?" Jacob grabbed my hand and pulled it back down.

"It's not exactly something I can prove."

"What do you mean?" he asked. "Do you think this was Dean?"

I exhaled in frustration. "No. Not Dean."

"I wouldn't be surprised," Jacob said.

"I'm not doing this," I mumbled, standing to my feet.

Jacob jumped up. "Do what?"

"I'm not listening to you rant about Dean."

"Look, I'm sorry. I'm a little concerned that someone was standing outside of my window last night. I didn't mean to upset you."

"I'm not upset, Jacob. I'm confused."

"Why?" he asked.

"Because you say you like Norah—but based on the way you kissed me, my gut is telling me you like me."

"I do like you," he said. "A lot."

"So you don't like Norah, then?"

"I do like Norah." Jacob exhaled. "I'm just—"

"You're what? Confused?"

"Yeah," he replied. "I guess so."

"Well then, maybe whatever this is should be done," I said, turning to walk away.

Jacob walked up behind me and grabbed me by my arm. "Whatever this is?" He laughed. "And what exactly is this, Sonny? Do you even know?"

"What is that supposed to mean?"

"I like you, Sonny. A lot. And there are things I can't explain to you right now. But that doesn't make me a bad guy. I've done nothing but throw myself at you since I met you. I've been texting you nonstop. I've been hanging out with you every weekend. You. Not Norah. You're the one who tells me halfway through our friendship that you and Dean have a thing. You're the one who's confused."

"Oh, so this is about Dean?" I shook my head in disbelief.

"Now it is," he replied.

"I didn't think I needed to tell you about Dean. He was in a relationship."

Jacob glanced at the ceiling. "And what? Now that he's not, it's okay to talk to both of us?"

"Dean and I are friends," I said.

"Is that why he spent the night with you?" he asked.

"How did you—"

"People talk," he said.

I listened as the cafeteria door swung open from down the hall. Students began spewing into the hallway.

"That's none of your business," I said.

"It is when you turn around and spend the night with me," he said, looking toward the cafeteria door. "You think that's okay?"

"Oh, so you're shaming me now?" I asked.

Jacob relaxed his shoulders. "No, Sonny. Of course not."

"I didn't mean to fall asleep at your house," I said. "It was an accident."

He clasped his hands and tossed them behind his head. "Was it a mistake?"

His question caused me to pause. I never considered there was a difference between the two.

"If it was a mistake," he said, "and you want to be with Dean, then just tell me and I'll leave you alone."

"I love Dean," I replied.

Jacob dropped his chin, his eyes searching for an answer in mine. "Do you like him?"

I opened my mouth, trying to find the right words, but they never came.

"Jesus, Sonny." Jacob rubbed his eyes with flat fingers. "Just tell me the truth."

"I like him, Jacob." My voice softened. "I always will."

Jacob stared into my eyes, then at the floor. He took a moment to gather his thoughts, then nodded before stepping backward down the hallway. I watched as he disappeared into the crowd of students.

I wanted to tell him not to go, because something in me wanted him to stay. But I knew asking him to would be selfish. The worst kind of selfish. The kind that's willing to break someone just so you can feel whole. And I wasn't willing to break Jacob any more than he already was.

"Did I interrupt something?" Kyle asked.

I looked beside me. "No," I said. "You didn't."

"I saw the pictures." Kyle shook his head. "Do you think Piper was behind this?"

I buried my face in my hands. "That's what I'm thinking."

Kyle pulled me into his shoulder with one arm.

"Are they that bad?" I mumbled.

"They aren't," he replied. "You were just cuddling."

"Like people will believe that's all it was," I said.

"I wouldn't be concerned about that," he replied. "I'd be more concerned with why Piper would do this. And why she'd be standing outside of Jacob's window."

"Isn't it obvious? She's paying me back for not dropping this." I pulled away. "Hey," I said, rubbing my neck. "You and Ari?"

He clenched his jaw. "Yeah. We're going to try to work things out."

"I see."

"I'll catch up with you later." He tapped me on my arm. "Don't worry about the photos. We'll figure this out."

Kyle turned around to walk to class and immediately stopped as Casey walked by. Her face was still red from crying, and her disappointed eyes sat meekly behind her glasses. She glanced up at him, pressed her lips together, and continued walking toward the end of the hall. He stared at her until she was out of sight, and although he didn't say a word, his sinking eyes said it all.

How can you tell when someone's fallen in love? Maybe you can't. But maybe, if you pay real close attention, love itself decides to speak.

13

DIRTY LAUNDRY

Dirty laundry—the worst kind of clothes. It's been said that the hardest stains to remove are the rumors that are aired about us. I believe whoever said that has never had to get mascara out of a white cotton T-shirt.

Westcott High's first basketball game of the season. A simple scrimmage—but at Westcott—every competition was overblown. And there was nothing simple about this one. The blue-and-white banners hung low from the gymnasium rafters, the parents filled the room with anticipation and intimidation, and the students filled the room with support.

"I can't believe we're doing this," I said to Winston.

We stayed behind in the hallway while people piled into the gym doors on Saturday evening.

"You okay?" he asked me.

I looked down at my white shirt, pressing my thumb against the black teardrop stain. "I've had a rough couple of days," I said as my fellow peers passed by me with judgmental eyes. "Everyone has seen those pictures."

"Is Dean pissed?" Winston asked.

"I think he's hurt," I replied.

"Don't worry." Casey walked up behind me. "You'll fix things with Dean."

"Yeah," I said as I thought about Jacob. "I know."

Winston checked his watch over the side of his soda can. "Where is Kyle? We were all supposed to meet here ten minutes ago."

"Probably somewhere with Ari," I said.

Casey looked down. "And Buckets and JC are meeting us near the office?"

"That's the plan," I replied.

Casey clawed her head with her frail fingers. It was painfully obvious that the war within her mind was spilling out.

"Jesus, both of you are out of commission?" Winston shook his head. "What is it with Westcott guys? They have to beat you across the heads with their flags before you recognize they're red?"

"I'm fine," Casey said.

I stared into her eyes. "You don't look fine."

"I guess I'm just confused," she said. "Kyle really opened up to me recently. I thought we were getting close." She paused. "He told me about the divorce."

My eyes narrowed. "What? When?"

"After the dance," she replied. "Once the two of you came back from Piper's house."

"I thought you couldn't find Kyle after the dance," Winston said.

"That's because he was in parking lot C," Casey replied. "He was leaned up against my car—waiting for me."

My mouth slowly began forming a smile.

"We sat and talked for hours," she said. "It sounds like he's been through a lot."

I towered over my sneakers with crossed arms, casually rocking back and forth on my heels as I looked down. "That was the worst year," I said. "Their divorce was rough on Kyle. He had to grow up pretty fast."

There was a brief moment of silence between the three of us as we all thought about Kyle, each of us for different reasons.

"Is that why he's such a good kisser?" Casey asked.

283

Winston choked on his soda. "Now *that* explains your mood."

"He kissed you?" I asked.

Casey scratched her bottom lip. "He just leaned over, slipped his hand on my neck, and kissed me."

"That's it?" Winston asked. "That's all it took?"

"That's all it takes." My mind flashed back to Jacob's lips.

"But I guess he and Ari really are getting back together." Casey looked down. "So that's that."

I stared at Winston as he mouthed the words *I told you so.*

Seriously? I mouthed back.

"I hope we can get into the safe," Casey said, interrupting our silent argument. "I'm ready for all of this to be over."

Just then, Kyle approached us with disheveled hair. His shirt was wrinkled, like he'd slept in it. "Sorry I'm late."

"Are you okay?" I asked him.

Kyle repeatedly ran his hands over his shirt, swallowing excessively. He reached into his back pocket and pulled out Principal Winchester's keys, then placed them in my hand.

My eyes narrowed. "Thanks?"

"Can I talk to you for a minute, Casey?" Kyle asked her.

Casey looked around the group. "Sure," she replied, following him to the other end of the hallway.

"You have one minute," Winston said as they walked away. "We have to go."

Kyle finally stopped, far enough away to make it difficult to hear their conversation, but close enough to where we could. His bloodshot eyes paced across Casey's face. "Are you upset with me?" he asked.

"Why would you think that?"

"Because you haven't been responding to my texts."

"I'm just really busy with my school work," she replied.

Winston and I shifted toward them.

"Busy with homework?" Kyle wasn't convinced. "Casey, we used to text every night."

"That was before you got back together with Ari," she said.

Kyle exhaled. "I figured that's what this is about."

"Would it be about anything else?"

I stared at Winston, and he at me, as we continued shifting.

"Look, Casey, I never wanted to hurt you."

"You didn't," she replied.

"Me and Ari—"

"Have history, and you and I have only just met," Casey interrupted. "You've been dating since the beginning of sophomore year. I get it."

"It's not that I don't like you," he said. "I don't want you to think this has anything to do with what you told me about your parents, or where you live, or anything like that." Kyle paused. "It's not you, okay?"

Kyle's voice was desperate, like he needed someone to understand him, and nobody could.

"Yeah," Casey replied. "Okay."

Kyle rubbed his eyes. "I should never have kissed you."

"You're really bad at the whole not-trying-to-hurt-people thing," Casey said.

Stick to the script, I thought.

"I didn't mean it like that," he said. "I definitely don't regret kissing you."

"What do you regret, then?" Casey asked.

Kyle swallowed. "Not meeting you before tenth grade."

I looked at Winston, my sappy eyes melting from their sockets.

"Can we still be friends?" Kyle asked her.

"Christ." Winston exhaled.

There was another long pause. I waited in suspense for her answer.

"I'm sorry, Kyle," Casey said. "I can't be friends with you."

Just then, Winston lunged toward Kyle. "Let's go!" He pulled him by the arm and led him away.

They walked ahead toward the office, leaving Casey and me trailing quite a bit behind.

I walked beside her, waiting for her to acknowledge the elephant in the hallway. She never did.

"Is he okay?" I asked.

"He'll be fine," she replied. "Once he realizes it was never going to work between us."

"What do you mean?"

"I'm pathetic." She laughed. "Look at me. Look at my life. My parents are junkies. I live with my brothers and aunt in a worn-down, Folk Victorian home with broken AC. The house is yellow, for God's sake. Yellow. Could it be any more tragic?"

"You are not pathetic, Casey," I told her. "Kyle doesn't care about that stuff. He told you so himself."

"Of course he does, Sonny," she replied. "It's cute to ride in on your white horse—until you see my wasted mother sitting on our couch for one of her supervised visits." She paused. "I'm not good enough for him."

"Kyle doesn't exactly have the picture-perfect family either," I replied. "And you know, for someone who hates the thought of being judged for what you don't have, you sure do judge others for what they do."

"What's that supposed to mean?"

"You don't want Kyle to dislike you for being broke, but you cut him no slack for coming from money."

"It must be so hard," Casey said, rolling her eyes.

I stopped in my tracks. "It's not as easy as you think, Casey."

She looked at me and paused, shaking her head before walking ahead. Kyle took a sharp right turn into the restroom, and Casey caught up with Winston at the front of the line.

I closed my eyes tightly, rubbing my fingers over my temples as I continued walking. "That girl . . ."

"Is trash?" Cliff walked toward me with a few of his friends, causing me to once again stop in my tracks. He wore a baseball cap and a bomber jean jacket; his hands were tucked into the pockets on his fitted khakis.

"What are you doing down here?" I asked him. "Are you too good to park in parking lot B like everyone else?"

"I avoid that parking lot," Cliff replied.

Lana flashed across my mind.

"What do you want?" I asked. "I'm sort of busy."

Cliff nodded in the direction of his friends. "I'll catch up with you guys in a minute," he said as they continued walking toward the gym.

"Oh, so you're staying?"

"Jesus, Carter!" Cliff smiled. "Would you lighten up? I just wanted to say hello."

"Hi, Cliff," I replied, my voice at an all-time sarcastic low.

Cliff laughed as if I were his personal entertainment. "You're starting to scare me, kid."

"Would you stop calling me 'kid'? You're half a year older than me," I said. "And I couldn't possibly scare you."

"Why's that?"

"Because you aren't scared of anything. You're a Violet, remember? You'll always be a Violet."

Suddenly, I wasn't so funny. Cliff dropped his smile, then glanced at his friends. He grabbed my arm, pulling me closer toward the office. "What the hell are you doing?"

"I overheard you and Ari's conversation in the hallway, Cliff," I said, pulling my arm away. "How could you do this to Kyle? We all know you kissed at the pool party, but this?"

"Jesus, Sonny." He leaned down. "I don't know what you think you heard, but—"

"Save it, Cliff," I whispered sternly. "That's not going to work anymore. I know what I heard. You and Ari have been hooking up ever since you and Lana broke up."

Cliff rocked back on his heels—like he always did. "I don't know what you're talking about."

"You need to tell Kyle," I said.

Cliff looked down at his sparkling white sneakers. "There's nothing to tell him."

"You can't be serious, Cliff."

"You need to stay out of it."

"Oh, I'm in it," I replied.

"You aren't."

"I know what you told Lana about you and Ari," I whispered. "About the summer before sophomore year."

Cliff leaned in toward me. "I told you not to bring that up again. Lana never should have told you about that." He looked at me, disgusted. "It's none of your business."

"That's beside the point," I said.

"Look, I made some mistakes, and I'm going to make up for what I did in my own way. But what I won't do, and what you won't do, is tell Kyle something that would do nothing but hurt him and destroy our friendship. If you care about him, Sonny, then keep your mouth shut."

Cliff turned around to walk toward the gym.

"Tell him, Cliff!" I shouted at the back of his head. "Or I will."

"Sonny, come on!" Winston hollered from the front of the hallway.

I walked toward the office, leaving my heated conversation with Cliff in the middle of the tile floor.

"Kyle's still in the bathroom," Casey said. "Let's wait."

"I'll go get him." Winston jogged toward the restroom.

"Here's a list of possible combinations." Buckets reached into his pocket; his green cotton jacket hugged his arms. "Important dates to the school and such. If it's a keypad—we'll try these. If it's a lock—well, we'll need to find the key."

"Unless the key is on this key ring," I replied, pulling Principal Winchester's keys from my back pocket.

"What are you guys doing?" Ari suddenly appeared from the shadows.

Buckets jumped. "Jesus, Ari! Could you whisper?"

"Because that would have been less terrifying?" she asked.

"What are you doing here, Ari?" I pointed in the direction of the gym. "The game is that way."

"I know. I saw you standing outside of the gym doors and then you all just disappeared. You couldn't look more suspicious if you tried. What gives?"

"We don't," Buckets said. "We aren't telling you anything."

Ari twisted the rings on her fingers. "Does this have anything to do with Piper?"

"What makes you think that?" JC asked her.

"Cliff told me she leaked his video," she replied.

"Don't you mean *your* video?" Buckets said.

JC walked toward her, dropping his head inches from Ari's face. "Piper framed me," he whispered.

I stepped forward. "JC!"

"She planted the answer key in my bag," he continued. "She set me up."

Ari crossed her arms; her gold bracelets were stacked on each one. "Piper? Why would she do that?"

"That's what we're trying to figure out."

"Why are you breaking into the office?" Ari waited impatiently for his reply.

"Because Mr. Russell left him a riddle," I said. "Which led us here."

"A riddle? What does it say?"

"Look, it's not important!" JC's impatience came out to play. "We're just trying to figure out what Mr. Russell wanted me to know. And I think the answers to my questions are right behind the safe's door."

"And you're what?" Ari squeezed her hips. "Going to expose her? You would never."

JC looked around the ill-lit hall.

"I guess you hadn't thought of that, huh?" Ari asked him.

Her question caused us all to pause.

"Is that what you want?" I asked.

He took a moment to collect his thoughts. "I want to wrestle again," he said. "No matter what."

I stared at JC as we both silently agreed to move forward. "Okay, then."

"I'm coming too," Ari said. "If Piper is capable of doing this, who knows what else she's capable of."

"Scared there are more videos, huh?" Buckets asked her.

I nudged him.

"Fine, Ari. You can come. But you can't tell a soul about this," I said.

She rolled her widened eyes. "Fine."

Suddenly, Winston approached the crowd. "He's gone."

"What do you mean?" I asked.

"Kyle's gone," he repeated. "He's not in the bathroom."

We collectively stared at one another in confusion.

"Kyle's in on this too?" Ari asked.

"You're in on this?" Winston asked her. "What are you doing here?"

"Where did Kyle go?" Casey mumbled.

"As much as I'd love to sit here and chitchat, we really should get this done," Buckets said. His loud voice commanded our attention. "I can't keep the cameras frozen for much longer. We'll have to do it without him."

I looked behind me down the hall, hoping I'd see Kyle's dark hair appear in the distance—but I never did.

"Ready?" I asked the odd group behind me.

Winston ran his palms against his jeans. "Is that rhetorical?"

With a shaking hand, I unlocked the office door with the key, then turned the knob and pushed the heavy door away from my face.

A gust of wind met us underneath the door frame. The office smelled of paperback books and antique furniture. I walked inside, and everyone else followed closely behind. We looked around the massive room. The white walls, covered with plaques, seemed to be closing in on us as we realized where we were.

"Are you sure about this?" Casey looked at me. "We can turn back."

I walked around the front of the main desk, glancing at the piles of paperwork, scattered pens, and stacks of folders. Just then, the safe caught my eye. It was sitting center on a small wooden table tucked underneath the desk. I stared at the silver box, unable to move, unable to do much of anything.

"It looks like there's a keypad and a lock." I lifted the list of possible combinations to my face.

The others shifted toward me. Ari grabbed the paper and keys from my hand and kneeled down next to the safe. She began trying every key on the ring at rapid speed— almost like she'd done this before. We all waited in suspense.

"The key's not on here," she said, placing them back into my hand.

I looked around the dark room. "Buckets, help me go through the desks." I sprang into action. "We have to find it."

For the next ten minutes, everyone moved in silence. The sound of beeps in my ear behind me eventually faded, and all I could think about was finding the key. I looked through the desk drawers thoroughly, and with each failed attempt, I lost a little more hope. My eyes scanned the room as I searched for another possible hiding space. Suddenly, I turned my head to the sound of loud thuds.

"Winston!" I yelled, pulling him away from the safe. "Smashing it isn't going to get it open!"

"Well, Ari doesn't know the combination," he replied.

She looked at him, frowning at his idiotic remark. "Of course I don't, you moron. If I knew the combination, you wouldn't be bashing the safe against the table."

"We can't open it, Sonny," Winston said. "We've tried everything."

"And we can't find the key," Casey added.

I looked at the clock that hung directly above the office door while running my hands up and down on the steel box. I let out a deep breath, realizing the last piece to our puzzle was just behind this tiny door. We were so close, but without knowing what Mr. Russell's riddle meant, we were still so far away.

Suddenly, the keypad caught my attention.

"I think I should go look for Kyle," Ari said.

"Good idea," Casey mumbled under her breath.

Ari stepped forward. "What was that?"

I ran my fingers over the safe's black buttons as I gazed intently at each one.

"I'm surprised you didn't think to do that earlier," Casey said.

"I'm surprised you have the nerve to address me," Ari replied. "After moving in on my boyfriend."

"Ex," Casey retorted.

Zero. I pressed down on the button.

"Kyle would never go for someone like you, Langdon," Ari said, looking her up and down. "And it has nothing to do with being a Cobalt or having an incredibly messed up family, which you do. You don't have enough guts to claim what's yours. If you did, you would already have Kyle."

Zero. I pressed again.

"How could I when you're always crawling back?" Casey asked.

"I don't crawl. I walk. With my head up and my fears on my sleeve. You think you're the only one who has problems? We all do. But I don't hide behind mine or use them as a crutch as to why a guy wouldn't like me. I don't let being a Cobalt stop me from getting what I want. Including a Violet. If you had any type of confidence in yourself, maybe you could get one too."

Zero.

"And which Violet is that, Ari? Because I'm pretty sure everyone in this room would say you're really in love with Cliff."

Ari stepped forward. "You don't know what you're talking about, little girl."

Once more. *Zero.*

"And you don't know what you want!" Casey shouted. "But maybe when you figure it out, you can let Kyle know. So he can move on without feeling guilty that he's walking away from the girl who's milking being his first love."

Ari's breathing became heavy.

"Yeah," Casey said. "The only crutch I see is you."

One.

I once heard that the average person loses fifteen socks a year when washing their dirty laundry. Over your lifetime, that's close to thirteen hundred socks floating in some mysterious oblivion, never to be seen again. And sometimes that's how the answers to life's puzzles are too. You search and search for that missing piece because your gut tells you it's there—but it's really just beyond your fingertips in that dark void where missing socks go.

14

TIME

Time—the one thing we all take for granted. I've always stood in awe that we as humans are able to convince ourselves we have enough of it, all the while knowing we're continually running out. If you ever get the chance, take a good long look at a clock. Watch the heavy hand tick by, knowing with every second that passes, you'll never get it back. Those daunting ticks can change a person. And so it did.

"Where did Kyle go?" I asked as we all rushed into the gym.

The team was warming up, with five or so minutes before their first big game.

"He couldn't have gone back to his dad's house without the keys," I said as we walked up the side of the blue bleachers, my blue jeans clinging to my legs.

Buckets pulled his tablet out of his bag. "Maybe he felt sick."

"Or maybe he bailed," said JC, who was wearing his wrestling jacket from the previous season.

We all climbed to the top bleacher and nestled into the row; Ari went elsewhere. After Ari and Casey's fight, it was probably for the best.

I glanced down at my phone. "I've tried calling him a thousand times. He won't take my calls."

"That doesn't seem like Kyle. He always answers your phone calls," Winston said, propping up his loafers in between two students on the row below us.

"I think we should hand this over to Jacob's dad," Buckets suggested. "He's the investigator. Let him figure out the riddle."

"We'll talk to Ron on Monday." I stared at Mr. Harrison from across the room. His face was filled with joy as he watched Jacob run up and down the court. "I'll ask him to meet us at the club for dinner."

"Can't we talk to him tonight?" Casey asked.

"No," I replied. "This is a big night for Jacob. I don't want to ruin it for him."

I looked down at the court. Jacob was shooting baskets on one end; Dean was talking to Coach T on the other. Their eyes were heavy, and it was painfully obvious I was the reason for both of their lackadaisical demeanors. Jacob's eyes suddenly met mine—and it wasn't the pleasant kind of meeting. He stared at me for a split second and then looked away. I never expected to start the year off down a boyfriend, and so quickly end up with two guys on my plate. The truth was—I wanted Jacob, and I couldn't explain it, not even to myself, but I also needed Dean. My sigh sang a shameful tune.

Suddenly, Winston nudged me on the leg. "Look at them."

I followed his gaze and realized he was staring at Cliff and Ari.

"It's almost as if they don't care who sees them."

"They're just sitting together," I replied.

"They're always together," he said. "I don't get it. It's like they want to get caught."

"I don't think that's it," I replied, unsure of how much longer I could keep their secret.

"They've spent weeks trying to convince Kyle that nothing is going on between them, but it's right in front of his face. You don't have to want to believe it to see it. It's beyond obvious."

I looked around the gym as the crowd settled. The teams were preparing for their game. The referees were discussing the rules. The coaches leaned over their clipboards. The scorekeepers were testing the scoreboard, and the students were gathering their signs. Everything seemed to be quieting down, and everything seemed to be in order. But no good event comes without a little trouble. And I hear once you solve one problem, you're merely steps away from your next.

"Winston . . . there's something I haven't told you."

Just then, I placed my hands over the sides of my face as the fire alarm pierced through both my eardrums. The sprinklers shot on, filling the gym with gusts of water and hysteria. Everyone started yelling and running down the bleachers. The moms tried covering their silk designer shirts, face paint melted down the cheeks of my peers, and the dads were likely in the corners somewhere, blaming the coaches for things outside of their control. It was pandemonium—Westcott style.

"Let's get out of here!" Winston yelled, pushing me toward the end of our row.

Buckets frantically shoved his tablet inside of his messenger bag. "I think I triggered the sprinkler system," he said as we all ran toward the exit door, which after a long wait, dumped us outside into parking lot B.

I ran my fingers through my wet hair, my makeup running down my face. "You think?"

Students flew from the doors, covering their heads. In the middle of the running crowd—we spotted someone walking. And they weren't walking toward us.

"Kyle!" Casey shouted, running toward his white Range Rover.

We all followed, but kept our distance.

"Kyle, wait!" she yelled again, taking the ponytail out of her hair.

"What do you want, Casey?" he asked.

"What is wrong with you?" Casey tucked her wavy wet hair behind her ears.

"Are we friends again?" His harsh tone was telling.

Casey attempted to dry her glasses with her sleeves. "Are you upset with me?"

He pressed down on the outer edge of his eyebrows. "No. I'm not upset with you, Casey."

"Then what are you?"

"I don't know," he replied, still pressing.

"You can't honestly expect me to just be friends with you," she said.

"I don't, Casey."

"Well then, what do you want from me?"

Kyle quickly glanced at me and then looked back at her. "I just want you to leave."

Casey's eyes narrowed. "Leave?"

"Just leave so I can't hurt you."

"Is that what you want?" Casey asked, tossing Norah's advice out the window. "You want me to leave you alone?"

They stared at one another, unblinking. I knew her question weighed heavily on Kyle's mind, because I knew that wasn't what he wanted. But he was stuck between what he wanted and what he'd always known—a battle I was far too familiar with.

"You're too good for me, Casey."

"Me?"

"Yes," he replied. "I'll ruin you."

"I doubt it," she said. "Can we just talk about this?"

Kyle stared at her in apology. "I'm sorry, Casey."

He opened the driver's side door to his car, but not quicker than JC, who slammed it shut.

"What the hell, man? Where did you go?"

Kyle turned around. "What do you care?"

"Why did you leave us hanging?" Buckets asked, tossing his messenger bag behind his back.

"Ky!" Cliff yelled as he approached the car. "What's going on?"

Ari followed.

"Did you do that?" Cliff asked, staring at Kyle's dry hoodie. "Did you set off the sprinklers?"

"Don't worry about me," Kyle said as he reached for his car door handle.

I grabbed his hand before he could open the door. We made eye contact, the kind that wouldn't let you look away.

"What's wrong?" I asked him.

The sound of distant sirens rang in the background as people gathered outside of the gymnasium door.

Kyle pushed my hand down. "Don't touch me, Sonny."

"Whoa!" Cliff stepped in between us.

"What the hell is your problem?" JC asked Kyle.

"My problem?" Kyle grabbed his bottom lip and smirked. "My problem is that you all think I'm some delusional idiot who doesn't see what's going on around me."

"What are you talking about?" I asked.

"You're not in love with me, Ari," Kyle said as he turned his attention toward her.

She sighed. "What are you talking about? Of course I am." Her voice was emotionless, like she'd reassured him of this a hundred times before.

"No." He shook his head. "No, you're not. You're in love with my best friend." Kyle tapped the roof of his car with his fingers. "Or I thought he was my best friend."

"Uh-oh." Winston cracked his knuckles.

"I am," Cliff said, stepping closer toward Kyle.

Kyle took a step back. "Get away from me, Cliff."

305

"No," Cliff said, getting closer. "Come talk to me."

"I said get out of my face!" Kyle shoved Cliff backward, nearly dropping him to the ground.

JC stepped in between them as I felt the familiar touch of Dean's hand. He gently pulled me aside, out of the direct line of impact. I looked down at my arm and then stared into his eyes.

"What's going on?" Dean asked me.

I couldn't talk, but my wide eyes likely spoke for me.

Cliff caught his balance and bounced back up. "You don't want to fight me, Ky," he said, brushing off his chest. "So don't do that again."

"I'll fight you if I need to," Kyle replied.

Winston slowly shook his head. "Grab the popcorn— the boys are becoming unhinged."

"Why are you doing this? Because you think your girlfriend likes me?" Cliff was becoming increasingly defensive.

"Because you two hooked up!" Kyle shouted.

Cliff ran his fingers through his blond hair. "I told you we didn't!"

"You're going to look me in the eyes and lie to me? Again?" Kyle rolled his hands into a ball. "I just heard you and Sonny's conversation."

I closed my eyes and exhaled.

"Yeah." Kyle looked at me, disappointment leaking from his pupils. "Next time you want to have a conversation like that, make sure there's more than a bathroom door between us."

Cliff stalled. "Look, Ky, there are things you don't know—"

"Oh, please tell me you aren't going to try to justify hooking up with Ari for months," Kyle said. "There's nothing you can say to justify that."

"Kyle—" I placed my hand on his shoulder.

He looked down at me. "How could you not tell me? We're supposed to be best friends, Sonny. How could you make me look like a fool all this time?"

"Please," Winston said. "Sonny hasn't made you look like a fool, Kyle; you've made yourself look like one."

Kyle nodded. "Is that so?"

"Yes, Winchester! We all knew it was Ari in the video!" Buckets stepped forward. "It was brutally obvious. You chose to pretend it was Lana."

"I chose to believe my best friend!" he shouted.

"And I was wrong!" Cliff expressed desperation in a last-ditch attempt to save his friendship. "I was wrong, okay? I made mistakes—"

"Oh God," Kyle blurted out, locking his hands behind his head and pacing the pavement. "Miss me with your mistakes, Cliff. Kissing once would be a mistake. These were choices."

"My choices," Cliff said. "No one else's. It's not Sonny's fault, and it's not Ari's. It's mine. I take full responsibility."

Ari crossed her arms. "Cliff—"

"No, Ari. It's my fault, okay? Don't worry about it."

Kyle nodded, staring into his friend's blue eyes. The history between them could fill the parking lot. It was strong and significant, and one would think a girl couldn't break it. A Cobalt at that.

"You think you can take whatever you want, Cliff. You've always been a taker." Kyle placed his hands into his pockets. "But you don't get to take her and get away with it." He looked Cliff up and down. "You're dead to me," he said, aggressively brushing by Cliff's shoulder on the way to his car.

Cliff let out a quick breath and wiped his lips; his eyes glistened in the moonlight. Whether it was tears or a reflection, I wasn't sure, but I was certain I had to do what I did next.

And here it goes . . . the second good thing I had known Cliff to do.

"Kyle, wait!" I shouted, grabbing him by the arm. "It's not Cliff's fault. Not entirely."

"Sonny, stop," Cliff demanded.

"No," I replied. "You don't get to call the shots anymore. It's done."

"What are you talking about?" Kyle asked.

I placed my hands on my head, pulling my hair back, my eyes stretching. "Cliff knew her first."

The whole group perked up in unison.

"What do you mean?" Kyle's eyes narrowed in on me.

"Cliff and Ari met when she moved to Westcott, the summer before tenth grade," I said, staring at Cliff. "The Zieglers moved into one of Mr. Reynold's condos, and Cliff and Ari met inside the lobby one day. They started talking and texting, and before they knew it . . . they had spent the entire summer together."

Cliff put his hands into his pockets and looked down at the ground.

"Cliff?" I said, suggesting he should take over.

He shook his head, opening and closing his mouth. Finally, the words came. "You came up to me two weeks into sophomore year and told me all about this incredible girl. And you lit up when you talked about her. I had never seen you that happy. I knew you were upset about your dad and—"

"Do not bring my dad into this!"

"You were going through a lot, okay? And I was excited for you to have a distraction." He paused. "When I asked you who the girl was, you showed me Ari's picture."

Kyle put his thumb and pointer finger on his eyebrows and exhaled slightly as he ran them down his face.

"So I did what I thought was right." Cliff shrugged his shoulders. "I took out my phone and deleted her number. And when Ari confronted me about ghosting her, I told her to go."

"Go where?" Buckets questioned.

"To you," Cliff said, staring at Kyle. "I told her to go to you. Because with everything you were going through, you needed her more than I did." He exhaled. "Look, Ky, I haven't been trying to steal Ari from you." He paused, shaking his head and trying to get the uncomfortable words out. Words Cliff wasn't used to saying. "I guess I've just been trying to let her go."

Kyle shook his head. "No. You would have told me if you liked someone. Especially if you two had been talking all summer."

"I didn't tell anyone, Ky. I was embarrassed."

"Of what?"

"Of Ari," Cliff said. "I didn't want anyone to find out I liked her. If that makes me a pretentious asshole, then I guess that's what it makes me. But that's the truth."

"You're right." Kyle looked at him, disgusted. "That does make you a pretentious asshole."

Cliff rolled up his sleeves. "Look, I know you can't understand this, but I'm doing you a favor."

Kyle nodded. "You see, those are fighting words."

"If you want to fight me, Ky, then let's go," Cliff replied. "But don't keep closing your eyes to the truth."

"Which is what?"

"She doesn't want to be with you!" Cliff shouted, clasping his hands behind his head.

"And how would you know that? Because you had a summer fling before tenth grade?"

"Jesus." Cliff exhaled slightly. "Because she wants to be with me, Kyle! Can you not see that?" He paused. "You say people think you're delusional? Well, maybe there's a reason for that."

"So you think because you gave Ari to me that it excuses you going behind my back and hooking up with my girlfriend?" Kyle asked.

"Both of you tuck your egos away," Ari said. "Nobody gives me to anyone."

Kyle stared at her. "So I was just your second choice? You were only with me because you were following orders from Cliff?" he asked. "You just let me waste all this time?"

"We became friends," Ari said. "And I did fall for you, Kyle. I did love you."

"Did you fall in love with me?" he asked. "Because those are two separate things."

Ari continued rocking back and forth, ignoring his question.

"Jesus, Ari, just tell me. Were you ever in love with me?" Kyle's voice softened as it took a dive toward defeat.

She slowly shook her head, her brown wavy hair falling down across her chest. "It's complicated."

"Ari—"

"I—"

"Just tell me!" Kyle yelled.

"No," she said. "No, okay? I don't think I was ever in love with you."

We all looked around the group at one another, afraid to breathe, afraid to move. It was the first time Ari had admitted to much of anything.

Kyle nodded. "And you?" He turned his attention to Cliff. "Are you in love with her?"

Cliff looked away, running his hand through his damp blond hair.

"Tell me the truth, Cliff," Kyle demanded.

Cliff kicked the pavement with his sneaker. "You don't want the truth, Ky." He tilted his head up toward him. "You never have."

Kyle grabbed his hood and placed it back over his head. He stared into Cliff's eyes, once again. This time, the history between them didn't seem so unbreakable. "Here's some truth for you." Kyle took a few steps back. "I'm off the team." He turned around and walked to his car.

"Kyle," I said, following closely behind him. "I'm sorry, Kyle. I wanted to tell you, but Lana made me promise I wouldn't tell a soul! Winston didn't even know!"

He opened his car door and jumped inside.

I stood in between him and the door. "Please talk to me."

"You know what, Sonny? Maybe you should worry about your own problems instead of getting involved in mine. You have two guys standing out there in the crowd somewhere, and they're both waiting for you to pick one."

"And you have an incredible girl standing out there, waiting for you to pull her out of the friend zone."

He quickly pulled his hoodie further over his head. "Move, Sonny," he whispered.

"Please just give me time to fix this," I pleaded.

Kyle started his car. "It's too late."

Time. The one thing we all take for granted. Sometimes, time is kind enough to be on our side. Other times, on its worst days, it speeds off without us.

15

DETOURS

Where would we be without detours? I'm not sure I've ever taken one that didn't end up being the better route. What are detours if not a better way to get to your destination? My mom once told me to look for the detours, because no matter the situation we face, there's always a way around it. Sometimes in life, not even the wreckage ahead is powerful enough to stop us from getting to where we're going. Sometimes.

As I stared at my bedroom ceiling fan, my vaulted ceiling reminded me I was as small as I felt. I listened as the blades pushed through the air, making a squeak each time they came full circle. Tears leaked from the corners of my eyes, gliding down the sides of my cheeks and into my hairline. My eyelids wanted to shut, but my mind wanted to think. I thought of the basketball game earlier that evening, and the three guys I had hurt throughout the start of my junior year. I thought of how insane it was that Cliff Reynolds had become my ally, and how sad it was that Kyle felt he had none.

I put my hands on top of my chest and exhaled, rolling over to grab my buzzing phone. My eyes narrowed as I checked the text. I jumped out of bed and opened my curtains to see Jacob's Jeep parked in my dad's driveway.

In no time at all, I was outside, walking toward him with intention. Jacob was leaning against the front of his car, wearing basketball shorts and a T-shirt.

I stood in front of him.

"Are you okay?" he asked.

I gave him a blank stare, knowing my eyes were swollen and my mascara was running down my cheeks. "Do I look okay?"

"Always," he replied.

The street light next to the driveway provided just enough light for us to see the outlines of each other's bodies.

"Why are you being so nice to me?" I asked.

"Sonny, it sucked to hear you say you like Dean. But I would never not be nice to you." He rolled his neck from side to side. "I bounce back quickly. Two hundred thirty-six scars, remember?"

I dropped my head, letting out the tiniest of smiles. "Look, Jacob, I never expected Dean to break up with Norah so quickly after you and I started talking. And when he did—I don't know—he just expected things to go back to normal."

"And did they?" he asked.

I wiped my face and tucked my hair behind my ears, trying to become a tad more presentable. "It was as if he never left."

Jacob nodded.

"But you came along," I said. "And you made me feel important. I never expected to like you, Jacob." I paused. "You're the new guy, for God's sake. No one likes the new guy."

He smiled.

"But I won't ask you to wait for me while I figure out my feelings for Dean."

"You don't have to," he replied.

"Friends?" I asked, holding out my fist.

Jacob grabbed my crunched-up fingers and slowly pulled me toward him. I fell into his chest, my hands resting on the hood of his car. Through his cotton T-shirt, I could hear his heartbeat, and I was certain he could feel mine. "Friends," he said, his hands warming my lower back. Then, gently, he pushed me back and wiped underneath my eyes with his thumbs.

"Thanks," I said.

"Sure," he replied. "But I, um, I really came here to talk to you about something else."

I stood up straight. "Okay . . ."

"I haven't been completely honest with you."

"I figured as much," I said.

Jacob chewed on his bottom lip, seemingly struggling with what to say next. "Claire was the first girl I loved, Sonny. And I haven't even thought of another girl since she died. But when I met you, I realized pretty quickly I could fall for you. And I got scared if I did, you'd fall for me too."

"And that's a bad thing?" I asked.

"Yes," Jacob replied. "You shouldn't like me, Sonny. You can't like me."

"How come?" I gave him a confused look.

"I'm just . . . I'm not . . ."

I poked my head toward him. "You're what?"

Jacob exhaled. "Look, I told you I liked Norah so you wouldn't like me."

"So you *did* lie?"

"Yes, but—"

"Why Norah?" I asked.

"I picked her at random," he replied. "I never saw her at Dustin's party. I saw her the first day of school. It was an added bonus when I found out who she really was—Dean's girlfriend."

"Added bonus?" My eyes widened. "Wow. You really didn't want me to like you."

"No . . . I did . . . I just . . ."

"I don't understand," I said. "Why shouldn't I like you? Why couldn't you like me?"

"I didn't want to hurt you. I—"

Suddenly, we heard the sound of a car engine zooming down my street. Cliff's black Mercedes pulled onto the curb; his tires came to a grinding halt. He jumped out of the car and walked toward me. Jacob straightened and stood in between us.

"Sonny," Cliff said, quickly walking up the driveway. "Are you not getting my texts? We need to go."

"Go where?" I asked.

"I'll tell you on the way."

"I'm not just going to hop in a car with you," I said. "Tell me where we're going."

"Would you just get in the damn car?"

"I'm wearing an incredibly wrinkled shirt. I can't go anywhere."

"It's never stopped you before," Cliff said.

I tilted my head toward him. "Seriously?"

"Here," Jacob said, reaching into the back seat of his car. "Take my hoodie."

He placed it in my hands as its appeasing scent rushed into my nose.

I tossed Jacob's hoodie over my head and quickly pulled it down.

"Thanks," I said to Jacob as he stared at me. "I guess I have to go." I threw my hair up into a ponytail. "See you later?"

Cliff walked back to his car, and I followed.

"Sonny!" Jacob yelled, still standing in the driveway.

I turned back around. "Yes?"

He took a deep breath, holding it in for a few seconds before exhaling. "Sometimes you have to look beyond the colors to see someone for who they really are." He widened his stance. "Not everything is as it seems, you know?" He shook his head, dropping it to his chest. "Even when it all seems black . . . there's always more just beyond it."

I paused, staring into his eyes with confusion.

"You know?" he repeated.

"What do you mean?" I asked.

Cliff lay on his horn, and I jumped in surprise.

I looked toward the Mercedes, and then back at Jacob. "I have to go."

"Then go," he replied.

"But what did you mean by—"

Cliff honked again.

"Just go." Jacob jumped into his Jeep. "You'll figure it out."

"Okay," I mumbled under my breath as I slowly broke eye contact with him. I then turned toward Cliff's sedan. I jumped inside and buckled my seat belt, the new car smell greeting me at the door. "What's going on?" I asked, trying not to touch anything.

"I could ask you the same question," he replied, slamming on the gas pedal.

My body slid back on his tan leather seats. The car was dark, but the dashboard was bright.

"Your dad never let me come over to see Lana at this hour," Cliff said.

"That's because he didn't trust your intentions," I replied.

He plugged his cell phone into his charger. "Smart man."

"Where are we going, Cliff?" I sat facing forward.

"You'll find out."

"I'd rather you tell me."

Cliff picked up an unlabeled bottle and took a swig. "That's because you're a control freak."

"Are you seriously drinking a beer?" I asked him.

He placed the bottle back into his sparkling-clean cup holder. "See. Control freak."

I crossed my arms and glared at him, shifting my body a little to the left.

"It's ginger beer," he said.

The more I got to know Cliff, the more he surprised me. "Well, it smells disgusting."

He sped through a yellow light; the pull of his engine was intense. He drove with one hand on the wheel, the other on his lap. His confidence was almost attractive, if he were anyone but Cliff.

"This is bringing me back to date nights with Lana," he said. "She complained, and I paid for dinner. Then I dropped her off and got no action because Coach Dirk was lurking from the window." He flipped his turn signal on. "I really miss those days."

"I know you're intending to come across as sarcastic," I said. "But we all know you're not over Lana. Or Ari, as it seems."

"Why do you take such an interest in my love life, kid?"

"I don't know. Something about watching a train wreck is too fascinating to turn away from."

"You aren't so good at love yourself," he said. "If you were, you wouldn't be wasting your time with Harrison when you really love Dean."

I glanced over at Cliff as he bit his fingernails.

"Why don't you worry about your own love triangle?" I replied. "You're in quite the mess yourself."

"Thanks to you." Cliff bit off a piece of his fingernail and spit it out of the window.

"No, Cliff. You're the one who hooked up with Ari behind Kyle's back. Regardless of who liked her first, it was still wrong. You should have just told Kyle that you were struggling."

"Maybe I should have, when I saw how quickly everything took a turn," he replied. "Their relationship was shit and I started to regret my decision."

"Well, I guess a bad relationship is what you get when one of the involved parties isn't truly into it," I said.

Cliff sighed loudly, pushing away from the steering wheel while sitting back in his seat. "Ari was in love with him, Sonny. She just hated she couldn't have me. I don't know why she told Ky she wasn't, but believe me—she was." He paused. "Just wait until he starts dating Langdon. You'll see Ari's love come out swinging then."

"Ari." I slowly shook my head. "That girl sucks at love."

Cliff rolled up to a stoplight. "Name one teenager who doesn't."

I stared out the front windshield, the impact of his statement running true through my veins. "So what stopped you from coming clean?"

"I started dating your sister," he said. "Nothing mattered after her."

"Did you cheat on Lana with Ari?"

Cliff took a sip of his ginger beer. "No. I would never cheat on her." He placed the bottle back down into the cup holder. "How is she anyways?"

I glanced over at him; his straight face stared ahead. "She's happy."

Cliff tightened his grip on the steering wheel and sniffed, shifting in his seat. I watched as he pretended to not be bothered by my statement, but I could tell it was no easy task. After all, the only thing harder than allowing yourself to care is *pretending that you don't.*

I looked away. "Now that Lana's gone, do you want Ari back?"

"Look, I don't want anything, okay? The only thing that matters to me now is fixing things with Ky." The light turned green, and Cliff slammed his foot down on the gas pedal. "And making sure he doesn't leave the team."

The back of my head hit the headrest. "What do two star-athlete Violets see in a girl like Ari Ziegler?" I asked. "I've always wondered that. I mean, she's not only a Cobalt, which no one would ever assume you'd go for, but she's a black-wearing, tattoo-having, vaping singer with an attitude." I paused. "Lana, I get. But Ari? What is it about her?"

Cliff cracked his knuckles against the steering wheel. "Maybe it's because she's everything I'm not supposed to be with," he said. "You learn to appreciate having choices like that when you're nothing but a machine to your parents."

"So you like her because your parents wouldn't approve?" I asked.

"No," he replied. "Because she made me feel like I didn't need their approval. That's hard to find."

We sat in silence for the next few minutes, neither of us saying a word. Eventually, it became brutally obvious where we were headed.

"Cliff," I said. "Why are we turning into the school?"

He sped down the long street and turned into parking lot C.

"What are we doing here?" I asked.

"Norah asked me to bring you." Cliff parked and unbuckled his seat belt. "Get out."

"Norah?" I looked over toward her car. "Since when do you listen to Norah?"

He opened his door and stepped outside. "Would you get out?"

I watched him walk around the front of the car, the parking-lot lights shining down on his face.

"Carter! Get out of the car!" he shouted.

"OH MY GOD!" I tossed my hands over my ears at the sound of Winston thrusting himself against my window.

I unbuckled my seat belt and opened the car door. "What are you doing?!" I shouted.

Winston tried catching his breath. "I've been kidnapped!"

"I'd hardly call that an abduction." Norah slowly walked toward us from her car, her heels pointy enough to poke an eye out. "You rode shotgun with AC blasting and full control over the radio."

I nodded. "Not partial?"

"What do you think?" Buckets asked as he appeared from the backseat.

Casey followed.

"He ate my Skittles too," Ari said, walking up behind her. "While I sat in the back." She glared at Winston.

"This is not a joke! She forced me into her car." Winston put his hand over his heart. "She wouldn't tell me where we were going!"

"You're fine, Winston." I rolled my eyes at his hysterics.

"Can someone tell me why we're in parking lot C on a Saturday night?" Cliff asked.

I looked at Cliff as he and Ari made awkward eye contact.

"It's the only place safe enough for all of us to meet," Norah said. "No one is here."

Just then, Piper's car slowly pulled into the empty lot. She parked beside Norah's car and stepped out of the driver's seat.

Norah tugged down on her peach-colored blazer. "Before you go and turn anyone in . . . I think it's time you know the truth."

Perhaps the only barriers strong enough to stop us from getting to our destination are the people who never wanted us to get there.

16

FRIENDSHIP

Friendship—that light yet heavy relationship that can slip through our fingers at any given point in time. The thing we all want. The thing we need. The relationship between two people who are appointed to one another—to take care of each other throughout life. Where would we be without it? Who would we be? And if one person stops caring, what would it be?

"The truth?" I asked Norah, rolling up my sleeves. "What is Piper doing here? You said you wouldn't rat."

"And I didn't," she replied. "Piper came to me."

The eight of us stood underneath the moon. The crickets chirping in the grass below gave melody to the evening's unlikely event, and the circle in which we stood was one soul shy of feeling complete.

"Shouldn't Kyle be here for this?" Casey asked. "If the truth is coming out, he deserves to be around to hear it."

"Maybe you should call him," Cliff said. "I think you're the only call he'll take."

"Doubt it," Winston mumbled.

I gave him a nudge to the stomach.

"I agree." Buckets pulled his brown beanie down on the back of his head. "Someone should call Kyle."

"I tried," Norah said. "He wasn't home when I drove by, and his phone is off."

"What about JC?" Casey asked.

"No." Piper stepped forward. "Nobody is calling anyone."

"What's the matter, Piper? Can't face him?" Winston tilted his head.

"You do know we already know the truth, Clemmons," Buckets said. "We're not interested in listening to you tell us that JC stole the answer key. That's horse shit, and you know it."

"Let the girl speak," Cliff said. "I'd like to get home."

Piper clutched her pearl necklace as if her life depended on it; she twisted the white balls around with her fingers.

"Principal Winchester approached me sophomore year as I was walking to my car one day. He asked me if I'd be willing to do him a favor."

Winston crossed his arms and raised a brow. "Principal Winchester?"

"He wouldn't tell me why he needed it, but he said if I agreed to the favor, he would help me out."

I stepped forward. "What was the favor, Piper?"

Her eyes scanning the pavement, she tried finding the words to say. "I did it," she admitted. "I put the answer key in his bag."

"Wait a minute," I said. "Are you saying that Principal Winchester gave you the answer key and bribed you into framing JC?"

Piper nodded.

"Why would Principal Winchester want JC kicked off the wrestling team?" Casey asked.

"I don't know," Piper replied. "I didn't ask questions."

"You didn't ask?" Winston laughed. "So you just happily agreed to setting your boyfriend up?"

"What could Principal Winchester have offered you to get you to turn on JC?" Buckets asked her.

Piper dropped her head. "A Princeton profile."

"Pardon?" Winston said.

"A Princeton profile," she repeated, but louder.

"What the hell is that?" Cliff asked.

"In short, it's an outline of what Princeton is looking for in admissions."

Norah smirked. "Why would you need that?"

Piper ran her fingers through her wavy hair. "Because I just do, okay?"

"Why?" Ari asked. "You're the smartest girl I know. You'll get into Princeton."

"You don't get it," Piper said. "I'm not like the rest of you."

"We know," Norah said. "You're better."

"No I'm not!" Piper's voice caused us all to stiffen up. "I struggle."

"With which Porsche to drive to school in the mornings?" Winston mocked her attempt to collect sympathy.

Piper continued running her fingers through her curls. "I struggle—"

"Christ, Piper, spit it out." Cliff tossed his hand out in front of him.

"You all think I'm so perfect—but I'm not," Piper blurted out. "I have to kill myself to get the grades that I do. While you're all out with friends on the weekends, I'm home studying. While you're dreaming at night, I'm up practicing for hours until my wrist is throbbing and my nerves are shot. I don't sleep. I hardly have time to eat. All

I do is study and practice. Nothing comes easy to me! Nothing."

We all looked around the circle at one another, unable to respond.

Piper pulled on her pearls; tears ran down her cheeks. "I know it wasn't right, okay? But when he offered me something that would take a load off my shoulders—having an itemized list of things I need to work on, rather than working on everything at once—I just jumped for it."

"I'm sure you could guess what Princeton wants," Casey said. "Why did you need the list?"

Piper bit her lower lip; she glared at us as if she resented every person standing there. "None of you would understand. None of you have tracking problems when you read, do you? None of you lose your place every time you go to the next line—and completely forget what you just read so you have to go back and reread the whole thing. None of you spent most of your childhood doing hours of vision therapy because your eyes have trouble converging and diverging or whatever. None of you have a Brock string hanging off your doorknob that you have to use every day to strengthen your eyes." Her hardened gaze traveled from person to person. "Your lives are so easy, and you don't even know it. Judge me if you want, but I needed that profile because I have to divide any task I do into chunks. It's something I've had to do since I was little."

She squeezed her moist eyes shut as her voice broke. "Writing is just as hard for me. I've been literally frozen over how I can tackle Princeton's entry essays. But with that list, I can make sure I have everything they want in there." She paused, setting her jaw. "Yeah, I know. . . . You think it's just common knowledge what Princeton wants, but it's not. Everyone who applies has good grades, talents, and extracurricular activities, just like me. I needed to know what would set me apart from everyone else." She looked around the circle with pleading eyes. "People would kill for that secret profile."

"Piper, you could have just asked me for help with your essays," I said, squinting at her. "You know writing is what I do."

"No." Piper shook her head violently as if I were asking her to jump off a bridge. "I didn't want you guys to know. I couldn't have you guys treating me like I was some charity case."

"You should still be ashamed of yourself," Winston said.

Ari exhaled loudly; her flat voice followed. "Jesus, give the girl a break, would you? We've all done equally horrific things. This is Westcott High. It's not exactly the dumping ground for the virtuous. The girl did what she had to. If I had to guess, it's nothing you wouldn't do if you were being bribed by your principal. We've all been stabbing each other in the backs for years. Let's not start acting high-minded, because at the end of the day, we're all just as screwed up as Piper."

"Was your dad in on this?" I asked her.

"Of course not," she replied. "He doesn't know about any of it."

"Hang on a minute." Buckets stepped forward. "Why is your garage-door code the code to the school's safe?"

"What are you talking about?" Piper asked.

"I typed it in, and it worked," I said.

"How do you know my garage-door code?" Piper asked.

"JC gave it to her," Casey said. "Sonny and Kyle broke into your house the night of the dance. They saw you on the golf course with a manila envelope and wanted to see what was inside."

Piper crossed her arms. "You broke into my house?"

"Stand down, Judas," Winston said. "You leaked Ari and Cliff's video—and the photos of Sonny and Jacob."

"What are you talking about?" Piper squinted her eyes. "I didn't leak those."

My heart dropped. "That wasn't you?"

"Of course not," she replied. "Why would I do something like that?"

"Really?" Buckets nodded. "You're noble now?"

Piper looked around the group. "Look, I know what I did was wrong, but I'm trying to make it right. I didn't leak anyone's anything."

Cliff stepped forward as he looked around the circle. "Then who did?"

Everyone's eyes made their rounds.

"I don't know," Piper said. "But I swear to you—I didn't do it."

"So Winchester gave you the profile?" Ari asked Piper.

"He tucked it inside of a catalog and told me to hide it. No one else has this profile. But he has connections."

I looked around the group.

"Wait a minute—why did you break into the school's safe?" Piper asked.

"Because Mr. Russell left behind a riddle on JC's doorstep. And he clearly wanted him to figure out what it meant. We thought it would lead us to evidence that linked you to the setup." I sighed. "But we still haven't been able to figure it out."

"What does the riddle say?" she asked.

"No one is safe at Geraldine's," Casey said.

Piper lifted her finger and dragged it through the air as if she were attempting to write the riddle out in front of her. "Is that why you were in Geraldine's? You were looking for clues?"

I nodded.

"What did you find?" Piper asked.

"Other than a creepy photo of a little boy standing in the middle of a field—nothing." Winston rolled his eyes.

"What was inside the safe?" Piper asked.

"Nothing." I dropped my head. "It was empty."

"That's the big bomb?" Norah questioned. "There was nothing in there?"

Cliff grabbed his bottom lip and laughed. "When did I become smarter than you, kid?" He stepped forward, smiling at me with his eyes. "Guy Penn's grandparents own Geraldine's. Ed and Dorie Williams—Mrs. Penn's parents."

My heart sunk.

"Guy Penn is the creepy boy from the photo?" Buckets asked.

"Her parents own more than a coffee shop," Cliff said. "They own a ton of real estate."

Buckets shrugged. "So?"

"There's one piece of land they've owned for over a decade and haven't been willing to sell, regardless of how many times my dad has tried to purchase it." Cliff paused. "The land the left wing is on."

"Guy's grandpa owns that?" Norah asked.

Cliff nodded. "The riddle led you to Geraldine's in hopes you'd see the picture."

"What about the safe?" Winston questioned.

"You got the riddle wrong," Cliff replied. "Russell wasn't leading you to the safe. Can't you read? He was telling you that no one is safe. He literally typed it out for you."

We cut our eyes at Norah.

"I told you I love puzzles," Norah said. "I never said I was good at them."

"What you're good at wouldn't help us here," Winston replied.

"Principal Winchester needed the land for expansion, so that the kids on the waiting list could finally get in." Cliff looked toward the sky, pacing back and forth across the pavement. "More kids, more money, more power." He smirked. "But Ed wouldn't sell it. Unless, of course, Winchester could secure his grandson a top spot on the wrestling team."

Piper placed her hand over her mouth.

"But Westcott's waiting list is full. So what's the only way a student can get into Westcott automatically?" Cliff asked.

"If their parent is a teacher," I whispered as everything began making sense.

"Which is why he fired Russell and gave Penn his job. It was the perfect exchange. Who would have suspected anything? A mom gets hired as the new English teacher, and her son tries out for the team when he realizes there's a spot open." He glanced at Piper. "Winchester found your weak spot, used you to frame JC, and tipped off Coach Dirk. JC gets busted with the answer key, then suspended, and Winchester's plan flies under the radar."

"Until Mr. Russell caught on," I said. "He figured it out. He knew."

"If you're so smart, why didn't you piece this together before now?" Winston asked Cliff.

"Because this is the first I'm hearing that Piper framed JC, or that there was a riddle left behind," Cliff replied. "I didn't think anything of it when Guy came to the school."

"Winchester framed JC for land?" Ari questioned.

"*Piper* framed JC for land," Winston corrected her.

Casey let out a quick breath. "And Principal Winchester ruined JC's life for it."

"Not his whole life," Cliff replied. "Just one wrestling season."

"He wouldn't do that," I said.

Cliff glanced at me. "Again . . . shitty humans."

"I'll turn myself in," Piper said, jumping toward the middle of the circle. "I'll go to the police."

"We can't trust you," Buckets said. "You've been trying to fool everyone for months. Struggles or not, you're nothing but a liar."

"I was desperate, okay? I wasn't thinking straight. Once I set him up, I thought I was in too deep. I didn't see a way out of the lie. And I didn't want to get caught at first, which is why I warned Sonny to drop it. But now that I know the truth . . . I don't care anymore." Piper wiped her eyes. "I never wanted to hurt JC. Not for Princeton. Not for anything." Her voice was convincing. "And I'll prove it. I'm confessing to helping Winchester. I'm exposing him for what he did to JC."

"When?" I asked.

"Monday," Piper replied. "I'll go straight to the police on Monday."

I looked around the safe-opening group as everyone waited for my reply. Dropping my chin to my chest, I reluctantly passed the torch. "Okay." I shook my head. "Yeah . . . okay."

"I'll do whatever I have to do for JC," Piper said. "For all of you."

Friendship. Where would we be without it? Who would we be? And if eight people started caring, what could it be?

17

LETTERS

Letters—those notes that bring us a wide variety of feelings and emotions. I suppose it depends on the content. Recommendation letters bring hope. Acceptance letters bring joy. Breakup letters—great pain. We all receive letters at some point in our lives. Most will be harmless. Some will be important. And then there are some that bring the greatest amount of fear that no reader, on their best day, would be able to shake. If you're real lucky, you'll never receive this kind of paper.

Sadly, it turned out we Westcott students weren't as lucky as we thought.

My head hung low as I walked through the school's parking lot on Monday morning. The sky had an unusual darkness to it, unlike any time before. The crows flew from light post to light post as the gray clouds slowly rolled over them. The building's red brick looked a little bit darker, and the ostentatious cars looked a little less important.

"Sonny!" A voice yelled from behind.

I turned around, my face matching the environment. "Hi," I said.

Kyle slowly walked toward me and pulled my head into his arms. "I'm sorry," he said, his chin on my scalp. "I was an asshole."

I pulled away and looked into his spent eyes; his remorse was notable. "Yeah," I replied. "You were."

"Do you forgive me?" he asked.

"Do you forgive me?"

"It wasn't your fault, Sonny. I don't blame you for any of this."

"I could have told you," I said. "I should have."

"You could have. But I understand why you didn't." He took a deep breath. "Truce?"

I looked down at my text thread with Jacob; I had three undelivered text messages.

Kyle nudged me. "Sonny?"

I ran my thumb across the screen. "Yeah . . . um . . ."

"Look, we have to make up," Kyle said.

I locked my phone, temporarily setting aside my confusion. "And why's that?"

"We only have fourteen more years before we walk down the aisle."

"Fine. Truce." I rolled my eyes and tried to smile. "But I'm so not marrying you."

"You don't know that," Kyle replied. He paused, the smile fading from his face. "Winston called and filled me in on everything from your meeting in parking lot C on Saturday night. I've been sick since yesterday, trying to digest the information."

I exhaled loudly. "I knew your dad was a little dark, but this? I had no idea he would do something so sadistic. What was he thinking? Using Piper to frame her boyfriend for a piece of land?"

"It's not all that shocking, Sonny," Kyle said as we both walked toward the front of the school. "I told you—he's just not a good man."

"That's an understatement," I replied. "If he did that to JC, are any of us even safe?"

"I've never felt safe with that man a day in my life," he replied. "I just can't believe Piper actually confessed."

"But not to leaking the video and photos," I said. "Which means someone else was trying to mess with us."

"Like who?" he asked.

"I don't know." I looked around the eerily empty parking lot. "Does it even matter anymore?"

He shrugged. "I guess it's not the weirdest thing that has happened in Westcott."

"True." I tapped my phone to wake the screen, glancing down to see if any texts had come through. "Have you talked to Cliff yet?" I asked him, realizing none had.

Kyle adjusted the hood on his sweatshirt. "No."

"Ari?"

"Nope."

"Casey?"

Kyle dropped his arms. "No. You're the first person I've talked to all weekend, besides Winston."

We walked into the double doors and plopped down on a nearby stairwell.

Suddenly, Winston came trotting down the steps and landed right beside me. "You two talking again?" he asked, adjusting his burgundy checkered scarf.

"Always," Kyle replied.

"So when exactly is this going down?" Winston asked. "Won't Piper have the police here first thing this morning?"

"I think that's the plan," I said. "Do you think your dad suspects anything, Kyle?"

Just then, Ari appeared from the side of the railing, giving Kyle a quick glance before walking up the steps; we all knew she was likely heading toward the music room.

I watched as Kyle lost himself in his own thoughts; his eyes were glued to Ari as they followed her up the entire flight of stairs.

I wanted to believe Kyle could eventually love Casey and fall out of love with Ari. Because every guy should know when it's time for them to leave. But that's the tricky thing about love. If you aren't the type to walk away, and you aren't the kind of person who moves on quickly, *you subsequently become the one who stays.*

"Ky?" I asked, attempting to reroute his attention.

Kyle shook his head. "No. I don't think my dad suspects anything."

Winston looked at me, his eyes filled with concern.

"I still can't believe your dad would use JC as bait for a piece of property," I said.

"Really?" JC asked as he took a seat behind me on the stairs. "Because now that I know he was behind this, it sounds exactly like something he would do."

"I agree." Buckets turned the corner. "I filled JC in on everything."

All of a sudden, Assistant Principal Clemmons came over the intercom. "If I could have everyone's attention, please. I need all students to report to parking lot C; please report to parking lot C for a mandatory fire drill. This is not an option. Please make your way to parking lot C." He paused. "Thank you."

His humdrum voice was telling, and I knew this was no routine fire drill.

We all stood up and walked out the door, making our journey toward the other parking lot. The students who were walking inside made a U-turn and walked the other way—Casey being one of them.

"Fire drill, huh?" she said. Her blue shirt was the perfect choice on a justice-seeking day such as this one.

"I can't believe this is finally going to happen," JC said as he cracked his knuckles. "I'll finally get to wrestle again, and this nightmare will be over."

"What about Piper?" Winston asked. "Do you plan to talk to her about what she did?"

JC stared at his dirty white sneakers as he placed one foot in front of the other, unwilling to answer Winston's packed question.

I remembered the sparkle in JC's eyes the day Piper succumbed to his desperate pleas to date him. The giddy conversation we'd shared when he realized he had fallen in love with her—like he was some starry-eyed ten-year-old. And the curved question mark of his shoulders the day he walked out of school and realized he'd likely never speak to her again. In that moment, as I watched JC trace his steps, I only hoped their love story wasn't finished being written.

Suddenly, unmarked black SUVs rolled down the winding street. We slowly turned our heads to the right and watched them pass by. They were in unison with one another, almost resembling a string of cars leaving a funeral.

"Here we go," I said, taking a deep breath in.

Kyle stiffened as if bracing himself for what was heading toward his dad.

"Someone from the police department must have called and told them to clear the building." Buckets snapped pictures of the SUVs.

"I can't imagine what's going through their heads right now," Winston added. "They probably think a student is about to be busted for something."

With narrowed eyes, I turned around and watched as policemen surged from their cars. "Little does Principal Winchester know—it's him."

"Wow. This is sort of intense," Casey said as she swung her arms back and forth. Suddenly, her cell phone went flying from her hand.

"You've got to stop doing that," I told her as we stopped in our tracks.

Casey turned around to grab it, but not quicker than Kyle, who bent down to pick it up.

"Here," he said, extending his hand toward her.

Casey took her cell phone from his hand. "Thanks," she said, looking down at the pavement for what seemed like minutes.

"You look pretty," he said, his voice low.

Casey looked down at her casual outfit. "If pretty is a two-dollar oversized T-shirt and a cheap pair of jean shorts —then sure." Her voice was overconfident, as if she were trying to cut the uncomfortable conversation short. "I guess so."

"That's what makes you pretty, Casey." Kyle's eyes traveled from Casey's sneakers to her messy ponytail. "I wish you understood that."

Casey's mouth opened, but no words came out.

Say something, I thought.

Kyle swallowed, then stepped forward in a last-ditch attempt to make sense out of his emotions. "Look, Casey, I —"

"I should . . ." Casey nodded in the direction of parking lot C.

He took a moment to gather his thoughts, collecting his scattered feelings from the ground after his attempt took a nosedive. "Yeah." He pressed his lips together and nodded. "Me too."

We both watched him walk toward the front of the crowd; neither of us said a word. But the breath that came from Casey's mouth was deafening, and although she stood unyielding in her decision to remain strong—I knew she had collapsed.

We finally reached parking lot C, the lot specifically reserved for overflow parking. On this specific day, it served another purpose.

We weaved through the crowd of students, confusion and gossip floating through the air like heavy clouds. They were impossible to push through.

Just then, Cliff, Ari, Piper, and Norah approached us.

I glanced over at JC. He was silent and had taken a few steps back, visibly shaken by Piper's presence.

"What's going on?" Piper asked. "What's with all the cop cars?"

I stepped forward. "What do you mean? Didn't you call the police?"

"Not yet," she replied. "I'm going to the station after school."

"Wait—what?"

Suddenly, I heard my name being called in the distance. It was subtle, but as it got closer, I realized who it was.

"Sonny!" Dean ran through the crowd.

I bobbed my head around to find him, which was no simple task.

"Sonny," he said, pushing through the last group of students. He stood in front of me, his breathing heavy.

I grabbed his arms. "What's wrong?"

"It's your dad," he said. His blue eyes paced across my face.

"What about my dad?"

"He's been arrested."

In that moment, the parking lot started to spin. Students' shirts were meshing together like a decoupage of colored paper, and their voices accumulated into a nondistinctive hum. I looked up toward the sky, but the sky was closing in on me. And I couldn't stop it from spinning. I couldn't stop myself.

"Sonny," Dean said. "Look at me."

My eyes danced across Dean's comforting lips; his words were in slow motion.

"Sonny." He grabbed my face.

I placed my hands on top of his, slowly shaking my head in hopes of making his statement untrue. "What . . . what do you mean . . . my dad?"

"Everything will be fine, okay? We'll figure this out."

I shook my head out of Dean's grasp. "What happened?"

"I don't know," he said. "I was walking into school as he was being placed into the back of a cop car. Ron Harrison was there."

And then, just like that, my heart sunk. "Ron Harrison?"

"I guess he was here investigating your dad," Dean said. "I don't know . . ."

I turned around to start running toward the front of the building, but Dean grabbed me back by the arm.

"Don't," he said. "I'll drive you to the station after school."

"I have to—"

"You can't miss a day of school," he said. "Your dad will kill you."

"He won't have a chance to if he's sitting behind bars." I turned around to continue running, but suddenly, Guy approached the crowd.

"Crazy morning, huh?"

I broke away from the circle; his voice lured me from the group like a hypnotic tune.

"Looks like everything came crashing down," Guy said. "They have a word for that—what is it called?" He stared into the sky as if searching through his vocabulary. "Oh yeah." He paused. "Boom."

My heart bursting through my chest, I stepped forward some more. "What do you want from me, Guy? What is your problem?"

The rest of the group gathered around us.

Guy leaned down and grabbed a stone off the ground, casually tossing it in the air as he spoke. "I was trying to be your friend," he told me, then looked around the group. "Can't we all just be friends?"

"With you?" JC shifted through the circle. "Do you know how you got into this school?"

Guy stared into his eyes. "Do tell."

"Our principal made room for your mom by firing our favorite teacher—in exchange for your grandpa's land." JC pointed toward the left wing. "That's the only reason you got in."

"Lucky me," he said, keeping intense eye contact with JC. "Because I really wanted to wrestle for Coach Dirk. He's the best wrestling coach there is." Guy glanced at me. "Well, he was."

"The only reason you're on the team is because Principal Winchester used someone to frame me and I got kicked off," JC told him. "Believe me—that's the only way you'd get my spot."

"Who on earth would frame you?" Guy asked him.

We all looked around the circle in silence as Piper looked away; her shame was showing.

"Don't tell me it was your girlfriend." Guy smirked. "I didn't think she was that easy."

JC lunged toward him and grabbed him by his collar.

"To manipulate, to manipulate," Guy said, grabbing hold of JC's hands.

"Get out of here," JC said. He released his grasp, giving Guy a little push.

"Sure." Guy tugged down on his shirt and gathered himself. He took a few steps back. "But before I go—" He reached into his bag and pulled out a stack of red envelopes. "These are for you." He handed a letter to me, Kyle, Norah, and Piper. When he came to the end of his stack, he stepped in front of JC, lowering his voice to a whisper. "You think I don't know how I got in here, *Jeremy Coleman*?"

JC froze.

"I just wanted *you* to know," Guy said.

Our eyes floated around in a trancelike state as we realized what his statement implied.

"My grandma always told me," Guy continued, inches from JC's face, "that in order to be the best you have to play smart." He twisted the stone around with his fingers. "But my grandpa told me you just have to play dirty." Guy smiled, taking a few steps backward. He tossed the stone across the pavement as if he were stone skipping. "I want to personally thank all of you for participating in my game. It sure was entertaining watching you run around town like the Boxcar Children, trying to crack my riddle."

"You couldn't meet me on the mat, Penn?" JC stepped toward him; his chest bumped up against Guy's as he looked down on his face. "You had to have your mommy pin me down?"

Kyle pulled JC away from Guy.

"Could've." Guy patted his messenger bag a couple of times. "Didn't have to." He took a few steps backward, smirking at JC before vanishing into the crowd of students.

The stillness in the air was palpable as we took a moment for reality to sink in.

"This was all for nothing." I dragged my Converse across the pavement, making vertical lines with my shoe. "Mr. Russell never left us a riddle." I shook my head. "He just left us."

"I'm sorry, Sonny," JC said. His anger hadn't quite left his voice. "I thought it was Mr. Russell's car."

"It's not your fault," I mumbled.

"Well, we tried!" Winston shouted, his not-so-perfect timing slicing through the thick air. "Anyone hungry? I could go for that panini from Geraldine's."

I glanced at him, slowly shaking my head in disbelief. My body felt as if I were flying through a dream. Nothing held enough weight to be real, but everything weighed a thousand pounds at the same time. And I couldn't process it all at once. I took a few steps back.

"Where are you going?" Winston asked me.

"I need to call my mom," I replied as I sat down on a concrete median, my arms wrapped around my knees, my head down. I was confused and heartbroken by my dad's arrest, and wondered how Ron was involved. I took out my phone to dial my mom, and then Lana, but was quickly interrupted.

"Sonny . . ." Norah proceeded to walk toward me.

I stood up.

"Here," she said as she opened her hand. "Jacob asked me to give this to you if he ever left."

I looked down at the small black box on her palm. "Jacob left?"

"I think so. He was only here temporarily while his dad was on assignment." She paused. "Didn't you know that?"

"Not exactly," I mumbled. "And I didn't know Mr. Harrison was here investigating my dad."

"What did your dad do?" Norah asked.

"I don't know," I replied, staring down at her hand.

"Well, Jacob isn't here," she said. "So I'm assuming they're leaving today."

I let out a lazy laugh and rubbed my face. "Guess so."

Norah glanced down at the box. "I didn't know what Jacob meant or why he asked me to do this. He just hugged me, said thank you, and walked away." She stretched her hand toward me. "He dropped this by my house last night."

I reached for the box, gently taking it from Norah—an unlikely delivery girl. I opened it to find a rainbow brooch and a folded piece of paper sitting center on top of a small black pillow.

I lifted the brooch and twisted it in circles with my fingers. It reflected in the sun as it spun around. Then, I reached for the paper and slowly unfolded it. My eyes skimmed the note.

"What does it say?" Norah asked.

The words swam before my eyes:

Sonny, when you wouldn't tell me what color you are,
I realized you aren't just one.
You're all of them.
I'm sorry.
—Jacob

"Wow," Norah said. "He seems super cringy."

"Yeah." I mindlessly ran my fingers over the brooch as my heart shattered. "He's the cringiest."

Norah raised her brows and turned to walk away.

"Hey!" I shouted, stopping her before she got too far.

She turned around with crossed arms, her paint-stained fingers digging into her skin.

"I'm sorry . . . about Dean."

Her head down, Norah dragged the bottom of her stiletto against the pavement, then looked back up at me. I waited for her reply—but it never came.

I placed the brooch back onto the pillow, yearning for the scent of musty cedar wood to sweep in from behind me. I could almost feel Jacob's eyes on my back, his hands on my waist, his lips on my lips. In such a short amount of time, his presence had found a way to haunt me. But there was something more haunting than the way he looked me up and down, the remembrance of his strong touch, or how it felt when our lips met. And that was knowing a careful girl like me got it all so terribly wrong.

As I went to close the box, it slipped from my weak hands and crashed onto the cement below. Just then, something caught my eye. I kneeled down to pick up the box and its contents—and to my surprise, I found another note. As I reached for the piece of paper sitting just underneath the black pillow, Jacob's statement from my driveway flooded my mind like a waterfall; and as I read the secret note, I drowned in his words. "What the—"

"She's a beauty, isn't she?" Principal Winchester asked, abruptly coming in from behind.

I jumped at the sound of his powerful voice, tucking the note into my pocket and stepping backward toward the others. His hands were in his dress-pants pockets, and his designer loafer was propped against the median I'd been sitting on. We followed his gaze and realized he was staring at the left wing.

"I remember when I first walked through the double doors of this school," he said. "Can't believe how much has changed."

Principal Winchester glanced up at the light post above us. "Parking lot C," he said, emphasizing each word. "Once the left wing is complete next month, this parking lot will be reserved for the junior and senior class." He nodded, still gazing upon the light posts. "It's a good thing I had security cameras installed last week. That Benji Randolph, with his longboard, is always up to something." He dropped his head, staring into the eyes of everyone in the circle. "Have to keep my eyes and ears on him."

I closed my eyes tightly, softly exhaling as the weight of our meeting on Saturday night fell onto my shoulders like bricks.

Cliff dropped his head and placed his hands into his pockets.

I stared at JC as he glared at Piper.

"Westcott isn't perfect," Winchester continued, staring at the school. "No school ever is. But I'm proud of how far it has come, and how far it will go."

I slowly tilted my head to the left to glance at Winston, then shifted my eyes to Buckets on the right and Casey across the circle.

"My school means everything to me, and I will stop at no cost to rebuild its reputation." Principal Winchester paused. "You kids understand that, don't you?"

We all nodded, so we wouldn't imply or suggest that we disagreed.

"Westcott means everything to us too, sir," Cliff said.

Principal Winchester slowly turned his head toward him. "Oh no, Cliff. Not Westcott." He grinned. "Bella View Day."

On that day—a day that will live in infamy—only one Crescent school survived the scandal—my school, Westcott High. And out of the ashes, for reasons unbeknownst to us, rose only one principal—*Principal Winchester of Bella View Day.*

Kyle stepped forward. "Dad, your old school closed down. This isn't Bella View."

"Of course it isn't, son." Principal Winchester's eyes narrowed in on him; his voice deepened. "Bella students would never be so stupid as to risk their futures by playing Nancy Drew—or spit on the SCC by breaking into the school's safe."

Kyle's face turned red as he swallowed excessively.

"You Westcott students don't deserve the prestigious platform a Crescent school gives you." He focused his attention on Piper, keeping his voice low so only we could hear him. "Look at you. The first chance you got at a fast pass, you jumped on it quicker than I could get the offer out. You sold your soul, and sold your boyfriend up the river, for an itemized list."

I looked over at JC, who was clenching his fists.

"I'd be careful saying you plan to turn me over to police," he continued. "Or anyone for that matter. You have a top-secret Princeton profile in your possession, with no proof whatsoever of who gave it to you. As far as I'm concerned, young lady, you stole it. Which means you'd never step foot inside their doors if they found out."

Tears emerged from Piper's lifeless eyes, rolled down her neck, and disappeared underneath her pearl necklace.

"And you two," he said, his eyes bouncing back and forth between Kyle and me. "Breaking into Principal Clemmons's house? What would your father think, Sonny?" He paused. "Son, what would your mother have to say?"

He then stared at the Cobalts. "You all have a lot of nerve. I open my arms to you, giving you the chance of a lifetime, and this is how you show me gratitude? I should cut you all from the student body like the dead weight you are."

He walked toward Norah. "A Chosen Ten. What a surprise you'd risk your seat for people who don't even like you. I'd be careful who you try to help."

He stepped in front of Cliff. "And if your father wasn't the biggest donor this school has, you'd be pulled off the team faster than you could say *privilege*. Of course, your privilege won't get you far anymore."

"Anymore?" I mumbled under my breath.

Cliff clenched his jaw, his crown clearly in question.

"What about me?" JC stepped forward. "You've already ruined me. I have nothing left to lose."

Principal Winchester stepped toward him. "I haven't ruined you, Mr. Coleman. Not yet. If you ever want to see a wrestling mat at Westcott again, you'll take back your suggestive tones and pathetic attempt at a threat."

We all stared at one another, accepting defeat.

"I don't want to hear about any of this again, understood?" Principal Winchester cocked a crooked smile. "Get to class," he said, giving his keys a shake in his pocket before walking back toward the double doors of the school.

We all stared after him in silence.

"This is all your fault!" Red-faced, JC lurched toward Piper.

Kyle grabbed him by the arm, but JC broke through.

"Why did you do this?" he yelled. "Why?"

I placed my envelope into Casey's hands as I shifted toward him. "Calm down, JC. People are staring."

"I made a mistake," Piper said, her chin trembling. "I'm sorry."

JC lifted his arms above his head, locking them with each hand. "A mistake? You screwed me over, Piper! You got me kicked off the team and suspended from school—and you watched as everyone turned on me. Why would you do that?! For Princeton?! Are you really that desperate for success?!"

Tears filled her eyes. "What could I have done? Imagine what he would have done to me if I'd refused!"

"Piper!" he yelled. "You could have come to me! You could have turned him into the police before you agreed to set me up, not after."

"Look, I came clean to everyone. I could have said nothing!"

"Well, maybe you should have," he said, reaching into his back pocket. He threw the envelope marked Jeremy Coleman at her feet. "Instead of doing all of this."

"I said I was sorry, JC."

"Yeah," he replied. "You really are."

"Calm down, Coleman," Norah told him. "Your veins are bulging."

"Guys . . ." Casey looked down at the contents from my red envelope, then stared at me with a mix of confusion and terror.

I swiftly walked toward her, pulling the sheet of paper close to my face; the words sent a chill through my bones:

Kyle Winchester
Norah Soros
Piper Clemmons
Sonny Carter
London Vanderbilt
Stella King
Alice Kennedy
Sawyer Ellington
Quinn Myers
Max Crimson

"What is this?" Buckets asked, staring over my shoulder at the paper.

"It appears to be the missing names from the Chosen Ten list," Winston said, hovering over my other shoulder.

"Who's Stella? And Quinn? Who are all of these other names?" Ari questioned.

Kyle quickly tore into his letter, cutting his eyes toward his fellow Westcott Awards competitors. There was an undeniable shift in the air—one that brought a gust of dread with it. Our linked gaze now took on a whole new level of tension as we all recognized the names on the list.

"Shit," Norah said as she stared down at her paper, her voice barely audible over the parking lot full of students. "You've got to be kidding me."

Cliff snatched the paper from Norah's hands. He smirked and tossed the letter onto the ground like a frisbee. "I knew it." He crouched down, his elbows digging into his knees. "I knew it was just a matter of time." He buried his face into his cupped hands. "They finally got through."

"Just in time for us to make it on Principal Winchester's shit list," Norah added.

Kyle wiped the sweat from his brows with trembling fingers. He paced back and forth and rolled his neck from side to side.

"What's going on?" Casey asked, reading our expressions.

For one brief moment, the members of our circle were no longer Cobalts and Violets. Or jocks and nerds. Or the Chosen Ten and the unchosen.

We were the same, crammed together in the exact same sinking boat, with ominous black clouds gathering overhead.

Cliff was the first one to jump ship.

He popped up, clasping his hands behind his head so quickly I thought his arms would fly off. "You know what, Sonny?" Cliff gave me a devilish glare. "I told you to drop it," he said, traveling toward me. "This was JC's problem— not yours—and you just couldn't stay the hell out of it."

Dean blocked Cliff from coming any closer. "Watch how you speak to her."

"Coming from you?" Cliff pushed Dean out of his face. Dean caught his balance with the help of Kyle.

"Don't even think about blaming Sonny for this," Kyle said.

"Don't pick and choose when you want to talk to me," Cliff retorted, glaring at him.

"You were on camera just like Sonny was," Kyle said.

"And you conveniently weren't," Cliff replied, towering over his former friend.

Kyle smirked. "Nobody called me to your little meeting."

"We called," Cliff replied. "You were too busy pouting over a girl who doesn't want you."

"Shut the hell up, Cliff!" Ari lunged toward him, shoving him in the chest with flat hands. "Just shut the hell up!"

"Oh, it's you two against me now?" Cliff asked.

"You barbarians!" Winston chucked his red ink pen toward the crowd. "Knock it off and tell us what's going on!" He walked toward the circle and bent down to retrieve his pen. "I'm going to need this back."

"They're coming." Kyle nodded.

Buckets rolled up his sleeves. "Who?"

The silence that followed was fraught with unanswered questions; nobody wanted it to be true.

"They're coming for their spots," JC said with a noticeable shift in his tone of voice. "The ones that were taken from them."

"And this is a message," I said, hovering over my list. "That our spots aren't safe anymore."

"None of us are safe anymore," Cliff added. "Just like the riddle said."

I slowly nodded, my eyes making their rounds across the parking lot. I was coming to the realization that the school I once believed could give me the world now had the potential to hinder me from getting it. "What do we do now?"

Norah broke through the crowd, beelining toward the left wing in her stilettos. Then she stopped, pivoted, and turned to look at us. "I suggest you pull yourselves together and get ready," she said. *"Here come the Royal Blues from Bella View."*

ACKNOWLEDGEMENTS

To my family: Thank you for your continued support, encouragement, and love. It'd be hard to do life without you guys—you sure do make it fun!

To my cast: Alec, Bryson, Catherine, Chris, John, Katalina, Lauren, Lucas, Mandi, Payton, Rebecca, and Tyler. Thank you for being a part of this ride and for bringing my book to life. You're all going to do great things in this world. I'm happy to know you!

To my editor, Andrea: Words fall short. Thank you for pushing me to push myself, for going above and beyond, and for believing in this story. You're a saint!

ABOUT THE AUTHOR

Westcott High is Sarah Mello's first self-published YA book. After high school, Sarah pursued her creative nature, which led her into the event industry. She opened a North Carolina wedding venue that she still manages today. However, she never forgot the words of her twelfth-grade English teacher: "You're a writer."

Sarah was born in New York and spent her first five years on Long Island. When she was five, her family moved to Charlotte, NC, where she calls home. If she isn't writing, you'll find Sarah helping people plan their special day at her wedding venue.

"After writing Chapter Three of *Westcott High*, I remember thinking how real it felt—as if I were watching my favorite TV show." Sarah goes on to explain the project behind the book. "Bringing my book to life in the way that I did felt like a new concept. I had never seen another author do anything like this, and it was scary at times. But I think there's something to be said about pushing yourself to try new things." Sarah even tackled her own book marketing. "I hope I've shown that you don't necessarily need an abundance of resources to pursue a dream. Just imagine your characters, grab some models and a guy with a camera, and establish a presence on social media. I've been so excited to get such positive reactions from YA readers."

67469984R00207

Made in the USA
Columbia, SC
27 July 2019